DEEP

SEA

Compiled & Edited by
Ben Thomas & D Kershaw

Black loom the crags of the uplands behind me,
Dark are the sands of the far-stretching shore.
Dim are the pathways and rocks that remind me
Sadly of years in the lost Nevermore.

Soft laps the ocean on wave-polish'd boulder,
Sweet is the sound and familiar to me;
Here, with her head gently bent to my shoulder,
Walk'd I with Unda, the Bride of the Sea.

Bright was the morn of my youth when I met her,
Sweet as the breeze that blew o'er the brine.
Swift was I captur'd in Love's strongest fetter,
Glad to be here, and she glad to be mine.

Never a question ask'd I where she wander'd,
Never a question ask'd she of my birth:
Happy as children, we thought not nor ponder'd,
Glad of the bounty of ocean and earth.

Once when the moonlight play'd soft 'mid the billows,

High on the cliff o'er the waters we stood,
Bound was her hair with a garland of willows,
Pluck'd by the fount in the bird-haunted wood.

Strangely she gaz'd on the surges beneath her,
Charm'd with the sound or entranc'd by the light:
Then did the waves a wild aspect bequeath her,
Stern as the ocean and weird as the night.

Coldly she left me, astonish'd and weeping,
Standing alone 'mid the legions she bless'd:
Down, ever downward, half gliding, half creeping,
Stole the sweet Unda in oceanward quest.

Calm grew the sea, and tumultuous beating
Turn'd to a ripple as Unda the fair
Trod the wet sands in affectionate greeting,
Beckon'd to me, and no longer was there!

Long did I pace by the banks where she vanish'd,
High climb'd the moon and descended again.
Grey broke the dawn till the sad night was banish'd,

Still ach'd my soul with its infinite pain.

All the wide world have I search'd for my darling;
Scour'd the far desert and sail'd distant seas.
Once on the wave while the tempest was snarling,
Flash'd a fair face that brought quiet and ease.

Ever in restlessness onward I stumble
Seeking and pining scarce heeding my way.
Now have I stray'd where the wide waters rumble,
Back to the scene of the lost yesterday.

Lo! the red moon from the ocean's low hazes
Rises in ominous grandeur to view;
Strange is its face as my tortur'd eye gazes
O'er the vast reaches of sparkle and blue.

Straight from the moon to the shore where I'm
sighing
Grows a bright bridge made of wavelets and beams.
Frail it may be, yet how simple the trying,
Wand'ring from earth to the orb of sweet dreams.

What is yon face in the moonlight appearing;

Have I at last found the maiden that fled?

Out on the beam-bridge my footsteps are nearing

Her whose sweet beckoning hastens my tread.

Current's surround me, and drowsily swaying,

Far on the moon-path I seek the sweet face.

Eagerly, hasting, half panting, half praying,

Forward I reach for the vision of grace.

Murmuring waters about me are closing,

Soft the sweet vision advances to me.

Done are my trials; my heart is reposing

Safe with my Unda, the Bride of the Sea.

Bride of the Sea H.P. Lovecraft, 1915

Table of Contents

Together

By Chris Bannor

When unknown sea creatures start turning up dead on the beaches of their new home planet, Dr. Danners and his partner Dr. Zian come out to investigate, only to find the source of the deaths is something from the deep-- and it might be coming for them.

The tranquil turquoise waters of Volos Bay sparkled under the twin suns of Gaia. The colour wasn't quite right to the eyes of the elders who had come, hearing of the planet's resemblance to Earth-Of-Old, but they smiled and told stories that the young took with a grain of salt.

After all, if Earth-Of-Old had been so perfect, why had they left?

Today, the surface of Serenity Ocean was calm and clear, living up to its name. Children played in the distance and their laughter, once contained in the echoing walkways of the ship, drifted over the sandy beach.

Adam Danners turned away from the view and to the matter at hand.

"Do you know what happened here?"

Zian LiuWei crouched next to a mass of sea creatures that had washed up on the shore. The beach was covered in jelly-like sacs with long branching arms and trailing tentacles.

"We don't even know what species this is." LiuWei stood and looked over at Adam. "We'll take some back to the lab, but I don't have any idea what happened here. We've categorised every type of sea creature and ocean phenomena we've come across since we found Gaia, but this is new."

"It's only been ten years," Adam reminded him. "Two since First Landing."

"Yeah. Which means we're back to research."

"No."

"Oh yeah," LiuWei taunted him. "We don't know what killed these. What I can tell you though, is that this is something from the deeper parts of the ocean."

"No."

LiuWei smiled. "We're going to the research station."

"I hate you."

"Yeah, yeah. Come on. Let's report in so we can get started."

"How can you stand that place?"

LiuWei stopped teasing and looked at Adam. "It isn't like the ship. We're not confined here. We can leave the station whenever we need to."

Adam nodded. "I know. I just…hate having to go back into a space like that." He took a deep breath and tried to get rid of the anxiety he felt at the prospect of recycled air and tiny shared living spaces. "But the job is the job. Let's finish up here, then you report in. I'll start making the arrangements."

LiuWei watched him a moment longer before he reached down and grabbed the box at his feet. "Samples or photographs?"

Adam smiled at that. "Like I'm touching those slimy looking buggers if I have a choice." He took the camera and began snapping photos of the scene. He had to bite back a laugh at the faces LiuWei made as he picked through the dead sea creatures to find the best array of samples to take to the lab. He grabbed what humour he could from the situation.

This was the third species to wash up on the beach, unknown and from the deep. Was it a natural phenomenon that they hadn't yet experienced? Or was there something else happening to their new home? As the ecological impact of their lives on Gaia was so closely monitored, everyone was clamouring for answers.

As much as he hated politics, he'd gotten himself embroiled in a hell of a situation. He just hoped they found an answer quick.

He really did hate breathing recycled air.

****

"Do you think it's really going to happen?" LiuWei asked as they stared down into the chambers of the Consortium.

Adam turned his back and rested against the glass. They could hear the ongoing debate but there was no need for them to be heard. They had no say. The arena was crowded today though, and Adam was grateful for the privacy his father's box seat provided. "It depends on who gets control. The politicians are trying to keep their jobs and the people are clamouring to get planetside. The scientists want to study it more."

"I know the debate. I asked if you think they'll let us planetside?" LiuWei was still looking at the proceedings

as President Danners began to speak.

Adam didn't turn back to listen to his father's words. He knew his old man's thoughts already; they'd argued it often enough over weekly dinners. "Yes. Dad's going to make some concessions that the politicians will hate but the scientists will flock to. It might take a few weeks to finalise, but they'll all agree."

LiuWei turned his eyes to him then. "You helped him find a compromise?"

"I told him the only way to get through to the scientific community. We've been studying for eight long years and everyone is tired of waiting," he said with a smile. LiuWei was one of the more vocal scientists who wanted to explore more, to get out into the field and get his hands dirty, learning the new planet. He wasn't the only one.

"How many teams will go down you think, before you and I get to land?"

They weren't senior scientists, but they were both well respected in their fields. They would have to wait for a few landings, if they followed protocol.

"I have never once used my father's influence to get ahead, to get more resources or more space in the labs. Like Hell I'm not cashing in on that now," he said with a grin. "Besides, I helped him find the compromise. I consider it my fee."

"How soon will we go down?"

LiuWei's enthusiasm was infectious and Adam smiled. "We'll be part of the First Landing."

***

The deep-sea research station, Poseidon, took two heliport rides, a long submarine dive down, and a day and a half to complete. Even with the public outcry to solve this event and open the waters again, it took time to make arrangements and get the samples to the right people. No amount of political pressure could speed up time, or bureaucracy.

The samples were handed off to the lab to get started and Adam and LiuWei were led to their bunks so they could get settled in and grab food. LiuWei wasn't one to unpack, so he left as soon as he set his bags down. When Adam entered the cafeteria, LiuWei was already at a table with a tray of fish and chips. Adam grabbed a burger from the unappetising list of food available and joined him.

"Stop scowling at your food," LiuWei hadn't looked up from his tray, but he knew Adam well enough to know his thoughts on the food at Poseidon. "It isn't the same as ship food. You can get the same burger up above."

"I'm aware. It's the air," he said. "All this recycled

air makes everything taste disgusting."

"You should probably talk to someone about that," LiuWei said as he forked another bite of fish off his plate. "You aren't the only one that's had a bad reaction to being confined after we landed."

"I'll get right on that. As soon as I have some time off and oh…yeah…someone wouldn't use it against my father in some sort of political manoeuvre."

"Confidentiality."

"Doesn't seem to count when you're the president's son. They don't have to know why I'm seeking counselling. Just the fact that I might would drum up drama for my Dad. He's got enough to deal with these days."

"What does he think about all this?" He waved his fork around to indicate the station. Adam knew what he meant.

"His concern is that something is happening that will taint the water and make it unusable for humans. What he believes is that it's just a seasonal occurrence, migration or mating seasons or something like that."

"So, he isn't worried."

"He's just worried we can't tell him what it is yet. It's happened on random beaches, so we haven't seen the actual occurrence."

"Only the aftermath."

"Exactly. He's trying to get eyes on the beaches to see if we can finally observe it."

"That's too much manpower."

"That's the issue," Adam agreed. "As much as we all want to figure it out, no one wants to stop their work to sit on the beach, nor do they want to give up their resources to watch a patch of water that isn't likely to do anything."

"So we're stuck here, researching the unknown animals and their cause of death."

"And hoping Poseidon's sensors can pick something up that no one else has."

LiuWei sighed. "This isn't going to be a quick one, is it?"

His partner already knew the answer, but it was an offer of condolence and not a question. It was a reminder that Adam wasn't stuck in a suffocating tin can on his own. He didn't bother to answer but turned to his bland meal. The quicker he got to work, the quicker he could get away from Poseidon.

***

Two days later, Adam was in a foul mood and there were no answers. No one knew why the new species of sea creatures had died and washed up on the shore, though it had happened each morning since they arrived. 5 beaches in total now. The only good news he'd heard from Lancaster was that the occurrences seemed to be moving north and they were using the five locations to pinpoint the next beach.

Poseidon was a deep-sea research station that had been built into the side of a massive ocean column. The entire outer wall was designed for observation of the surrounding oceans while allowing the inner sections to function as living quarters and the non-scientific operations of the research station.

When Adam walked into the conference room, there were only two empty chairs. He nodded to the people he knew and took the empty seat next to LiuWei.

"They're already pissed you're here," LiuWei whispered when he leaned close. "You could have showed up on time."

"When the president calls, you don't tell him you need to hang up."

"You do it all the time."

"When my Dad calls. When the president calls, I don't."

LiuWei's eyes widened at his words, but Adam brushed it off by mouthing "Later" to him as Director Camilla Lancaster walked in the door. At least he'd managed to beat her there.

"The president is growing impatient. I don't particularly enjoy being on the other end of that man's bad mood, so what do you have to tell me?" She didn't bother with formalities. For all the years that Adam had known her, she'd always been blunt. It helped get to the heart of matters, but she was a political nightmare. She didn't hold her tongue and Adam had been watching her and his father trade barbs since First Landing. The only reason she'd ascended to her current position was that she was so loved by the scientific community.

"Whatever it is, its path seems to be heading north," the scientist across from Adam answered. Adam hadn't met him yet, but the scowl on LiuWei's face told him all he needed to know. He trusted his partner's instincts and judgments as much as his own.

"Yes, but have you figured out what beach will be affected next?" the Director asked.

"We still don't know what it is," one of the others added. "We can guess which section of beaches based on the previous events but there is inconsistent data."

"What is consistent?"

"It's coming for us."

Adam looked at his partner and LiuWei answered the question he hadn't voiced yet. "It's coming *to* us. Whatever this is, if the path remains the same, then it will come to us."

"We aren't coastal," the scientist across the table scowled.

LiuWei scoffed but no one took heed of it. The two must have a history, and a well-known one, for everyone to ignore them. "If I was tracking the beach locations, I suppose it would be a problem, but since these are deep-sea creatures washing ashore, we've been tracking an alternate event."

"Go ahead, Dr Zian," the Director said.

"We found some strange occurrences in the ocean currents that I believe are causing the deaths. We've had the Nerites and Amphitrite redirected from their exploration sites since they are the two closest survey drones we have. Amphitrite is trying to catch up to the phenomena we're tracking, and Nerites is following in the wake to see if we can find the disruption sites and what we can learn from them."

No one said anything and LiuWei continued. "But what we know so far is that it's moving in a straight line for us."

"What could cause that though?" Dr Aaron Campfield asked. "I can't think of anything that could."

"That's the problem, isn't it?" Adam asked. "We settled this planet without enough knowledge. We're finding new things every day, new discoveries that are amazing, and some that are just straight-up dangerous.

People balk at being kept contained in small areas when we have a whole planet to explore, but we don't know what else is out there. And the oceans that feed us are even less known to us. Who knows what sort of things are out there?"

"We don't know anything yet," Liu Wie continued to address Director Lancaster. "It could be a fault line on the ocean floor that has been dormant. It could be some form of gargantuan sea creature from the depths we've yet to explore. Science Fiction is as apt to give us the truth as science right now. We don't have the facts. Hopefully, once the Nerites and Amphitrite get to their locations, they'll have something more for us."

"I want all available resources turned to this, under the direction of Dr Danners and Dr Zian." She held her hand up to cut off the fast-growing uproar. "Specific research projects continue as you are, but any equipment that we can spare and any personnel to track it will be given immediately. And if they come to you and ask specifically for something, give it. I don't care how crucial you think your project is. We have a priority to understand this phenomenon and make certain the oceans are as safe as we think they are. Thank you."

It was a clear dismissal for everyone, though she remained standing by the table. When LiuWei began to stand, Adam tapped his wrist and shook his head. His partner nodded and kept his seat. When the room was cleared, Director Lancaster closed the door and looked back at them.

"You really believe this is coming at us?"

"I do," LiuWei said.

"Should we be evacuating Poseidon?"

"There was no sign of debris on the beaches. At this point, there is no reason to believe that whatever this is has caused destruction to the area. We'd see dead sea plants, rocks, shells, all sorts of other marine life it was tearing up the ground."

"You think it's a creature?" Adam asked.

"I think it's coming for us. That's all I've got."

She let out a deep breath, then looked at Adam. "What's with your father? That call was not a normal check-in."

"He hasn't said anything to me," Adam said, "but Dad's under a lot of pressure to open the beaches back up. Our agricultural programs haven't been as successful as we hoped, and we're relying heavily on fishing and marine harvesting for the colony's food supply. If we can't settle this soon, we'll have to start rationing. People aren't going to handle it well. They want to expand and if they decide to move away from the walls, there is only so much we can do without turning Gaia into a military state."

"Why the hell did we agree to come down so early, anyway?"

She knew the answer already but Adam was tired and he hated having to stay behind to play liaison for his father when Lancaster was taking advantage of the fact that he was there to answer for him, instead of asking the man himself.

"You know damn well why. We didn't have a choice."

***

"What the hell happened today?" LiuWei asked as they finally found solace in their quarters. The spaceship had always seemed too small, but today it was even more so. Adam felt the walls closing in whenever he turned a corner. He knew it was the reports he'd read. His father wasn't a scientist, and he trusted very few to give him straight answers, so Adam read every report the president was briefed on.

"I'm fine," he lied.

"That was a panic attack, Adam. I've known you since we were kids. We grew up together. You have never had a panic attack before. What the hell is going on?"

"You know the scientific community is still holding out, trying to keep us from landing yet." LiuWei just

nodded. *"They handed my dad a report today that ended the debate. We'll be landing as soon as we can make arrangements."*

"That's great," LiuWei's voice showed his confusion, though. *"That's what we wanted."*

"The ship has had a major malfunction. When we land, we won't be coming back up. We'll dismantle the Asteria, but this is it. Whatever we find on the planet, we have to make it work. Our trip just ended."

LiuWei leaned back against the wall and closed his eyes as his head dropped back. "Damn."

"Yeah. We wanted to land and slowly expand once we could make sure areas were safe enough, but this means landing everyone in a very quick timeframe."

"This could be suicide."

"Genocide," Adam reminded him. *"We are all that is left of the human race. If we can't make this work, we all die."*

LiuWei nodded. "Yeah. Alright. Good reason for a panic attack."

Adam looked at him for a moment, then suddenly let out a laugh. It wasn't funny. It was a horrible thing, but LiuWei had always been able to lighten the load for him and he couldn't help but let out the exhausted relief at having shared this with someone. LiuWei smiled like he always did when he got Adam to let his guard down, a small smirk that knew too much and said he knew how to use it too.

He did. And Adam was never more grateful that LiuWei had befriended him all those years ago.

He continued to laugh until he wasn't able to stay upright anymore and LiuWei pushed him back into his bunk.

That night he dreamed of terrors on the planet and exploding metal, but whenever he woke, LiuWei was watching over him. It gave him the strength to face the nightmares once again.

***

Adam walked into the main research station to a bank on monitors, all tracking the movements of one of the droids. "What are we looking at?"

Dr Campfield looked over his shoulder at him and nodded back towards the screen. "The Nerites found the first location."

The monitor showed a site devoid of life. It looked like some areas had been scraped clear, while in other animals had died while still clinging to rocky surfaces. Some were half-buried in the sand while others seemed to have just fallen to the ocean floor and never moved again. Scavengers were moving in, but it had taken them a few days to enter the affected area. Whatever had passed had scared them away.

"I really don't like the look of this."

LiuWei was sitting at a station in a corner of the room and he motioned both Adam and Dr Campfield over. "You're really not going to like this," he said. The small monitor at his workstation showed the movement of Amphitrite.

"What am I supposed to be seeing here?" he asked.

"Her catching up," LiuWei said. "We used the suspected time of the events to deduce a speed and Amphitrite should have been able to catch up by now."

"We should be seeing something by now."

"Yes," LiuWei agreed. "We should be able to see whatever this is, but we can't. It's not even fast enough to catch its wake. As devastating as the area Amphitrite is going through, the waters are already calming back into natural patterns. It's coming fast."

"And it changed speed," Campfield said.

"It's not an event. It's a creature," Adam realised what LiuWei was driving at, and he saw the dawning horror in Dr Campfield's eyes.

"Let's take this to Lancaster."

***

"What can we do?" Campfield asked when they finished telling the Director what they'd found.

There was a moment of pause before LiuWei said, "Evacuate the station. At least all non-essential personnel in case this goes poorly."

"You don't seriously believe some giant creature is coming at us with the intention of destroying us?" Director Lancaster said.

"I believe we are on an alien planet with not enough research—"

"We have eight years of research from the spaceship! Not once in all the years we were tracking from above did we see anything like that. Not once since First Landing, two years ago. You think it was hiding?"

"Or hibernating," LiuWei didn't back down from Lancaster's rant. "We observed from space, but we weren't down here. Poseidon is only a year old and our research under the sea has just begun. No matter what this is, how can we not do everything possible to make sure lives are not at risk? At least ask if people want to wait it out on the surface!"

Director Lancaster held her hand up. "What will your father do?" she asked Adam.

"Call him and ask."

"I'm asking you."

"I can't answer that. I'm not the president and I don't

speak for him."

"You do it when it suits your purposes."

"I do it when you ask for his mood. I can't speak for the president about something like this. Hell, he won't be able to speak for himself until he's heard from a half dozen other people, anyway."

It was only a partial lie. He knew his father would tell Lancaster to offer evacuation to anyone that wanted it. LiuWei's suggestion had been used before and it was popular with the people. There were too many unknowns to balk every time something might happen, but offering optional evac instead of ordering a full evac meant they kept everyone informed and were doing their best to keep the human race alive. Even if no one believed in the threat that LiuWei mentioned, they were covering their bases by offering.

Director Lancaster wasn't happy with his answer, but there was nothing else she could say. He didn't work directly under her. He and LiuWei worked as an independent investigation team for the Consortium. And at the end of the day, he was his father's son and not the man himself.

"Excuse me, gentlemen, it looks like I have a call to make."

She left the room and Dr Campfield stayed behind with them. "Do you believe they'll evacuate? That if she offers, they'll actually leave?"

Adam shook his head.

"Dr Zian?"

"No. We might lose some of the support staff. Maybe a few people will take it as a surprise holiday, but mostly people will stay. Too many research projects going on and no one will want to lose the time or trust someone else with their work."

"We scientists are a stubborn bunch," Dr Campfield said.

LiuWei smiled. "Meaning you won't be leaving?"

"Something of this significance is coming at us and you expect me to leave?"

"No, I suppose not."

Adam shook his head. "You're all a bit crazy. If it wasn't my job to stay, I'd be off Poseidon in a heartbeat."

Dr Campfield laughed but he walked to the door. "I'm going to try to track the currents. We don't have a lot of sensors in the path we believe it's taking, but if I can get one or two repositioned, I might be able to find it and see how fast it's going."

"Thank you, Dr Campfield," Adam said. The man waved him off like it was nothing and went back to work.

"Adam, you don't have to stay."

He turned to look at LiuWei, whose face was entirely devoid of amusement. He was as serious as Adam had ever seen him. "What?"

"I know how much you hate it here. You don't have to stay on Poseidon to track this. I can stay here and relay the information to you. There is no reason for both of us to be here. If this hits, if it really is something coming at us, at least one of us would be on land to-"

"Don't. I'm not leaving. If you think that way, then you leave." LiuWei tilted his head slightly and glared. "Yeah, exactly. So don't mention it again." They stared at one another for a moment before Adam finally smiled. "Don't we have better things to do?"

LiuWei shook his head. "I do. You should probably make a call as well. Or be prepared for one. You know as soon as she hangs up he's going to ask for your expert opinion."

"Our expert opinions."

"Which are the same this time."

"Alright, I'll let you skip the call. Go find something new for me to tell him. Something with less horror attached this time," he said, trying to keep things light.

"I'll get right on that."

***

Four A.M. was never a good time to be awake.

Adam scrambled out of his room and nearly fell back

as the ground under his feet shifted. He was caught by LiuWei who'd emerged behind him. "What the hell was that?"

"Earthquake?" LiuWei said.

When Adam looked over his shoulder at him, he knew neither of them believed it. LiuWei pushed him off his chest and they both took off at a run towards the main monitoring room. There were always a few people supervising the station and the equipment, even in the dead of the night. They ran into the room and found they weren't the only ones who'd made the mad dash. "What happened?" Adam yelled over the other voices.

"We can't see what hit us."

"What do you mean hit us?" he asked.

"A wave of some kind," one of the overnight crew said. He recognised her as one of the junior scientists. The most promising of the younger generation of scientists, but still getting the experience that would allow her to have her own team someday. "Sensors around Poseidon went down in formation, but it was too fast to get out any kind of warning."

"What's causing the wave?" he asked.

LiuWei had already gone to a workstation as the door behind him opened to a host of scientists, including Dr Campfield and Director Lancaster.

"Update!" Lancaster yelled.

"We were hit by a wave of unknown origin. Sensors are offline around the station," he answered.

"Let's get Proteus and Pontus primed for launch," she said.

"Isn't it late to try to get people out?" he asked. He'd argued with her and his father about the need for the evac but neither had listened. The president hadn't even listened when Zian LiuWei called and - besides his son - he was his most trusted scientific advisor.

"I'm sending them to see what this is," she snapped at him.

"Redirecting all the outlying sensors and drones back towards the station," LiuWei called back to them. "Amphitrite is almost in range and Nerites is close behind."

"I thought Nerites was researching the path," Adam asked as he went to stand behind LiuWei.

"I called it back last night after I spoke with the president," he said. "I sent it back on a straight path instead of trying to follow."

"Good call," Adam said grimly.

"What the hell is that?" someone yelled and Adam looked up at the main monitor to see the wave coming towards them again. The whole station shook with the impact and the room went silent for a moment, then erupted into noise again as everyone began trying to make sense of what was happening.

"Observation." LiuWei said.

"What?"

"I'm going to the observation deck." He wanted to argue that it was the most exposed and vulnerable part of the entire complex, but he couldn't deny how much he wanted to see what was out there with his own eyes and not through a monitor. They ran out of the room and he waved his station radio above his head as the Director tried to get him back. She could yell at him through the radio if she wanted.

***

Unlike the monitoring lab, the observation deck was quiet. The people who were there were watching the waters with trepidation. No one wanted to voice their concerns and Adam felt more than one pair of eyes on his back, waiting for answers he couldn't give.

"They won't catch up in time," LiuWei said softly. "We're going to be blindsided by whatever this is."

"If we survive this, remind me to tell my father 'I told you so'."

"If we see him again, I'm likely to get arrested for punching the president."

Adam looked at LiuWei beside him and his lips

twisted up into a smile at the statement. He wasn't sure he was joking, but he needed the levity at the moment.

"Please don't get arrested."

"I make no guarantees," but he was smiling too.

"It's coming again!" Someone yelled and most of the people in the observation deck left, but Adam couldn't. Maybe it was stupid, but they had nothing, and he wanted to know.

"It's not the same," LiuWei whispered as he leaned forward. They walked to the window and watched as something began to move closer to them. It was a wave, but not the same as it had been before.

"Is that—" He didn't have time to finish his question as the first of the creatures slammed against the window. They both jumped back and watched as the window was inundated with the same animals they had found on the beach. The station shook with the impact, but they managed to stumble against each other and keep their feet.

The window held without damage, though they needed to have engineers look at it. If it happened too many times, he wasn't sure it wouldn't lose integrity.

"Well, we know it's the same phenomena," Adam said wryly.

"Dr Danners?" The radio in his hand went off and he opened up the channel to Dr Campfield.

"The observation deck is fine. A little knocked around from impact, but everything is holding up."

"All our cameras showing the outside have been damaged or are covered," the doctor said.

"They were the same ones we found on shore," he answered before they could ask. "It looks like they might have gotten caught in those earlier waves."

"Or maybe the waves were to cause this," LiuWei suggested.

Adam looked out at the surrounding water. The lights that ran the distance of the station had been knocked out and they couldn't see anything beyond the dim lights that the observation deck threw off.

"We have nothing else, Campfield," he said. "If we see something coming, we'll let you know."

"We'll let you know when we need you back," the other man said before he turned the radio off.

Adam let out a deep breath. "This is insane," he said softly. "What is this? What is causing this? Do you really believe some kinds of Godzilla-like monstrosity is out there?"

He knew the answer, but he needed to hash it out again.

"Earth's history had periods of gigantism, and marine life has always had its larger creatures. The reasons for gigantism to succeed are the same here as they were on Earth."

"It's far fetched."

"It fits the facts better than anything else we've got. Why are you fighting this so hard?" LiuWei demanded.

"Because if you're right, we're stuck here with over a hundred people and a creature that is either hostile or unaware of the damage it's causing us."

"She should be evacuating us," LiuWei said. "The Pontus and the Proteus could start making trips up to the surface."

Adam nodded. "We've got to convince her to send the others away."

"And hope whatever this is doesn't take a departing vessel as a sign of aggression."

"It's coming again!" The radio came to life and Adam looked out the window. Instead of the wave that had crashed into them the first time, or the sea creatures that had last hit, when the impact came, it was with a fleshy body covering the window. The impact caused them to jolt together. They hadn't been able to see it very well without lights, but it clung to the window and they could see the suckers keeping it attached to the surface.

"Oh my god," Adam whispered in awe.

LiuWei stepped closer to the window and Adam followed. "It's...Adam?"

"Yeah, I see it too."

"This is a tentacle."

"Yeah."

"It's a fucking tentacle."

Adam opened up the channel of the radio. "Campfield, are you there?"

"We're here," he answered.

"Danners, what's happening?" Lancaster's voice came over the radio. "We don't have any visuals."

"It's one of the creatures. It's…enormous. There's a tentacle on the window of the observation deck. Just a tentacle, and it's covering most of it."

"Did the Proteus and Pontus launch yet?" LiuWei asked.

"Pontus is leaving now."

"Don't send Proteus."

"We need to know what's out there," Lancaster argued.

"We need a way out," LiuWei snapped.

There was no answer over the radio, but Adam knew the words had gotten through.

"We need to get back to them," LiuWei said. "She's going to get us all killed."

"We have no indication this thing actually means to h—"

The tentacle across the window began to undulate slowly, and they watched as an arm worked down over the window beside it.

"It's just like the others. The arms are similar to a sea star, but with tentacles like some of the jellies on Earth."

"Those are carnivorous."

"So how do we get it off our station?"

"Maybe we just leave it alone?" Adam suggested. "If it can't find food here, it'll move on."

Even as he said it, the creature began to move again. It didn't move off though. Instead, they watched as it pressed more firmly against the window. "Oh hell," Adam said as he grabbed LiuWei's hand and began to pull him towards the doors.

"It's trying to open our shell," LiuWei said as they both turned to run. The doors closed behind them, and they ran through the hall towards the nearest hatch. Adam hit the alarm, and they reached the security door just as they heard a loud pop.

"Breach!" The radio called out from where Adam had hooked it on his belt as he ran.

They shoved the hatch closed and turned the wheel to seal it up. He didn't want to think about how many other people might have been on the other side. The observation deck had been empty, but there were other offices and labs down there. He hoped because of the hour that they'd been empty.

Adam stood with his hands on the wheel, but LiuWei grabbed the radio from his belt. "The hatch has been closed. Adam and I both made it."

"Get up here," Lancaster said.

LiuWei put a hand on his shoulder, but before he could react, something ran into the other side of the door.

"Lancaster," Adam took the radio back as they ran. "Get everyone as deep as you can. It's trying to come through the door. We need to seal off everything we can just in case."

"Already working on it," she said.

A second later the emergency alarms went off, calling for everyone to head to the shelter. They ignored the order and returned to the monitoring room. "What's happening?" Adam asked.

"We're in the dark. We just don't know," Lancaster said. "The Pontus left the bay, but we lost contact almost as soon as it left."

"They're here!" LiuWei called out from the workstation he'd gone to when they entered.

"What?"

"Amphitrite and Nerites. Nerites is just at the limits of its vision, but Amphitrite can get us a visual."

"Put it on the screen," Lancaster said.

A second later the monitors were filled with the image LiuWei had been suggesting. On top of the pillar they had built their research station was a giant sea creature. Jelly-like sac and tentacles of a giant jellyfish, but around the rim were sea star-like arms. It was beautiful if it didn't have one arm and two tentacles jammed into their observation room, and the Pontus caught in one of its tentacles. The submersible was cracked in two.

"No," Lancaster whispered.

"It knows we're here," LiuWei said softly. "It's going to hunt us down."

"No," Campfield denied. "Just because it found the Pontus doesn't mean we can't get out with the Proteus."

"It broke the ship. Why do you think it decided to crack the windows of Poseidon?" LiuWei demanded. "It learned there is something edible inside our ships! It's going to hunt for food now."

Alarms went off in three sections and Campfield switched his workstation monitor to the cameras. "It's coming through," he said, his voice calmer than it had been since this began. "It's going to kill us all."

"Hell no," Adam said. "I'm not getting eaten by an overgrown mutant jellyfish sea star."

"We need to get to the secured area. When you sent the alarm, did you send the code to the president?" Adam asked.

Lancaster looked at him but shook her head. "No.

It's… It's too late."

"On it," LiuWei said before Adam even had to ask.

"You need my code," she protested.

"I'm the partner of the president's son," he snarked as his fingers moved over the keyboard, sending the message. "You think I don't have my own emergency code to get Adam to safety if anything happened?"

Adam would protest about his need to be taken to safety, but right now he was just grateful LiuWei had a code. He had his own as the president's son, and while he knew his father liked LiuWei, he hadn't known he'd given him that clearance.

"Let's go," LiuWei stood from the monitor and they all ran to the door.

"We can get to the Proteus and get as many people out as we can," Lancaster said.

"No, head to the deepest room and wait for help," LiuWei countered.

"This is my station," Lancaster snapped. "Follow orders or stay and die. We won't wait for you."

LiuWei pulled Adam to a stop, but Lancaster and Campfield kept running.

"LiuWei?"

"You saw the Pontus. Anyone in the Proteus is just going to be its next snack."

"What else can we do?"

"Hide, until it moves on. If we can get deep enough, I think we can outlast it. At least until your dad can get to us. I redirected Nerites and Amphitrite's video feeds to Dr Jackson. He'll help your dad find a way to get to you."

The alarm overhead changed and Adam cursed. "What the hell is she thinking?" he asked. They started to run then, but they could both hear the mechanics all around them. The lifeboats, submersibles that could fit up to six people, were being launched. They were intended to be a safety measure to help them escape in case of emergencies, but they were slow moving and not easily manoeuvrable.

"They'll die," Adam said softly. "Is she panicking?"

"Or making a diversion for the Proteus?" LiuWei asked.

"She wouldn't," Adam said. "She…no."

They ran on, trying to make it to the bay before anyone else took a lifeboat. It was too late though. The lifeboats were all gone, and the majority of the community had been loaded onto the Proteus.

"Get in here!" Campfield yelled.

Adam was torn, but LiuWei gripped his hand hard. "It's a death trap," he called back to them. "The president will send help. We can last it out in the emergency centre."

"We can't! Nothing is going to stop that thing!"

"Get in here, Danners! If Zian isn't coming, then leave him behind!" Lancaster tried again.

"Adam, please," LiuWei shook his head.

He looked at the others and he took a step back. He looked at LiuWei and nodded. "We'll wait it out. I trust you."

"There is no second chance!" Lancaster yelled.

"Campfield… Aaron. You can stay," LiuWei countered.

The doctor stood just behind Lancaster and he could see the indecision in his face. Lancaster didn't give him another choice though. She pushed him back into the ship and closed the door.

"Damn it!" LiuWei cursed. He didn't wait though. He pulled Adam towards the door. They had almost made it when there was a loud screech behind them. They both turned back in horror as a tentacle reached up through the water chamber and wrapped around the Proteus.

"Run," Adam nearly tripped as he ran into LiuWei. They both turned again and heard the metallic crash of the ship being destroyed. The sound of water crashed through the room and they ran faster, trying to get to the next safety hatch. They ran through and stopped to close the hatch before racing on again.

They ran until they reached the one room that had

been built in case of the utmost emergencies. There was no one else there, just the two of them. Everyone else had tried to escape through the lifeboats or the Proteus.

Over a hundred people, dead in a matter of minutes.

LiuWei closed the last hatch, a series of three that led into the innermost chamber. When he was done, he pulled Adam down onto the floor in the farthest corner from the door.

There was no noise from the station itself, but they could hear the groans of metal being put to too much strain. Of water rushing where there should be none.

There was nothing they could do. They would have died on the Proteus. They were probably going to die now…waiting for rescue that would take too long to come.

Adam let out a shaky breath and pulled his knees up to his chest. LiuWei sat at this side, and that was the only comfort he had. LiuWei had never broken a promise to him in all their long years together. This was the ultimate promise. He reached over and entwined his fingers through LiuWei's. He closed his eyes and waited.

***

"I thought I was going to die," Adam cried into the young man's shoulder. They had to be close to the same

age, but the other seemed so much braver.

"Of course not. I'll protect you," he said.

Adam looked up and the other smiled. "I'm LiuWei. You don't have to worry about anything."

Adam sniffed. "I'm Adam."

"I'll keep an eye out for you, Adam," LiuWei promised. "And I'll teach you to defend yourself."

"Yeah?" he liked the sound of that. He got teased sometimes, because his father was a politician. He wanted to be able to protect himself, even if he was only 6.

"Of course. We're best friends now. If we're going to have each other's backs, you have to learn how to protect me too."

"Yeah!" Adam cheered up at the thought.

"Good. Don't ever worry, okay. I'll always come get you. 'til death do us part. Like the adults say."

"That's marriage, silly."

LiuWei smiled. "It's a promise. We'll be together, Adam. Always. And even if it comes for us, we'll be together. We'll die together."

CHRIS BANNOR is a speculative fiction writer who lives in Southern California. Chris learned her love of genre stories from her mother at an early age and has never veered far from that path. Chris has been published in anthologies by Black Hare Press, Reanimated Writers Publishing, Blood Song Books, Iron Faerie Press, Zombie Pirate Publishing, EMerry Publishing, and Eerie River Publishing. Her stories range from horror and science fiction, to romance, fantasy, and steampunk. When Chris isn't writing, she enjoys movie marathons, binge-watching TV shows, musical theater, and road trips with her family. Otherwise, she is a general homebody who lives with her two teenagers, a cat, and a dog.

Bibliography

100 Word Zombie Bites: An Undead Anthology, Reanimated Writer's Press, 2019

APOCALYPSE, Black Hare Press, 2019

Bad Romance, Black Hare Press, 2020

Best of Iron Faerie Publishing 2019, Iron Faerie Publishing, 2020

BEYOND, Black Hare Press, 2019

Clockwork Dragons, Zombie Pirates Publishing, 2020

Dark Solstice, EMerry Publishing, 2020

Dark Valentine, EMerry Publishing, 2020

Drive, Eerie River Publishing, 2020

Fatal Faeries, Nocturnal Sirens Publishing, 2020

Forest of Fear, Blood Song Books, 2019

Forgotten Ones, Eerie River Press, 2020

HATE, Black Hare Press, 2020

Hawthorn & Ash, Iron Faerie Press, 2019

LOVE, Black Hare Press, 2020

OCEANS, Black Hare Press, 2020

Twenty Twenty, Black Hare Press, 2020

UNRAVEL, Black Hare Press, 2019

Connect

Website: www.chrisbannor.com

Facebook: www.facebook.com/chrisbannorauthor

They Watch, they whisper
By Joel R. Hunt

When a crew of infamous pirates find a slaughtered merchant vessel, they rejoice at the riches found within. Only their cabin-boy Ollie notices the dead men who watch them take it.

Ollie's oar cut through the water like a mortician's knife. He half expected the sea to bleed.

His was one of three pirate dinghies rowing across motionless waters towards an equally static merchant vessel. The night was clear, lit all around by a full moon that made the ocean gleam like a mirror, yet so far, it appeared that the dinghies had gone unnoticed. Ollie prayed it would remain that way. He had seen plenty of death in his two years at sea, but tonight was the first time he was expected to fight.

The first time he was expected to kill.

Captain Goldthumb, never one to shy away from danger, stood at the prow of the foremost dinghy, grappling hook in hand. His namesake glinted in the moonlight, a sharp jut of metal to replace the thumb he had lost years before. Whether that digit now rested in the belly of a kraken, a trophy case in the Tower of London, or the eye of his traitor father's skull, Ollie couldn't say. He'd heard each story sworn as honest fact, yet in two years of sailing with the captain, he'd never dared to ask the man himself.

Almost a dozen others sat dotted between the vessels, each one a killer, but only one struck as much fear in Ollie as Captain Goldthumb. Sat beside him on the dinghy's port side, Bart the Barber rowed in silence. Many in Goldthumb's crew killed for coin or for duty. Not Bart.

Bart killed for pleasure.

As if sensing his thoughts, the pirate glanced over.

"Nervous?" he growled.

Ollie shook his head, and Bart let out a humourless splinter of a laugh.

"Liar."

As the three dinghies came to rest beside the ship's starboard hull, Ollie slid his oar from the water, while Bart swapped his for a grappling hook. Across from them, Captain Goldthumb was swinging his own hook back and forth, feeling the weight of the thing, and the third dinghy's sole occupant, Big Jin, rose like a leviathan hefting a hook in each hand.

It all seemed too easy. Surely the crew wouldn't all be sleeping at the same time? Where were the lookouts?

Suppressing a shiver that had nothing to do with the cold, Ollie tugged on Bart's sleeve.

"What if it's a trap?" he whispered. The older pirate snarled and pushed him back.

All eyes were on the captain now, waiting for his signal. It came as a nod, almost imperceptible in the moonlight, and without a second's pause, four hooks sliced through the air. Each latched on to the bulwark above, cracks of thunder in a silent night. If the ship's occupants hadn't been aware of them before, those sounds were all the alarm that they needed. Captain Goldthumb was the first to begin the ascent, with Bart and the rest following his lead. They crawled up the hull like spiders, dirks already in hand as they spilled onto the deck and out of Ollie's sight.

Ollie tensed, waiting for the screams. He imagined

the crew, resting in their hammocks, waking to the pain of a dirk in their guts. He imagined them opening their eyes to Bart the Barber's wicked smile as he gave them the final shave of their lives. He imagined a cabin-boy, no older than himself, shivering in the bilge and praying not to be found by the killers invading his ship.

But there came no screams.

Instead, calm voices spoke back and forth. After a time, Stowaway Sally's face appeared over the bulwark.

"She's already been hit," the woman called down, "No souls as we can find. Raft up and come aboard."

A few years ago, Ollie might have rankled at being given orders by a woman, and an American at that, but he had since seen Sally's skill with a flintlock. Her late husband had seen it too, after raising his hand to her one too many times. Ollie had no intention of following him to the grave. Nodding back at Sally, he took one of the dangling ropes and fastened the dinghy tight. The older cabin-boy Peter did the same with the captain's dinghy, to which the third, now empty, had already been tethered. With the boats secured, Ollie heaved himself up and began to half-push, half-walk his way along the hull. His bare feet struggled to find purchase, and several times he slipped and cracked his knee against the wood, but he persevered, grateful that none of the other pirates were witnessing his struggles.

"Brace yourself," said Sally as he reached the top of the rope. Taking a deep breath, Ollie rose over the bulwark and took in the scene.

It almost knocked him back into the ocean.

A dozen dead men lay sprawled across the deck, alongside disembodied chunks that might belong to a dozen more. Some had been shot. Some cut open. Some, it seemed, had been beaten and chewed as if by a wild beast. Blades and guts and sightless eyes all glistened in the moonlight, and everywhere that Ollie looked was washed in blood. It lapped at the bodies like a crimson ocean, given new life by the ripples of the pirates' footsteps. The boards themselves were swollen with it. These dead men would forever be part of their ship.

Steeling himself, Ollie hopped over the bulwark and planted his feet in the blood. He had no wish to disrespect the dead, but anywhere he walked on this deck would be through what once was inside a living man.

"Boy!"

Ollie ran to Captain Goldthumb's side. The other pirates were disappearing below deck, no doubt searching for anything left behind by the monsters who had slaughtered this ship, but the captain remained on deck. He surveyed the faces of each dead man in turn, though his expression was as closed and cryptic as ever.

"Captain?" said Ollie. The captain rubbed the bridge

of his nose, then clapped a hand on Ollie's shoulder. The cold metal of his thumb dug in uncomfortably.

"Check for survivors," said Goldthumb, "and for valuables."

"Yessir," said Ollie, though he lingered by the captain's side as long as he dared. He was no stranger to picking pockets – indeed his skill in that endeavour had led him into Goldthumb's service in the first place – but weaving through the streets pilfering handkerchiefs felt a world away from stealing the last belongings of butchered men.

It was slow work, and Ollie had little enthusiasm for it. The eyes of each corpse lay wide open, so they seemed to be watching him as he pried open their cold fingers for rosaries and lockets, or dipped into their slack mouths to liberate golden teeth. Once, a small silver coin slipped through his fingers and landed in the pool of blood below, and Ollie glanced over his shoulders to check the captain wasn't looking before he left it there and moved on.

Yet, roaming from corpse to corpse, Ollie found himself increasingly unnerved by the state of the dead men. One was tied belly-first to the mast, with his head twisted around so his chin rested on his spine. Another had his torso split open just below his rips, and his own arm rested inside, clutching his heart. Another still had half a dozen dead rats stuffed in his gaping mouth, his throat bulging and ready to burst. These men hadn't just been killed. They had been defiled. There was evil at work here.

Ollie didn't want to see any more. He bundled up his meagre treasures and set off to find the captain.

"Oliver."

He stopped.

It came to him like a breeze on a windless night. Someone had whispered his name. Quiet enough that it might be his imagination, clear enough that it might have been spoken into his ear.

Ollie peered through the darkness, trying to make out any human shapes that looked to be alive. He found none. He was alone among the corpses.

"Oliver."

He spun, searching in every direction for the speaker.

"Is…is that you, Bart?" he asked. When he got no reply, he tried again; "Peter? Sally?"

"Oliver…"

It seemed to be coming from the stern of the ship, though that was as empty as all the rest. Ollie took a hesitant step forward. Paused. Listened. Took another step. Paused. Listened. As Ollie made his slow progress across the deck, the whispering became more regular, yet at the same time less distinct. It no longer sounded like his name. It sounded like a dying animal.

On the stern side of the mizzenmast, Ollie found his answer. A wheezing, wounded sailor was propped against the beam, clutching his breast pocket as if it were the only thing holding his body together. Blood poured from uncountable wounds, adding to the flood the man was sitting in. Watching it flow out like that, Ollie could have believed that this one sailor had coated the entire ship. Only his face had been spared from bloodshed, though it was disfigured by old war-wounds; half of the man's nose was missing, crumpled away into a mound of scars that clenched and twisted with each laboured breath.

"You're alive," Ollie said, giving voice to his own wonderment. The half-nosed man flinched and glared up with wild eyes. Fury fell away to confusion, and then to fear.

"It can't be…"—the man gasped—"You… you…"

"Calm down," said Ollie, alarmed by the man's fevered passion, "I ain't here to kill you or nothing like that."

But even as he was speaking, the fire in the half-nosed man's eyes flickered away. He let out a last, ragged breath, before settling back against the mizzenmast and moving no more.

Ollie had never watched someone die before. He didn't know what he should do. He thought of making a prayer to God, but he hadn't spoken to God since joining

Goldthumb's crew. It didn't seem right. Unsure of what else he could do, Ollie stood and was about to move on when, between the man's fingers, something glinted. He wasn't holding his chest, Ollie realised. He was clutching an amulet. Pressing it into his heart as though willing it to become a part of him. The chain was dangling down, caught up in his tattered shirt, and from the quality of the chain alone Ollie could tell the amulet was valuable. He crouched down and touched the man's hands. Still warm. It felt rotten to take it so soon after the poor sailor had died, but if Ollie waited much longer, those fingers would start to go stiff, and then he'd have a devil of a time getting it free.

He gave the half-nosed man a gentle shake, just to be sure.

"Mister? You're dead, ain't ya?"

Ollie took the lack of reply as all the permission he needed. He pried away the fingers and slipped the amulet into his own hands. It was warm to the touch. Perhaps not surprising given how tightly the half-nosed man had been clutching it, but it felt warmer even than his fingers. It was heavier than Ollie had expected from its size, too, although perhaps that was normal for more expensive jewellery.

It was a curious amulet, a disk of shining gold inlaid with a gemstone Ollie had never seen before; the thing was a deep blue-black shade, and it seemed to ripple and flow in the meagre light of the moon. In fact, no matter how still Ollie held the amulet, the colour of the gemstone never seemed to settle. Then Ollie noticed the writing carved along the golden rim. Strange letters that seemed at once both English and foreign. He turned the amulet over in his fingers, squinting hard at the words as his vision blurred.

He felt a certainty in his heart that if he could just make out what the amulet was telling him…

"Oliver."

Ollie looked up and screamed, collapsing backwards into the blood. The half-nosed man was sat inches from his face, mouth open, eyes accusing. He must have slumped forwards while Ollie wrestled the amulet from him.

In the dead man's glassy stare, Ollie watched his own panicked reflection.

"Boy?" came Goldthumb's voice from across the ship.

"Weren't nothing, Captain," Ollie called back. He picked himself up and stashed the amulet in his pocket, stuffing it deep beneath the bundle of other stolen items. The eyes of the half-nosed man didn't leave him, accusing in their stillness, but Ollie forced himself to step past the body and return to the others at the ship's centre.

He walked as fast as he dared over the slick, crimson boards, because whichever direction he looked, he saw the eyes of the dead. Each body he had stolen from, even those he would have sworn were lying face down as he rifled through their pockets, now appeared to be watching him as he passed. Ollie clamped his own eyes shut, yet still their wide, white eyes watched him through the black. From an eternity away, further than the stars and deeper than the ocean, they whispered to him.

"*Oliver… Oliver… Oliver…*"

"Ollie!"

He jolted awake just as he crashed into Captain Goldthumb, nearly knocking the man down. The captain clipped Ollie with a sharp backhand, the metal making his head ring.

"Watch your step, you clumsy oaf!" Goldthumb snapped.

Without a word, Ollie handed over his bundle, which the captain inspected with disinterest before pocketing. He didn't ask about the other item in Ollie's pocket, which suited the boy, who shrank back as Sally marched back onto the deck.

"Captain," she said. "The hold's full of cargo, as if she only set sail yesterday. And the cannons, they ain't been fired. Stacks of powder in the magazine, none been touched. If it were pirates what done this, there weren't no fight, and they didn't take nothing as we can tell."

"Strange," said Goldthumb. He turned to Ollie. "Find any survivors?"

"No Captain," said Ollie, "No survivors."

"Them who done this might've flown a British flag to get close," said Sally. Goldthumb shrugged. It was of no concern now.

"Take as much of the cargo as we can carry," he said. "Leave the powder. We've enough as it is."

The crew had been waiting for the order, and after it was given they wasted no time. Big Jin was the first to rise from the hold, carting a chest under each arm. The rest were hauled out with a pirate at each end, then eased onto the overburdened boats below. As Ollie watched the progress, he felt a presence over his shoulder, and clutched his pocket tight. The amulet was still there, heavy and warm.

"Quite a haul," Bart said through a razor grin. "Quite a haul."

Ollie nodded. He squeezed the reassuring weight of the amulet and didn't let go until Bart had moved on. When Peter called up that the dinghies would take no more, the pirates clambered back over the bulwark and down the ropes, leaving Ollie, Goldthumb and a few stragglers on board.

"*Señor Pólvora!*" cried the captain. A lanky, olive-skinned man sauntered across the deck.

"*Si, Capitán,*" Pólvora replied.

"If the Royal Navy find this ship, they'll come hunting for whoever did this. And I don't think they'll take my word on the matter. Safer for everyone to send her down to Davy Jones, eh?"

"Ah, *si Capitán*, for this they have left me much to play with," said Pólvora, "She will not go quietly, I fear."

"I expect nothing less from you. Just give us time to get to a safe distance."

The Spaniard made his way below deck as Ollie and the others returned to their dinghies. Being the last to clamber over the bulwark, Ollie was greeted with one last view of the crimson deck and its soulless inhabitants, with no living man in sight. Shards of ice pricked his spine as he spotted a dozen faces, mangled and torn, staring directly back at him.

"Oliver."

Ollie scrunched his eyes closed and climbed down the rope as fast as he dared. Once he was inside the dinghy, Goldthumb gave the order to cast off, and the two cabin-boys untied the ropes that bound them to the ship. Ollie's fingers were fumbling as he worked, and it took him longer than it should have done, but the crew were still revelling in their bounty and no one chastised his sloppiness. He took his seat in silence, tracing the weight of the amulet inside his clothes.

"Find anything good?" Bart asked as he plunged his oar into the water. Ollie forced himself to let go of his pocket and pick up his own oar.

"Not really," he mumbled.

The sea was just as motionless as when they had boarded, disrupted only by the stroke of the oars, but now a distant fog was closing in. Ollie could see it swirling and writhing, blown by a wind that didn't reach the ships. It reminded him of the gemstone in his amulet. He itched to see it again.

But not while the others were around.

After a minute of rowing, Pólvora appeared on the ship's deck. He dived into the sea, looking for all the world like a bird of prey swooping down for the kill, and then emerged to swim towards the dinghies. Goldthumb ordered Bart and Ollie to hold position so that they could pick the Spaniard up while the other dinghies returned to *The Silent Flight*.

"Good," said Bart. "We'll get to see the show."

"Are we far enough?" asked Sally, and Bart shrugged.

They didn't have to wait long. While Pólvora was still crawling through the water towards them, a deafening crack tore through the air, ringing Ollie's skull worse than any cannon he'd ever heard. The port side of the ship erupted in flame, hurling splintered wood a mile out to sea and sending a shockwave through the water. Ollie gripped the side of the dinghy to keep himself from falling overboard. Then the roar of the explosion was replaced by the groan of a thousand dying beasts as the deck fractured and the mast collapsed. Bodies were flung into the water before being quickly buried in shattered barrels and torn rigging and broken pieces of the ship.

A moment of silence followed, though perhaps there were noises Ollie missed under the powerful ringing in his ears, and it seemed that the vessel might stay afloat despite the damage. Then it lurched like a wounded animal and began its slow descent into the unfathomable depths below.

Bart gave a standing ovation, whooping and cheering at the night's sky, while Sally scanned the waters around them.

"Where's Pólvora?" she asked. "Did he get far enough from the blast?".

"*Si, si*, I am here," the man said, emerging by the dinghy's side. His face was wild and alive, and he was grinning almost as much as Bart as they pulled him aboard. The four of them watched for a while as the broken ship sank further below, with Pólvora narrating which section of the vessel was likely to collapse or break away next, but after a time, Bart lost his patience. He pushed an oar into Ollie's hands, and the two of them began to row back to *The Silent Flight.*

They had been rowing for a minute when they were interrupted by a sudden sound.

"Help!" came a cry from the wreckage, "Ollie, help me!"

Ollie jolted in his seat, standing and scanning the waters. He heard the splashing before he saw it – two desperate hands flailing as they struggled to stay afloat.

"Man overboard!" Ollie shouted.

"Where?" asked Bart, squinting through the dark. Ollie pointed at the splashing, alarmed to see it getting weaker with every passing second.

"There! Right there!"

The dinghy turned around and, led by Ollie's directions, rowed towards the sinking arms. By the time they were close enough, the man was face down in the water, unmoving. There was hope, though. Ollie had seen men brought back from drowning long after they fell still. He practically jumped over the side of the dinghy to grasp one arm, and Pólvora reached over for the other. Together they heaved the body aboard.

Ollie recognised that half-nose in an instant. He leapt back as if the man's skin was fire and clasped the amulet in his pocket with both hands. Not a second later, Sally gasped, and Bart swore under his breath. Pólvora had dragged the rest of the body on board. What little of it was left.

The explosion had torn the half-nosed man in two, splitting him from beneath one armpit down to his opposite hip.

Ollie shook his head.

"No…" he said. "I saw him… I *heard* him…"

Before he could say any more, a hand grasped Ollie's collar and another slammed into his jaw. Ollie doubled over, clutching his throbbing face. Bart dragged him close so that they were face-to-face, the older pirate's rank breath washing over Ollie.

"Stupid blight!" Bart snarled. "Wasting our time for a corpse, you mangy rat."

He raised his hand to strike again. Ollie flinched, but the blow didn't come. Bart's anger had washed away, and now the man was staring with a growing hunger at Ollie's pocket. At the amulet. Without thinking, Ollie moved to cover it, and at the same time Bart reached out with calloused fingers.

"Bart," Sally said. He blinked, and the hunger was gone, replaced by a deep, sharp frown.

"Throw that damned thing to the fish and let's be done with it," he snapped. He released Ollie and shook his head as Pólvora rolled the half-nosed man back into the sea. Without another word, they rowed back to *The*

Silent Flight, where the sounds of celebration were just beginning. The older pirates hoisted up the remaining chests as Ollie secured the dinghy to the ship, and then Bart and Pólvora clambered out.

As Ollie made to follow them, Sally rested a hand on his shoulder.

"I saw it too," she said. "The splashing."

"Did you hear him calling out?" Ollie asked. "Calling my name?"

She shook her head, but there was a softness in her eyes, a willingness to believe. Perhaps the man had still been alive and died from his wounds after that last surge of effort. It was hardly a comforting thought, but it made Ollie feel surer of his senses.

As Ollie clambered back onto the deck of *The Silent Flight*, his breath caught in his lungs. For the briefest moment, he saw the glassy eyes of a dozen dead men staring at him from across the deck. He blinked, rubbed his eyes, and the dead men transformed into Goldthumb's crew, watching him emerge onto the ship. Their gazes lingered uncomfortably, frozen in the middle of speaking and toasting one another. Ollie's hand dropped to his pocket, where he gripped his amulet. Some of the crew's eyes followed the motion. Then, one by one, they returned to life, turning from Ollie and back to their conversations as if he had never been of interest to them.

Ollie staggered across the deck, unsettled by the brief attention of the crew, and set off at a march towards the gun deck. He caught Bart watching him pass, and when Big Jin crossed his path, the giant man seemed to linger, his meaty fingers twitching. Ollie thrust both hands deep into his pockets, gripping the reassuring warmth of the amulet, and lowered his head in the hope that any further attention might slide right over him.

He heard the dead man's whisper again, *"Oliver."*

"What?" asked Peter, spinning to face Ollie.

"I ain't said nothing," Ollie mumbled, pushing past.

By the steps to the gun deck, Captain Goldthumb was speaking to Rangi, the tattooed navigator.

"The stars aren't right, Captain," the old man said, scowling upwards. "I've never seen these constellations before. It's as though something has draped over the sky…"

"Well, do what you can with it," Goldthumb said. "I want a course set before this fog catches up with us."

"Aye, sir."

That done, Goldthumb turned to address the rest of the crew. Ollie paused, inches from the steps.

"We've got richer tonight lads, and no mistake!" Goldthumb shouted, grinning at the cheers that answered him. "You know what comes next. The treasure's been pooled, and each of you gets a share. Let none say that

Goldthumb doesn't reward loyalty!"

The next cheer was followed by a press of bodies towards the hold. Ollie let himself be carried with the crowd, keeping a firm grasp on his pocket, until he was able to peel away unnoticed. He had no interest in the rest of the treasures they had stolen from the merchants. He had his reward already, and he didn't intend for it to fall into any other hands.

At the far stern of the gun deck was a scupper hole that had been blocked for as long as Ollie could remember. He crouched down out of sight and brought out the amulet. Even in the dingy light of the gun deck, its gold glimmered and its gem swirled. The warmth of it spread through Ollie's hands, clawed up his arms, flowed into his chest. The words along its edges begged to be read. The whispers demanded to be heard. If he could just spend a little longer clutching it to his heart, perhaps –

Footsteps from behind.

"Ollie?"

His heart jolted. As fast as he could, he dug his hands into the slop that clogged the scupper and pressed the amulet deep inside. Then he scraped the filth back over it and wiped his hands on his vest. It would be safe there.

Taking a deep breath, Ollie clung to the wall and crawled as close as he could to the nearest cannon, popping up there instead of above the scupper. A few yards away, Pólvora stopped in his tracks, his expression one of surprise and suspicion.

"Ah, *Señor Pólvora*," said Ollie with forced cheeriness. "I was just checking on things down here."

Pólvora looked him up and down.

"You are wanted by the *capitán*," he said.

"Right. I'll go, then," said Ollie. He waited for Pólvora to lead the way, but the man didn't move. Eventually, Ollie shuffled out from behind the cannon and made his own way across the gun deck. He felt Pólvora's eyes on his back the whole way.

Arriving at Goldthumb's cabin, Ollie knocked, surprised to have Peter open the door almost immediately. The other cabin-boy gestured for him to enter. Inside, Ollie found Captain Goldthumb sat on the far side of a long table with two places set for a meal. Knives and forks and silverware that Ollie couldn't even name covered the table, centred around a number of fresh and delicious plates that Peter was now setting out.

"Ollie," Goldthumb said with a smile. "Won't you join me for dinner? Please, take a seat."

Goldthumb had never invited Ollie to dinner before. There was something unsettling about it, though of course Goldthumb's practiced face revealed nothing of his intentions. Ollie lowered himself into the nearest chair, tensing for danger.

A rabbit sitting by the grinning face of a fox.

"Peter, some wine for our friend," said Goldthumb, and the older cabin-boy obeyed without a word. Ollie plucked at his pocket, missing the reassuring weight of the amulet, as Peter brought a bottle over to him and poured a generous glass. Goldthumb leaned on the table, dismissed Peter and helped himself to some fish.

"You liberated some nice items tonight," he said.

"Thank you, Captain," said Ollie.

"I was surprised that you weren't celebrating with the rest of the crew once you got back. We shared the spoils, like always. You missed out on that."

"Yes, Captain."

"You didn't want any of the treasure? Perhaps you feel rewarded enough, hm?"

Ollie opened his mouth to reply, but before he could speak, Goldthumb slammed his fist into the table.

"Stop that infernal whispering!"

Ollie flinched, drawing back in his chair.

"I weren't whispering, Captain," he said.

Goldthumb turned to Ollie as if he had only just noticed him. He cast a cautious eye around the room.

"Of course," mumbled the captain. "Of course…"

He delicately piled more food on his plate and gestured for Ollie to do the same. Then, after a single bite, Goldthumb steepled his fingers and continued.

"Some of the crew have been talking, Ollie. They think that it's not healthy for a—quiet, damn you!—a young deckswab such as yourself to be alone so much. You should be sticking with the rest of us, learning the trade, don't you agree?"

Ollie gaped. It was as though the captain were arguing with someone who wasn't there. Or who no one else could see...

"Ollie?"

"Oh. Yes, Captain. I agree, Captain."

"Good," said Goldthumb. "That's good. Life at sea is all about sharing, you know. We share our work. We share our knowledge. We share our treasure. It's important to me—I said quiet!—that my crew are all working together."

"Yes, Captain."

"Because that's where we all end up, you know. Together. Far, far below the ocean's waves. There's a great cave deeper than the world itself, and older than the stars. Every wreck and sunken sailor finds its way there. Such a wondrous place. And the people there, ah, such people! Thousands of them, gathered in that cave. Millions! They dance and twirl and writhe. They watch. They bloat."

"Yes, Captain."

Goldthumb stood, enraptured by his vision.

"I can send us there, boy," he breathed. "I can send us there tonight!"

A hand shot out, and with a clink of metal on metal, Goldthumb was suddenly holding a long, gleaming blade. Ollie jumped out of his chair, heart pounding, as the captain advanced around the table.

"Captain!" he said, raising his hands. "Please don't! Something's wrong, you ain't yourself!"

"All I need, Ollie,"—Goldthumb panted, prowling ever closer—"is what you stole from me!"

He raised the knife. Beyond the wall, someone yelled, and a moment later Peter burst through the door.

"Captain Goldthumb! Pólvora's turned mutinous! They caught him trying to scuttle us down in the magazine!"

Goldthumb's intensity dissipated in an instant. His face crumpled in on itself, from wide-eyed wonder to stoic pragmatism.

"Where is he?" the captain asked.

"On deck. They're holding him down and waiting for you, Captain."

Goldthumb nodded. He tossed aside his knife and marched out of the room without giving Ollie another glance. Ollie sank against the wall, trying to calm his pounding heart. Soon, however, his panic was replaced by a new fear. As Goldthumb strode up towards the deck, where Pólvora's deranged screams drowned out the heckles of his captors, Ollie ran instead to the gun deck, hopping down the steps three at a time and racing to the scupper. But he knew what he would find before he got there. He felt it deep in his heart, like part of his soul was missing.

The muck of the scupper had been clawed away, and Ollie's amulet was gone.

"*Oliver…*"

He didn't need to follow the whispers. He knew who was responsible.

By the time Ollie was back on the top deck, a crowd had gathered around the scene, and Ollie had to push his way to the front. Several men were holding Pólvora in place, standing him before the captain for judgement. The Spaniard was shirtless and wild, straining like a captured animal against the men holding his arms. Gunpowder coated his hands and flaked from his hair.

"*¡Tenemos que devolverlo!*" he cried at the sky. "*Tenemos que devolver el collar del diablo!*"

"Where is it?" Goldthumb snapped. "Where is the amulet?"

"*¡Es el collar del diablo! ¡Desde el profundo, desde el profundo! ¡Debemos devolverlo! ¡Todos debemos devolver al profundo! ¡El diablo tiene este barco y nos hace bailar! ¡Nos hará bailar, girar y hincharnos desde* *el profundo!*"

The words continued to pour from Pólvora's mouth without him taking a breath. To Ollie, who didn't speak a word of the language, it was meaningless. But there were other clues that Ollie could piece together. The amulet couldn't be being worn; Pólvora's chest was exposed and his leggings, thin and light, clearly weren't carrying the amulet's weight. Yet the man's lips, Ollie noticed, were bleeding, and his throat bruised. Ollie's eyes lingered on the man's stomach.

"It's…" Ollie started, before catching himself. Goldthumb turned and glared at Ollie. As he did, a sudden understanding lit his eyes like cannonfire. He drew out his dagger and gripped Pólvora's jaw.

"I'll have it back, you dog!"

Pólvora screamed as the knife plunged into his stomach. Again and again the captain sank his steel into the man's innards, turning and twisting the blade with each stab. Once Pólvora's stomach had been reduced to shredded rags, Goldthumb hurled the knife to the deck and stuck out his thumb. He pushed his hand inside, squirming and flexing, until deep within Pólvora's body, the clink of metal on metal could be heard. Ollie stepped forwards. At last, with a sickening squelch, Goldthumb pulled the amulet free. It dripped with viscera, yet the gemstone remained clean. Pólvora's writhing body collapsed to the floor as the captain turned to his crew, face ablaze with victory.

"It's mine, you whispering devils!" he screeched, "The amulet belongs to me! If any of you tries to take it, I'll split you open and let the buzzards have you!"

Goldthumb looked to each of them in turn, prowling from side to side, daring any challengers to approach. No one moved. No one spoke. Not even when they saw Big Jin lumber up from below deck and stride over. The captain sensed rather than saw him, and turned already mid-rebuke.

Big Jin didn't wait for a word to leave Goldthumb's mouth. He raised the cannonball that he had tucked into his monstrous hand and brought it around in a wide arc. It hit Goldthumb's head with the force of a tidal wave. The captain's skull crumpled. His body sprawled like a discarded rag doll. From his twitching fingers, the amulet hurtled and bounced once – twice – across the boards, coming to rest by the taffrail.

The crew took a collective breath.

Then the butchery began. The pirates fell on one another in a fury, cutting and punching and firing their way through the crowd to get closer to the amulet. Only Ollie wasn't fighting. He ducked and weaved between the melee, dodging blades and using his small stature to his advantage. He approached the amulet almost unnoticed, reaching out to pluck it from the boards.

His fingers closed on empty air. He didn't see who snatched up the amulet, being knocked to the deck by their fist and landing heavily. Before he had time to stand, a shot rang out, and the thief collapsed next to him.

"It's mine!" Sally screamed.

But she needed to reload. Moving on instinct alone, Ollie grasped the amulet from the dead man's fingers and bolted across the deck. Everywhere he ran, eyes snapped to him, as though he were calling out for their attention.

"The boy has it!" someone shouted, and the crew turned as one to face him. Ollie kept running. Another shot punched through the air, and splinters rained down where the bullet embedded itself inches from his head.

"*Oliver.*"

Reaching the doorway, Ollie leapt from the deck to the bottom of the steps in a single bound, falling into a painful roll but managing to scramble upright. A door opened ahead, and Peter's face peered out.

"In here!" he called.

Ollie slipped through the gap and slammed the door closed behind him. He and Peter held their breaths as footsteps charged past, shaking the floorboards. On the deck above, a scream was cut short. Peter wedged the door closed with a piece of wood and the two boys sat against it.

They waited for some time, listening to the sounds of violence from above and below. Once, someone tried to force their way through the door, but a shot rang out and a heavy body slumped to the ground.

"They've all lost their minds," Ollie whispered.

"They have," said Peter, "but not us."

Ollie frowned. There was an intensity to Peter's expression that made his neck prickle. He gripped the amulet tight.

"No," he said slowly. "Not us."

"I can't hear screams anymore," said Peter, "I think they might all be dead. Just us left. So… there's no harm in…showing me…"

Ollie shuffled so that his pocket was further from Peter's fingers, but the boy lashed out a hand and gripped Ollie's wrist.

"Let go!" Ollie cried, squirming to get free. Peter grabbed Ollie's collar and pulled him closer. His eyes were ablaze.

"It whispers to me!" he said. "I hear it! I hear it in you! Show me the amulet! Give it to me!"

Ollie swung his free arm and smashed Peter's head against the door. The boy crumpled with a groan. Ollie hopped over his body and wrenched the wood free from the door. He burst through and slammed it behind him. His first instinct was to flee further into the bowels of the ship, but he heard movement there and decided to head up.

An oppressive silence gripped the deck. In all directions, bodies lay sprawled where they had been cut down, with their stomachs opened and their limbs impossibly angled. Dead eyes glistened in the moonlight and seemed to follow Ollie as he scrambled along the slick boards. A lone figure stood ahead. Ollie crouched to the side, hoping to remain unnoticed, but the man's attention wasn't on him. He was facing away, hands loose and empty by his sides.

Through the dark and the thickening fog, Ollie recognised the frailty of the figure's shape. It was Rangi, the tattooed navigator. He didn't seem to be a threat, perhaps couldn't be if he tried, but Ollie had to be sure. He crept nearer. Soon, he was mere yards away, approaching the man from behind. If Rangi knew he was there, the old man didn't show it. He rambled to the sky, as though the moon herself was listening.

"Do you see?" he wheezed. "How they dance among the black. They hide their true selves, slink against the darkness, knowing we won't find them. But they've always been there. They will always be there. Watching us. Whispering their names. Listen. Listen to the light from the moon. Do you hear them?"

Step by silent step, Ollie made his way around Rangi.

There was a pool of blood by the man's feet, shimmering in the moonlight, but whether it was his or belonged to another, Ollie couldn't tell. It was only when he reached the man's front that it became clear. A cold dread filled Ollie's soul, and not even the warmth of the amulet could banish it. Sensing him for the first time, Rangi's head snapped down like a marionette cut loose. Crimson tearstains drenched his cheeks, and his empty sockets locked onto Ollie.

"Do you see?" the blind man hissed.

Ollie stumbled back and crashed onto the deck. He gripped his amulet tighter.

"Get away from me!" he cried.

"They dance around the stars," the man went on, "Twirl around the moon. But never cross it, for then we would see them. We would know of their presence, writhing against the black. They do not let us witness. But they are there. They have always been there. Watching even now. Do you see them?"

"Shut up!" Ollie screamed.

"Do you see? How they twirl and dance and—"

Rangi's voice gurgled into silence as a blade sank into his neck. The old man didn't even flinch. Blood poured from his opened throat, yet as the last of the colour drained from his tattooed face, his eyeless stare never left Ollie.

His lips never stopped moving.

Do you see? they asked in silence, *Do you see?*

Bart pushed the dying man aside and thrust his dirk towards Ollie. His face was split by a dagger-like grin, but his eyes held only hate.

"Gimme that amulet, you little wretch," he spat. "Throw it over and I'll gut you fast. Don't make me wait."

"Don't take another step," Ollie said, pushing himself up on shaking feet. "I'm warning you!"

Bart laughed. His chest heaved and the sound echoed out, harsh and joyless, until it seemed to Ollie that every corpse on the ship was laughing along too. Bart waved his dirk and took an exaggerated step.

"Missed your chance," he said. "Now I'll gut you slow. Real slow."

He lunged. His wild swing tore through Ollie's vest, narrowly missing the boy's skin. Ollie jumped to the side, scrambling under some rigging and trying to put as much distance between himself and Bart as he could. The man was fast, though, and used to chasing down quarry. As Ollie rounded the mast, Bart was already waiting for him, and only an urgent change of direction saved him from another swing of that deadly blade.

He leapt over Stowaway Sally's corpse, ignoring her glassy eyes as they followed him.

"Oliver."

"Shut up!" he cried.

Seeing barrels ahead, Ollie scampered over to them, hoping to get behind before Bart could spot him. The sharp laugh that trickled after his footsteps told him that it was already too late. Bart was close. Ollie span, glancing in every direction, trying to spot the pirate in the dark. He couldn't see a single living soul.

This was his chance. While Bart was hiding, Ollie could find a weapon and protect the amulet. Scouring the deck, his gaze fell on Sally, her trusty flintlock in hand. One shot from that, and Bart would be a dead man. Ollie ran over and began to wrestle it from Sally's cold fingers. It was almost free when the slightest creak sounded from behind.

"Gotcha!"

Ollie leapt back. His leg caught on Sally's corpse, and he crashed down beside her. Bart's dirk swung where the boy's neck had been moments before. Desperately, Ollie tried to untangle his limbs from the stiff body, but Bart was too fast. With a snarl, he sank his blade through Ollie's foot, and the boy screamed. The next thrust brought the dirk into his gut, where Bart let it rest.

"It don't belong to you," he whispered, gripping Ollie's jaw and pushing it up to expose his neck. "It calls out to me. Whispers my name. An' when I slit your wretched throat, you will too!"

As Bart pulled his dirk from Ollie's stomach and pressed it against his neck, Ollie flung out his arms. The amulet in his fist crunched against Bart's nose. Hot blood poured across Ollie's fingers. Bart's dirk hit the boards with a dull clatter as the man reeled back, swearing. Without thinking, Ollie grasped for it. Lifted it. Lunged.

It slid into Bart's neck as though returning to its sheath. The man's eyes shot wide open, his lips trembled, and his hands batted weakly at Ollie. He swayed from side to side, as though trying to pull himself from the blade, and then he let out a single rasping breath.

"Oliver."

He collapsed.

Ollie dropped the blade and scrambled back, ignoring the pain and the blood streaming from his stomach. He curled around the amulet, cradling it like a newborn, and stroked its warm, crimson surface. All the dead men would be watching him, he knew. Let them watch. They would see that the amulet was his. His and no one else's.

For aeons he lay there, listening to the whispers of the corpses. The whispers from the deep. There was no other sound.

Not until a cry came from the sea. At first, Ollie thought they had finally come for him, to take him to the caves that Captain Goldthumb had spoken of, where he could dance with his amulet for eternity. But then he heard voices. Footsteps. These were living men, and they had come for his amulet. Ollie curled around it as tightly as he could, pressing it into his chest.

"Boy?"

A hand gripped Ollie's shoulder, and he was rolled onto his back.

"Don't fear, boy," said the man. "We're not here to hurt you. We have a doctor on board. Come with us and we'll get you patched up."

Ollie peered at the stranger through bleary eyes. As the man's features became clear, Ollie shrunk back, clutching the amulet to his heart, horror carved into his face.

"You're… you're dead!" he croaked, crawling away on shaking limbs.

The man before him frowned, wrinkles appearing around his half-nose. He matched Ollie's slow retreat, step for step, and reached out with an open palm. He looked about to speak, until his eyes drifted down to Ollie's amulet and lingered. A dry tongue ran along the half-nosed man's lips.

"What do you have there, boy?" he whispered.

Ollie's fingers tightened. The metal bit into his skin, blood seeping from his clenched fist. It was warm and heavy in his hand, and he would no sooner relinquish it than he would his own beating heart.

"I think you should…hand that over," breathed the half-nosed man, eyes dancing like a devil in the night. "I'll keep it safe for you."

"You're dead…" Ollie rasped again.

The half-nosed man lunged for the amulet, cracking Ollie's head against the deck as he fell upon the boy. Ollie's tried to resist, but a weakness was overcoming his muscles. The half-nosed man forced Ollie's arm against the creaking planks until it stopped pushing back and clamped the boy's mouth shut. Ollie writhed once. Twice. Then fell still.

By the time a voice called out through the darkness, he was certain.

"No life below deck. Find any survivors up here?"

The half-nosed man gently released his grip. Then, with due reverence, he closed Ollie's eyelids and drew back.

"Not a soul," he said.

Footsteps announced the approach of the second sailor.

"Let's not linger, then. I'd bet a month's wages this forsaken vessel is cursed."

"I dare say you're right," said the half-nosed man.

Slipping the reassuring weight of the amulet into his breast pocket, he followed his shipmate to the bulwark, grasped the ropes they had tied there and clambered back to their boat. Together, the men sank silent oars into an unmoving ocean and rowed away into the night.

JOEL R. HUNT is a writer, proof-reader, ex-teacher and part-time human currently residing in the UK. Among his other hobbies of eating, breathing and crouching in dark corners, Joel constantly plans stories and screenplays - a very small number of which actually get written. Most simply languish in his ever-growing 'Unfinished' folder, which is now approaching a mass capable of generating gravitational pull.

Joel's genres of choice are horror and sci-fi, although the odd bit of sentiment does manage to sneak in between the freakishness and disturbing twists. He hopes in time that he might earn a living from putting words on a dead tree in a particular order, or at least earn enough for the occasional cup of tea and vegetarian full English breakfast.

He also wants some pet rats, but that's neither here nor there...

Bibliography
ANGELS, Black Hare Press, 2019
BEYOND, Black Hare Press, 2019
Deep Space, Black Hare Press, 2019
MONSTERS, Black Hare Press, 2019
Objection to Perfection, The Gentleman Press, 2012
Sirens at Midnight, NBH Publishing, 2019
Sweek Flash Fiction Book (Part 3), Sweek Publishing, 2019
Sweek Flash Fiction Book (Part 4), Sweek Publishing, 2019
Sweekstars 2018, Sweek Publishing, 2018
WORLDS, Black Hare Press, 2019

Connect
Twitter: @JoelRHunt1
Reddit: JRHEvilInc
Amazon: amazon.com/-/e/B07SBX6G3W
Goodreads: goodreads.com/author/show/6439719.Joel_Hunt

Torsaaker's Reef

By Jonathan Inbody

When the aging submarine HMS *Hope* sinks to the ocean floor after a mysterious collision, the crew will discover there are worse things out in the black water than they could have ever imagined...

I: Scuttled

I never liked the water, but after the Great War I learned to resent the land. Worse than either was the mix of the two; the mud, where countless men fought and died like rabid animals in shallow trenches. Germans, Brits, the French, it made no difference; an entire generation of God's favoured sons had been abandoned to a muddy hell, where they drowned in their own blood and choked on gaseous death. I saw men ripped open, holding in their innards like scarecrows losing their stuffing, men gone blind from mustard gas crawling in twisted heaps through fields of barbed wire, men desperately running into No-man's-land with a wild-eyed longing for the release of death. With each lost friend or putrefying enemy corpse I watched with hollow eyes, the hatred for man's world simmering in my heart grew hotter. I yearned for solitude, isolation, freedom from the industrial depravity spreading across Europe. That was how I came to be stationed on the *HMS Hope*.

We were all of us wartime survivors, physically whole but spiritually mangled aboard a ramshackle submarine; mindlessly performing our duties as ghosts aboard the Flying Dutchman of the modern age. Captain Frakes was the best of us, and the one of us who had seen the worst. As a commanding officer his missing leg hardly mattered, and with the able-bodied Lieutenant Valerian at his side it mattered even less. Frakes was respected by the men, loved and fearfully obeyed like a father who was unafraid to loosen his belt. Valerian was young and thin, an officer borne of officers who had never seen the devastation of total war. He was somehow still truly alive, a believer in a loving God and a purposeful universe. For the rest of us, with the lone exception of Chaplin Marsh, hope was only a thing to have ripped away by the end of a bayonet. God had died with us in that trench, drowned in mud and blood and the acrid stench of gunpowder.

The *HMS Hope* had once been one of under a dozen, the experimental R-Class flagship of a slowly expanding fleet of submarine hunter-killers. But now the world was changing. There had been uprisings and unrest in South Africa, Egypt, even Ireland, and in the aftermath of a worldwide war Britain had lost a step. The *Hope* was now a barely functional relic, one of an underfunded fleet endlessly patrolling the oceans as a token attempt to trick the world into believing in our rapidly fading power, and the men that crewed her knew it. We were misanthropes, exiles; lost souls left to dwell beneath the world's surface waiting for an enemy that would never arrive. The world had left us behind, and we were content to wander aimlessly beneath its depths.

I awoke one morning to the sound of the engines, rumbling gently through the steel walls as I slowly rolled out of my cot and dressed. What day was it? The month was October, that much I knew, but as each day slid into the next with alarming malaise, I learned that keeping track of the date was a fool's errand. We were making a wide arc through the Pacific between the Pitcairn Islands and the west coast of South America, patrolling broadly as we waited for the change of seasons. Frakes spent most of each day locked in his quarters, acknowledging his redundancy at the same time as he mourned it. Valerian handled most of the *Hope*'s daily operations, delivering the same instructions to the officers on the bridge every day and instructing Barca what food to prepare for the crew.

I passed Valerian in the cramped corridor and gave him a casual nod, which he returned with a faint smile. The formalities of rank had fallen away slowly at first, then collapsed all at once, and by now hardly anyone even kept up appearances. Valerian and I were the only officers who took tea with the men, and despite his lack of experience he was liked well-enough. Most of the officers regarded him as an exasperatingly well-intentioned younger brother, and I was afraid that in the social hierarchy I was thought of as something of a distant uncle.

Doctor Copeland stepped to the side of the thin corridor to let me pass, pressing himself against the metal wall. "Good morning, Miller. How did you sleep?"

"Terrible," I replied gruffly, stepping past him and ducking into the mess hall.

Inside, Chaplin Marsh sat alone at a table with his

hands folded, whispering a quiet prayer. At the table next to him, the lanky Peltz and broad-shouldered Garrity played cards, glancing over at where Barca was finishing up breakfast in the kitchen. I patted Marsh's shoulder as he finished his prayer, then walked over and sat down next to Garrity and Peltz.

"Ensign Miller," Peltz said with an acknowledging nod, flaring his hand of cards out so I could see what he was working with.

Garrity leaned back in his seat and hid his cards, then looked back towards the kitchen. "We're getting hungry out here, Barca!"

Barca stepped out of the kitchen with two metal plates and walked over to the table, where he placed them down in front of Peltz and Garrity. Bacon and scrambled eggs; thank God for homestyle cooking.

"You hungry, Miller?" Barca asked, starting back towards the kitchen.

"For your cooking?" I called after him. "Always."

Garrity looked down at his plate. "What? Are we rationing bacon?" He pushed his chair out from the table and headed for the kitchen, passing Barca as he returned with my breakfast.

"Careful!" Barca yelled back to him. Garrity waved him off, pushing aside the swinging door as he disappeared into the kitchen. As the door swung closed, I could hear the bubbling of hot grease. My nostrils filled with the smell of cooking bacon, and I smiled as Barca slid the plate over to me.

"You spoil us, Manuel," I said with a smile, stabbing a piece of bacon with my fork.

"I do my best!" He replied cheerfully.

Peltz nudged my shoulder. "Hey, while Garrity's in the kitchen, would you mind showing me his cards?"

I smiled and shook my head. "A gentleman never cheats."

He chuckled. "Who the hell accused me of being a gentleman?"

The sub suddenly lurched violently to the side, jarring us out of our chairs and sending us sprawling to the metal floor. I looked over at my upturned plate of breakfast and sighed, then looked over at where Peltz had landed face-first next to me.

A bloodcurdling scream came from the kitchen. Barca pulled himself up to the kitchen counter as Garrity stumbled out of the swinging door and into the mess hall, clutching his face with both hands. Hot grease was spilling down the front of his shirt, and as he screamed again, the smell of burning flesh returned to my nose.

Steam rose off of his face and hands in a small cloud as he threw himself to the floor, scratching at his face in an attempt to remove the burning grease covering it. His fingers were coming away with strips of sizzling flesh as his eyes darted back and forth in panicked anguish, watching as we stood frozen all around him.

"Mr Barca! Bring water!" Marsh yelled, breaking the stunned silence of the room. He rushed over to Garrity's side with a towel, then pulled Garrity's burning hands away from his face and began to wipe his face.

I turned and saw Valerian run past the door to the mess hall, rushing forward to the bridge to find out what had caused the jarring stop. I would be needed, too.

"Take Garrity down to sickbay!" I barked at Peltz as I ran to the door. "I have to find out what's going on!"

"What do you want me to do?" Marsh asked.

"Say a prayer."

Peltz pulled Garrity up to his feet, then slung an injured arm over his shoulder and began to walk him towards the door. I turned and ran down the hall after Valerian, dodging around a few fallen crewmen in the middle of regaining their bearings.

The inter-sub communication speaker buzzed to life. It was Frakes. "All crew, brace for impact!"

I clutched a nearby beam. A loud scraping rose from underneath us and the sub lurched violently backward, almost pulling me off my feet despite my handhold. In the corridor ahead of me, Valerian fell forward to the ground, caught himself with both hands, then righted himself and continued running. The spry bastard: I was almost jealous.

I started cautiously forward as the scraping underneath us slowed to a stop, then ran down the corridor and emerged into the bridge. There, Frakes and the navigation crew were recovering from the crash, pulling together scattered charts and fallen equipment.

Valerian retrieved Frakes' crutch from the ground and handed it to him, steadying him with one arm as the Captain regained balance on his lone leg.

"What happened?" I asked, pushing past two navigators as I approached the Captain.

"We were climbing to get above a reef and something snagged the propeller," Frakes replied, straightening his hat. "We've run aground."

"*Run aground*? Where?"

"The ocean floor," he said grimly. "We've hit bottom."

Valerian and I exchanged a worried look as Frakes hobbled towards the navigation crew. "Bellman, what's our status?"

"We have power, but no propulsion," the nervous man replied, tossing aside a pair of broken glasses. "We're dead in the water, at least until we can fix the propeller and some of the underside damage."

Frakes put a strong hand on the man's collar. "I'll

say when we're dead. Where are the divers?"

"Peltz was just in Mess," I offered. "Should I get him?"

Frakes nodded. "And fetch Garrity for the comms. We need to get in touch with the rest of the fleet."

"Garrity was injured," I replied. "Splashed with hot grease after the first upset."

"What about the other comms officer?" Valerian asked from nearby.

"We're short one," Frakes bitterly corrected him. "Garrity works alone."

By the time I reached the back of the sub, Peltz was putting on his diving suit. He fastened a pair of clasps on his sleeves, then moved up to his shoulders. "What's the damage, Miller?"

"Propeller maybe. Could be more."

He swore under his breath. "Why couldn't we have crashed *after* breakfast?"

I handed him his diving helmet, and he put it on then motioned for me to fasten it into place. As I snapped the bolts into place and pulled tight the restraints, Chaplin Marsh stepped into the corridor. His face was chalk white, and his eyes were filled with a familiar emptiness. Whatever state Garrity was in, it was grave.

"Are you alright, Marsh?"

He slowly shook his head. "Strips of flesh…curling

up and falling off. It smelled just like the bacon…*it made my mouth water*."

"You've seen worse, Marsh," I said firmly. "We've all seen worse. Keep it together; the men are going to need you for morale."

The Chaplin nodded, then stumbled past me as I finished securing Peltz's diving helmet into place. "You're ready to go."

Peltz reached up with one gloved hand and opened the circular glass panel at the front of his helmet. "Hell of a morning, huh?"

I nodded. "Hell of a morning."

A few minutes later, Valerian and I stood on the other side of the airlock door, waiting for Peltz to return from outside. Valerian glanced quickly around for any lingering enlisted men, then looked at me with visible worry. "You've been in bad situations before. What do you think our chances are?"

"Our *chances*?" I replied with wry bemusement. "We're stuck on the bottom in the middle of the ocean and our only comms officer took a shower in hot grease this morning; what do you think our chances are?"

"I'm being serious."

"So am I," I replied flatly. "If everyone keeps their heads, and if someone can use the radio, *and* if there's another sub close enough to us, we may be alright. But if we can't get in touch with anyone, or if no one is close enough…"

Valerian swallowed nervously. "Why are you so damn calm?"

I cast him a sidelong look. "I've seen enough death to know panicking won't keep it away."

I left him to wait for Peltz and headed back towards the bridge. I needed to talk to Frakes; it wasn't like him to be so hands off in an emergency. Valerian was already cracking, and we would need more than any information Peltz could give us from his underwater walkabout. We needed leadership, the kind only Frakes had the gravitas to give.

I stepped into the bridge to see the Captain leaning forward on a table with both hands, silently staring out the glass panel into the black ocean ahead of us. "How are you feeling, Captain?"

Frakes turned his head to glance at me, then looked back at the viewing panel. "Something to say, Ensign Miller?"

"The men are nervous, sir. Valerian more than most. We need you."

He sighed heavily. "That pistol you carry, do you have it on you?"

I nodded, patting the hidden holster under my armpit. "Do you think we'll need it?"

Frakes smiled faintly. "Can you hear it, Miller?"

"Sir?"

"Listen."

A soft creaking moved across the top of the sub towards the back of the bridge. It seemed intentional, somehow, a series of regular pushes and knocks as if something outside was checking for structural weaknesses, moving from one end of the ship to the other.

"There are men outside," he said quietly, holding intense eye contact with me. "They're trying to get in."

I frowned. "*Men*, sir?"

"Can't you hear them?" Frakes asked, putting a hand on his holstered sidearm. "They're whispering out there, chattering back and forth in a hundred languages."

I shifted uncomfortably. "Captain, I really don't think-"

CRACK! The ship's hull above us crumpled and broke inward, pouring tons of black water into the bridge. The raging current swept me off my feet and roughly slammed me into a navigation table. As I struggled to pull myself back to my feet, I looked over to check on the Captain. The water had pushed him back into his chair, where he sat staring at me.

Frakes smiled wearily and gave me a mock salute, then drew his sidearm and shot himself in the head.

II: Pressure

"We're taking on water!" I yelled as I sloshed out of the bridge and into the corridor. "Everyone to the back of the sub!"

Another loud crack echoed through the sub as a stretch of hull to my left broke inward. Water streamed in as if fired out of a cannon, hammering a sailor into the metal wall and knocking him immediately unconscious. I barked unheard orders at another crewman, straining to scream over the racing water, then turned to look down the corridor behind me. A pair of sailors stumbled through the knee-deep water, pulling themselves forward on any sturdy piece of metal they could find. A third leak sprang behind them, rocketing freezing water into their backs and knocking them forward to their knees.

I rushed down the corridor and grabbed one man's hand, then pulled him to his feet and reached for his companion. I took hold of a limp hand and pulled the man's head to the water's surface. His eyes were closed and his mouth was hanging open as a cloud of blood spread in the water around his half-smashed head, and as I let go of him, I couldn't help but wonder if he wasn't one of the lucky ones.

A limp figure in a diving suit slid into the sub through one of the leaks and roughly crashed into the metal wall. *Peltz!* He must have been pulled in from outside. I waded over to him and grabbed him with both hands, then began to drag him through the water towards the bulkhead door. If I could just get to the other side, if we could only force the door closed… Peltz woke with a start and began to thrash, swatting at my arms with his gloved hands. I tore his helmet off and tossed it aside, then grabbed him by the collar with one hand and slapped him with the other.

He stared up at me, pale-faced and wild-eyed, his voice shaking as he began to speak. "It's a graveyard out there; a hundred sunken ships, scattered across the ocean floor! And the reef, tangled all around them… I could hear it *talking*!"

"Peltz! Snap out of it! We have to move!"

He reached up and clutched my shirt with a shaking hand, then pulled me closer and harshly whispered. "We're in Hell, Miller. *We're already dead!*"

A long, rust-coloured shape slithered into the sub through the rushing torrent of dark water, coiling and writhing as it moved through the water towards us at an alarming clip. It wound around Peltz's leg at lightning speed, then tightened its grip like a constrictor around prey, sending a loud snap echoing through the corridor as it shattered his bones.

Peltz screamed and clutched at my shirt, shaking his

mangled leg in a desperate attempt to free it. The spindly tentacle wound further up his waist and emerged from the rising water. It had the texture of sponge-like coral, but with a disturbingly fleshy colouration. It was covered in tiny, red-flecked holes, and as the end of the strange tentacle reached up for Peltz's uncovered face, I stumbled backward in horrified shock. The porous tentacle was split into five prongs at the tip, each reaching out like an independent finger of an unearthly grasping hand.

The fleshy-coral hand grabbed at the front of Peltz's face, digging its spindly fingers into and through his flesh, breaking through the front of his skull and caving it in. His screams turned to wet gurgles as the monstrous hand pulled out the mashed pile of skin, bone, and grey matter and tossed it aside into the water. It found a handhold at the caved-in hole that had once been his upper jaw, then grasped it tightly and began to drag him down into the rising black water.

Peltz reached out for my hand as I watched in horrified awe. His twitching hand pawed at mine, then went limp and fell into the water beside me with a dull splash. Under the water, I watched as the bulk of the coiled tentacle wrapped itself fully around his body, then tightened again. I could hear the dull snaps and cracks of his bones above the sound of rushing water, and I finally regained control over my faculties just as the fell tentacle pulled him fully beneath the black water's surface and quickly dragged him out of sight.

I whirled to look at the bulkhead where a sailor was struggling to close the door as black water rushed into the next section of the sub. I called out to him desperately and began to pull myself through the water towards where he stood white-knuckle-clutching the door. I was shaking, less from the freezing water than from mortal fear, and with each second of desperate struggle against the rising water came another pang of terror at the thought of another tentacle lurking in the water around me.

The sailor at the bulkhead pulled me through the half-closed door and went back to pushing. Behind the door were two more men, and with all four of us pushing we finally managed to hold the door shut. I spun the wheel handle and sealed the door, then took a step back. I could hear the water rushing against the other side, but for now it seemed likely to hold.

Someone screamed from the other side of the door, pounding their fists against the metal as they begged us to let them in. I looked at the nearest sailor and shook my head. Even if we could get it open, there was no knowing if we could close it again.

The pounding on the door suddenly stopped, and I hoped that meant the man on the other side was dead. The alternative was too bleak to even consider, but I knew the thought would be back to haunt me the next time I laid down to sleep.

I led the sailors to the mess hall and collapsed into a chair, catching my breath as I looked around for familiar faces. Doctor Copeland ran back and forth between injured sailors, quickly bandaging open wounds and checking for concussions. There had been less than thirty of us onboard, but now the group of survivors couldn't have numbered more than fifteen.

Valerian and Chaplin Marsh walked through the door, holding up the bandaged Garrity between them.

"We've lost the bridge," I said shakily. "And the captain. Peltz too."

"Then we've lost the radios," Marsh said quietly.

I shook my head. "Garrity's cabin has the backup equipment. Is he conscious?"

"Barely," Marsh replied. "Copeland's got him on something for the pain, and even when he's awake enough to talk all he does is scream."

Valerian looked around the mess hall at the scattered survivors as the colour drained from his face, then looked back at me. "What happened on the bridge, Miller?"

I chuckled darkly. "Well, let's run through it, shall we? Frakes shot himself, the bridge is under water, and we had to seal the bulkhead even though I knew there were men alive on the other side."

He stared at me wide-eyed.

I let out an exasperated sigh. "It had to be done, or we'd be swimming right now."

"You murdered them," Valerian said, his voice quivering with fear and anger.

"I saved everyone else," I replied flatly. "It's *triage*. You'd know that if you'd been to war."

He fell silent, letting me catch my breath as he went to check with Copeland. Marsh laid Garrity on the cold floor beside me, draping his coat over his chest as he whispered a prayer. Across the room, Barca was passing out small tin cups of water to the survivors.

Soft creaks spread across the metal ceiling above us, and the mess hall fell silent. The grasping tendril that took Peltz was still out there, and I knew it wasn't alone. How many of them were out there in the black water, testing the *Hope* for weaknesses so that they could peel it open like a tin can and feed on the helpless meat inside? No, not *feed*; it hadn't devoured Peltz, only crushed him. What did it want?

A worse thought crossed my mind, and I tried desperately to stifle it. But it kept rising, smashing itself against my battered senses until it was the only thought I had left. *What was the grasping thing attached to?*

Valerian's eyes met mine from across the room. Things were dire, and if we didn't keep control, they were bound to get worse. The men were restless, injured, frightened; it wouldn't take much to turn them from fear to anger. I idly wondered how many tranquilizers we had in sick bay. Enough to suppress a mutiny?

"Everyone able to work, get yourselves together and report your names and duties to myself or Ensign Miller," Valerian announced, failing to hide the dread in his voice. "We're going to gather supplies, hole up in mess hall until we can call for help."

A few murmured acknowledgments came from the crew as Valerian crossed the room and sat down next to me. "How was that?"

"It'll do," I replied, pushing down the panic in my chest. "At least for now. We need to wake Garrity, get in touch with the fleet."

Valerian frowned. "Do you think he's capable?"

"He has to be."

"But—"

"We don't have time to *bicker*!" I whispered harshly. "There's something out there, and it's trying to get in! It's like living coral or something; it took Peltz right out of my hands, crushed him before I could even blink. Whatever course of action we're going to take, you need to *take* it! You don't have the luxury of hesitation anymore, Lieutenant."

We sat in silence for a few seconds, letting the

tension simmer as Valerian made his decision. Then he took a deep breath, put his shoulders back, and rose to his feet. "Copeland, get Garrity awake. We're making a distress call."

A half hour later, Marsh and Copeland held Garrity up in his seat while I switched on the radio equipment. We had carried him down the cramped corridor to the communications room, jostling him every few seconds in an attempt to jar him out of his painkiller-induced stupor, but he was no more conscious now than when he had been lying on the floor. He mumbled and moaned as we adjusted him in the seat, placing his bandaged hands on the transmitter.

"You've got to try, Garrity," Copeland said quietly, nudging Garrity's shoulder. "You don't have to talk, just get us to the right frequency and Miller can do the rest."

Copeland looked up at me, and I nodded.

"Garrity!" Copeland said loudly, shaking him by his shoulders. "We're dead in the water; don't you want to go home? Just get us in touch with somebody! Anybody!"

Garrity moved his hands slowly, running them over the equipment to get his bearings before flipping a pair of switches. Then he reached up for the frequency dial and began to turn it. Marsh grabbed the headset and put it on, anxiously listening as Garrity scanned the ELF band.

"It's just static; nothing's breaking through," Marsh

said quietly. "Wait; there're voices!"

I grabbed Garrity's hand and held it still on the dial.

"Can't make out what they're saying," Marsh continued. "Something about- *oh God*. It's Frakes."

The blood ran cold in my veins. "Marsh, if you're putting me on…"

"I swear to God. It's the captain's voice, low like he's whispering from behind all the static…he keeps repeating…"

"What's he saying?" Copeland asked fearfully.

"*Let us in.*"

I pushed Marsh aside, grabbed the headset, and slammed my hand down on the transmitter. "Mayday, mayday, this is Ensign Miller aboard the *HMS Hope*. We are dead in the water, sitting on the ocean floor. We need immediate assistance. Our Captain is dead, along with most of the bridge crew. I'll repeat the message once, then follow up with coordinates. Over."

Copeland reached over for the maps as I waited for a response. After a few seconds, I repeated the message again. "Mayday, mayday, this is Ensign Miller aboard the *HMS Hope*…"

Garrity slumped over in his chair as Marsh got up and began to pace the room. Copeland threw aside an outdated map and closely examined the chart underneath. "He hasn't been marking latitude and longitude. If we could get to the bridge-"

"The bridge is *gone*," I replied darkly.

Marsh let out a nervous laugh as he paced behind us, shuffling his feet as he ran a hand through his hair.

"We are unsure of our location. If you're receiving please respond!"

Static hissed through the headset. There was nothing, not even the voices Marsh had heard. It was as if the world had gone silent, abandoned us to the vast blue morgue of the ocean or sacrificed us to a wrathful Poseidon. I slammed my fist into the nearby wall.

Marsh began to pray quietly as Copeland made sure Garrity was still breathing. There must have been other frequencies, more ways to get across an SOS, but if there were Garrity was in no shape to explain them to us.

"Is he alive?"

Copeland nodded. "He just needs to rest."

"Marsh; I want my message repeated every other minute, and I want you to look for any of Garrity's notes that might help us."

Marsh stopped pacing and gave me a distant look.

"I need you to stay here, repeat the distress call. Call for us if anyone responds."

He stared at me, pale and half-vacant, then slowly nodded.

When I returned to the mess hall, I could feel a

growing tension in the air. Valerian and Barca were sitting alone at a small table in the corner, while on the other side of the room the surviving crewmen were having a whispered argument. I sat down next to Valerian and shook my head.

He cursed under his breath. "Are we out of range?"

"We shouldn't be," I replied. "But we couldn't hear anything, not even chatter… and I think Marsh is cracking up."

Barca leaned in close to me. "I know what you saw on the bridge."

I shot Valerian a withering look, then turned back to the cook. "I don't know what I saw, I just know that what I *thought* I saw doesn't make any sense."

"'*Living coral*,' that's what you said," Valerian said.

Barca nodded. "Torsaaker's Reef."

I furrowed my brow. "What's that?"

"A myth," Valerian interjected.

"A story," Barca corrected. "A ghost story spread by Spanish sailors. The story goes that there was a Dutch explorer who was travelling along the coast of South America. Abbe Torsaaker had an interest in folklore, along with naval history, and he joined up with pirates to investigate an infamous patch of ocean near the Pitcairn Islands. It had been considered holy ground to the ancient Tayu; the battleground in a war between gods. Do you know about the Tayu?"

I shook my head.

"I'm not surprised," Barca replied. "They had been exterminated by the Aztecs before the conquistadors even set sail for the Americas. The Tayu believed in a family of incestuous gods, each being responsible for the creation of a part of the world as well as holding dominion over one of the primal forces of reality. Ithratol was the god of vegetative growth and hidden knowledge, the twin gods Ko ruled over earth and sickness, and the goddess Yetalka held dominion over the ocean and over the souls of the dead."

"And Torsaaker knew the legend?" I asked.

He nodded. "According to the Tayu, while man was living in mud huts and caves, the goddess Yetalka was hoarding the souls of the dead. The elder gods went to war, supposedly in the exact spot where Torsaaker was now looking. For hundreds of years, the spot had been known for disappearing ships, mysterious shipwrecks… the usual sailor's tales, but shipping records bore it out. So Torsaaker went there with a hired crew, planning to spend a week there surveying the area for the causes of the story; maybe there was a half-submerged atoll or hidden shoals or something. On the second day, his ship sunk. The survivors refused to talk about what they had seen, and Torsaaker himself withered away in a German monastery, babbling deliriously about what he had supposedly witnessed."

"What was it he saw?"

"A living reef, made of human flesh; the stitched together bodies of drowned sailors animated by the souls of the damned."

A chill ran up my spine to the back of my neck. "That's just a ghost story, Barca; just something to scare sailors. There's no truth to it."

He looked at me, slowly taking in my quivering voice and pale face. "If you say so."

I looked over at Valerian, who glanced between the two of us nervously. "Do you believe any of that?"

"Of course not," he replied unconvincingly.

A few crewmen on the other side of the room rose to their feet and started toward us. The man at the front, who I knew conversationally as Brooks, held a large wrench at his side. He cleared his throat to get our attention, then lifted the wrench and rested it in his other hand as if threatening to use it. "So, what's the plan?"

"The plan?" I asked, turning to face him as I considered our chances. If it was outright mutiny, we'd be torn to shreds. But if it was only a few of them, maybe-

CRACK! Brooks slammed the end of the wrench into the side of my head, sending me sprawling to the metal floor. Valerian leapt to his feet, holding his hands out in an attempt to keep the mutineers back as Barca helped me back to my feet. I put a hand to my temple and brought it back wet with sticky blood.

"What do you think you're doing?!" Valerian shouted at the men.

"We need someone in charge who'll *do* something!" Brooks barked back. "We're going to die down here!"

"You're welcome to take your chances outside," I muttered, feeling at my bleeding head to make sure my skull wasn't cracked.

Brooks scoffed. "Look at you; a pair of gutless bastards and their loyal wog."

Barca leapt forward and punched Brooks in the gut, then grabbed him by the collar and threw him into a nearby table. One of Brooks' fellow mutineers drew a small knife from his pocket, jabbing it at Barca to force him back from his fallen leader.

I turned to Valerian, who was standing stock-still with a look of blank panic on his face. "Do something, goddamnit! You have to stop them!"

Valerian stepped forward and grabbed the shoulder of the man with the knife. The man whirled and stabbed him in the stomach, then pulled it back and stabbed him again. Valerian stumbled backwards and fell to the floor, holding his wounds with bloody hands as the mutineers closed in.

I looked around the room in a desperate search for friendly eyes. The rest of the men watched us silently, uncomfortable with participating in the mutiny but clearly in favour of it. That was it, then.

I reached into my coat and drew my hidden pistol, then pointed it at the mutineers with a firm hand. "Back off! Any sudden moves get a bullet."

Brooks looked at me, then looked past me over my shoulder. The other mutineers followed his gaze, then Barca did the same. I turned my head to look at the open doorway behind me, where Chaplin Marsh stood quietly watching us, his hands covered in dark red blood.

"What happened, Marsh?"

"There are demons here," he replied quietly. "Powers, principalities…unclean spirits. They tried to possess me, make me do things I didn't want to do."

"Who?" I asked, turning the gun towards him.

"The voices from outside. The corrupted souls of the damned. They wanted me to let them in so they could claim us for the devil. I resisted, but Garrity was so *weak*. I had to kill him, you see; he was trying to bring the fleet here. That's what it wants; more bodies, more flesh for the tangled pile. And Copeland…he tried to stop me, and I just… God help me, he's dead too."

He looked up at me holding the gun, then behind me at the mutineers, Barca, and the bloodied Valerian. For a moment he looked almost confused. "I did the right thing, didn't I, Miller? I saved their souls from Hell."

"Put your hands up, Marsh," I said as I moved my finger to the trigger.

He giggled deliriously and took a step towards me. "How many bullets do you have in a little gun like that? Enough for everyone?"

I cocked the pistol. "Just one."

He smiled crookedly. "Save it for yourself."

A loud creak spread across the top of the sub. The crew fell into terrified silence as we looked around in fearful anticipation, and Marsh's giggle rose into a full-throated laugh.

That was when the mess hall ceiling caved in.

III: No Man's Land

A raging torrent of water blasted down through the caved-in hole in the mess hall ceiling, crushing Brooks and one of the other mutineers with a wet crunch. The crew began to scatter in a panicked scramble for the door, shoving and trampling each other as they sloshed through the rising icy water. I stood beside the door with my gun drawn and scanned the panicked crowd. Where were Barca and Valerian?

Thick, coiled tentacles of rust-coloured flesh

slithered into the mess hall through the torrent of black water and lashed out like striking vipers at the fleeing men. A burly crewman's arm was instantly ensnared and snapped, then used as leverage to pull the man screaming beneath the water's surface. Another fleshy tendril wound quickly around a metal table and effortlessly crushed it, then slipped down into the rising water to continue the search for its prey.

I aimed my gun at the nearest tentacle with a shaking hand and tried to get up the will to shoot it. I only had one shot; I'd have to make it count. Suddenly, a barrage of intrusive thoughts tore at the back of my mind. No, not thoughts. *Voices.* I could hear them inside my head, speaking in more languages than I could count. Then one rose above the others, and a chill ran down my spine as I recognised whose it was.

"Join us, Miller," the voice of Captain Frakes said warmly. "It hurts at first, but then it's Heaven."

Another voice rose to the top of the bubbling thoughts; this time it was Peltz. "The dead feel no pain…no sorrow, no grief, no guilt… The dead are never alone."

I clutched my ear with my free hand, screaming as I tried to push the voices out of my head. They felt sharp somehow, as though they were digging their claws into my mind in an attempt to get a grip. I fell back into the wall and slid down into the freezing water, waving my gun back and forth in panicked confusion. The screaming in my head reached a fever pitch, battering my senses with a deafening cacophony of countless voices as the black water rose around my head. I put the gun underneath my chin and put my finger on the trigger. They weren't going to take me, not while I still had a choice.

A hand plunged into the water and grabbed my collar. Barca pulled me out of the water and threw me against the wall, then looked at my almost catatonic expression and slapped me. "Snap out of it, Miller! We can't stay here!"

One of the coral tentacles shot out and wrapped around his arm, then tore it off with a wet rip and pulled it into the water. Barca screamed and clutched the stump with his remaining hand as deep red blood poured down his side. I reached out and grabbed him, pulling him towards the door as I held my gun out towards the tentacles behind us.

"Don't let it take me, Miller," Barca begged weakly. "*Please*. Kill me."

I pressed the gun to his forehead and closed my eyes, my finger hovering just above the trigger. I knew I could do it; I had done it before, but it never got any easier.

A tentacle shot out of the water and wrapped around

his chest, then flexed and crushed his ribcage. He opened his mouth to scream and blood dribbled down his chin as his eyes begged me for release. Then, as fast as it had arrived, the tentacle receded, pulling Barca out of my hands and beneath the surface of the rising water.

I turned and ran out of the mess hall, sloshing through the knee-deep water rapidly filling the corridor. All around me, panicked crewmen were pushing each other, throwing themselves against sealed bulkheads, and shouting out in anguished fear as the voices invaded their minds. There was nowhere to go now, nothing to do but wait to be taken. There was no escape, no way to flee but - *the diving suits*! Peltz had been taken wearing one, but there was still one left!

I scrambled down the corridor, waving my gun to keep away the panicking sailors. Behind me, I heard a familiar tearing of flesh and splintering of bone; the fleshy tendrils were out of the mess hall now, winding down the cramped corridor and mulching the men as they continued their feast.

I shoved past a half-closed bulkhead and stepped around a screaming sailor, then grabbed a low-hanging metal pipe and pulled myself down the flooding corridor. I ducked into the storage room and rushed to the far end, where the remaining diving suit would be sitting next to the airlock. I turned a corner around a pile of stacked boxes and froze. Lieutenant Valerian sat next to the airlock on a metal bench, holding the diving suit with one hand and clutching his bleeding stomach wounds with the other.

He looked up at me, then down at the gun at my side. His face was pale and covered in a cold sweat, and as I began to raise the gun, he chuckled darkly. "I think you and I had the same idea."

I pointed the gun at him. "I need the suit, Valerian."

A sad smile spread across his sweat-covered face. "You can take it; I don't have the strength left in me. I rather think I'm done for."

I took my finger off the trigger, then lowered the gun and handed it to him. "I'll trade you."

"That's kind," he said weakly, taking the gun from me with a shaking hand. "Do you really think you can survive out there?"

"I'll take my chances," I replied. What *had* I thought I'd be able to do with the suit? I had been running on pure survival instinct, fleeing a predator like a frightened animal, and now that I had a means of escape I found myself at a loss as to what use it could be.

As if reading my mind, Valerian laughed again and shook his head. "Better to die out there than in here."

"Let's hope."

Valerian shivered. "Is this what death feels like?"

I nodded.

He winced. "It's cold."

I began to put on the diving suit as the black water rose around us. I clasped the gloves and boots into place, then heaved the diving helmet over my head and put it on. As I fastened the bottom of the helmet to the neck of the suit, Valerian motioned for me to open the glass panel so he could see my face.

"You want to live, don't you?" he asked, holding steady eye contact with me.

I thought about it. "I guess I do."

He smiled. "First time in a while?"

I laughed, then quickly finished tightening the restraint belts. I put a gloved hand on the airlock door handle and began to turn it, struggling against the force of the rushing water to open it.

Beside me, Valerian held up a hand and gave me a mock salute, then raised the gun and put it under his chin. "I'll wait until I hear the outer door open; that way I'll die knowing you have a chance. If you can't get away… give it Hell."

I nodded. "Godspeed, Lieutenant."

I flipped the glass panel shut and stepped into the airlock, closed the door behind me, then turned and began to open the outer door. As I pushed it open, the airlock began to fill with pitch-black water, rushing around my ankles and rising past my knees as I instinctively held my breath. It passed my shoulders and finally covered my head, then filled the room and the pressure stabilised. It would be a moment before my eyes adjusted to the dark, but for now, all I could do was step out into the black.

I stepped into the doorway and looked down at the ocean floor a few meters down. A muffled gunshot came from the sealed door behind me. Good on you, Valerian; you were one of the lucky ones.

I pushed myself forward and out of the airlock and slowly fell to the dark seabed, kicking up a cloud of dust as I landed. I waited for the water around me to clear, and as it did, my jaw fell open.

All around me were sunken ships, sticking up over the flat seabed like jagged mountains on a blue horizon. There were galleons, steamships, even longboats, each sitting derelict in the undersea graveyard. Vibrantly colourful fish darted in and out of the splintered hunks of wood, nipping at patches of seaweed and swimming in schools around the outside edges of the field of shipwrecks.

I turned to look at the *Hope*, and for a moment I was struck by how right it felt that it had come to rest here. It was just another wreck now, a sunken ship crewed by the damned and abandoned. The top of the sub had been caved in and ripped outward, and as my eyes followed the floating bits of wreckage up, I felt my breath catch at the back of my throat.

A roiling mass of twisted tentacles coiled back and forth around the edges of the sub, pulling drowning sailors out into the black ocean. There was no head, no animal, only thick tentacles of flesh coral that connected to a brain-like bulb at the far end of the gigantic thing. It was almost indescribable, like a hundred-fingered hand reaching out mindlessly for something to grasp. A huge arm-like tendril stretched from the brain-bulb back into the blackness of the ocean, and I wondered grimly if it *was* a hand, stretched out from some ungodly thing just out of sight in the distance.

I slowly walked across the ocean floor towards it, watching in horrified awe as it tore apart the sub. The more I stared at it, the less sense it made; it had the porous, rocky appearance of coral, complete with outcropping branches and crests, but it bent and stretched like boneless flesh in an almost octopoid tangle of tentacles.

The voices began to stab in at the edges of my mind. I could hear them all now; Peltz, Frakes, Marsh, Brooks, warmly begging me to join them. But where were they? Inside that thing?

A thrashing sailor fell to the seabed just in front of me, writhing as one of the flesh coral tentacles tried to wrap itself around him. No, not tentacle; branch. Hand-like appendages split off the tentacle at various points, each grasping for the fallen sailor. A shape something like a torso and head rose from the end of the tentacle, and a twinge of horror-struck my gut as I recognised it. The man-like barb wasn't a coincidence, or some sickening mockery of the human form—it was Frakes, reaching out for the fallen sailor with rock-like arms. The hole he had shot in his head was still there, and inside I could see a wriggling mass of coral. He hadn't been consumed; he had been assimilated. His body was part of it now, sewn into the tentacle like part of a patchwork quilt of flesh. All around him, grasping arms and unblinking eyes dotted the surface of the tree-trunk tendril, along with gnashing mouths and spore-like ears. It didn't just have the appearance of flesh; it wore flesh as a cloak around its nerve-like core.

The thing that had been Frakes grabbed the fallen sailor's arm, then reached out with his other hand and shoved it down the sailor's throat. A swarm of eel-like centipedes emerged from the tiny holes covering the Frakes-thing's body and scuttled down onto the sailor, then began to dig into his skin and tunnel through it. Within seconds, they had sewn him into the flesh coral, weaving in and out of his hollowed body as they finished stitching him into place.

The huge tentacle lifted up from the ocean floor and rejoined the writhing mass of coiled flesh as I watched silently, struggling to keep the countless voices from consuming my mind. They were babbling now, begging me to join them in the coral, promising me it was Heaven. I hoped there was nothing left of who they had been, only the poor imitations of human interaction by an alien consciousness. They were only bodies now, just flesh absorbed into the wriggling mound that used them as anglers to attract its prey. It was Heaven, Hell, God, the Devil, all of that and more, but also somehow it was less. It was Death, undiscerning and ever-oncoming, an all-consuming force of amoral nature.

The huge fleshy arm at the end of the tangle of tentacles flexed, pulling itself up towards the brain-like bulb where the tentacles met. Behind it, a shape was pulled out of the darkness of the open ocean and into my vision, dragging behind the fleshy arm like the shell of a hermit crab. It was a gigantic skeleton, monstrous in shape and hideous in form, with sharp spikes that branched out jaggedly from each massive bone. The fleshy arm was attached to a half-destroyed skull, where another bulb-like mound of wriggling flesh pulsed from inside. It was as if the brain of the gigantic corpse had come alive, grown outward like an ever-expanding nervous system still tethered to its skeletal shell. Maybe it had.

Whatever it had been before, the tangled mass of flesh dragged the picked-clean skeleton behind it as it finished its search of the *HMS Hope*, content that it had consumed all the souls onboard. Swarms of fish followed behind the dragging skeleton, weaving in and out of the reef-like bones like desperate scavengers at a rotten whale fall. Could it be called a creature, or was it more appropriate to call it a place? It was a massive, self-contained ecosystem of parasites and symbiotes built around the corpse of an abyssal god, sustained by the never-ending consumption of its principal inhabitant; the mindlessly hungry, ever-grasping coral. It was almost beautiful in its perversity, a sunken profanity against a rational universe. It was only doing what it knew how to do, what all life was programmed to do at its most basic level; feed, grow, survive.

I stared at Torsaaker's Reef for what felt like an eternity, taking in every inexplicable detail with an almost religious awe. There *was* a god, I decided, or at least there once had been. What a shame it wasn't ours.

I turned to look at the sub and my eyes fell on the torpedo tubes. A spark ignited at the back of my mind. I started running across the ocean floor, bounding over floating bits of torn metal and ducking underneath wriggling tentacles of flesh. I wasn't going to be like them; just another nameless body swallowed up by Death's greedy gullet. I was *alive*, goddamnit.

I reached the *Hope* and began to climb the sheer side of the submarine, grabbing at outcropping rivets or jagged bits of broken metal as I scrambled up towards the torpedo tubes. I had avoided the dead god's notice so far; the voices held at bay in my head by an almost serene acceptance of oncoming death, but as I got closer to the torpedoes, I heard them begin to scream.

"Do you feel that?" I yelled. "It's called fear!"

The mass of tentacles shot out through the black water towards me, reaching out for me with the hands of a hundred-thousand drowned men as I pulled myself up into the tube. I slid my gloved fingers underneath the panel on the closest torpedo and started to pry it open, gritting my teeth as I strained against the thick metal.

"Fear is what keeps us apes going! It's why we build, fight, breed; because we know someday, we'll be dead and gone! You'd know that if you actually learned anything from all those men you pretend to be!"

I saw vacant faces appear at the end of the torpedo tube, sticking out like man-shaped barbs from the huge tentacles. I saw the nearly headless Peltz, the skull-shattered Frakes, the one-armed and hunched over Barca. Their mouths hung blankly empty as their voices shrieked inside my mind, and their coral hands began to stretch down the tube towards my metal boots. There were more behind them—the hollowed-out bodies and minds of countless drowned and shipwrecked souls.

"Go on, try the same old trick; I've seen plenty of dead men! But I'm not dead just yet, and I've got a lesson about life I want to teach you."

I put my feet up onto the torpedo, using them as leverage as I tried again to pull open the panel. Finally, it sprang open, knocking me back into the wall of the tube. I dived forward and reached into the torpedo panel, feeling for the detonation switch.

Suddenly, I felt the torpedo tube buckle and bend inward as one of the coral tentacles pulled it free from the rest of the *Hope*. At the end of the half-smashed tube I could see the writhing mass of living coral, pulling me closer and closer like the last remaining crumb of a messily devoured meal.

I smiled, hovering my finger above the detonation switch as I waited for it to bring me closer. "This might not kill you, but it'll sure be one hell of a black eye. See, that's the truth that a god would never know, the lesson you're about to learn; death is inevitable, and pain is universal. Maybe it shouldn't be, but it is…and it's about time you felt some of it."

The faceless thing folded outward around the half-smashed torpedo tube, surrounding me with a grim kaleidoscope of petrified dead men on a multitude of gigantic tentacles.

"Or to put it another way, if I can adopt an American turn of phrase…"

I flipped the switch.

"I daresay life's a bitch."

JONATHAN INBODY s an author, filmmaker, and podcaster from Buffalo, New York. He writes surrealist horror, scifi, fantasy, westerns, and pretty much anything else that can have monsters in it.

He can be heard every other week on his improvisational movie pitch podcast X Meets Y, and his scifi horror anthology podcast Gray Matter is coming soon.

Bibliography
ANGELS, Black Hare Press, 2019
APOCALYPSE, Black Hare Press, 2019
BEYOND, Black Hare Press, 2019
Grievous Bodily Harm, Zombie Pirate Publishing, 2019
MONSTERS, Black Hare Press, 2019
Raygun Retro, Zombie Pirate Publishing, 2020
Treasure Chest, Zombie Pirate Publishing, 2019
UNRAVEL, Black Hare Press, 2019
What If?, Black Hare Press, 2019
WORLDS, Black Hare Press, 2019

Connect
Amazon: amazon.com/author/jonathaninbody
X Meets Y Podcast: xmeetsy.libsyn.com

The Rashatek

By K.B. Elijah

In a desperate attempt to salvage her scientific career with the discovery of a new sea creature, Dr Ryka Patel accidentally stumbles across something much bigger—and horrific—that lurks in the ocean's depths...

Salted crackers.

That's all I could think about. My mouth watered at the imaginary taste my mind had acutely conjured in mocking tantalisation: the crisp bite, the tang of the salt, the savoury aftertaste.

"Salted crackers." This time I'd spoken my craving aloud.

"Indeed," my companion said. In true Nadia style, she didn't ask what I was talking about.

"You feel like salted crackers?"

"No."

"Well, I do."

"Did you even pack any?"

I scowled at the brightly lit dashboard in front of me, cursing my thoughtlessness. "No. But I brought the cream cheese and the marshmallows this time."

"Then eat those."

I rolled my eyes. Nadia didn't understand cravings. "I wanted the marshmallows *last time* we came down," I explained, "and the cream cheese the time before. But this time I want salted crackers, and we don't have any."

I probably imagined the sigh that followed my words. Nadia didn't lower herself to such emotional exasperation. Her voice, whenever she spoke, was expressionless.

"I know," I added, "it's always something obscure and never the same craving twice. I'm difficult that way. But that's why you like me, right?"

Silence.

"Do you want me to shut up about the crackers?" I

asked.

"That would be...preferable," Nadia said. "Considering we are currently 4,717.5 metres from the surface, let alone anywhere near a food store. Perhaps we can focus on the mission?"

The mission. It sounded so glamorous when she put it that way, like it was an epic quest to save the world, when in reality we were floating around in a little submersible hunting fish.

Not just any fish. I like to think humanity has progressed far enough by 2143AD that I could catch a fish without resorting to such desperate measures. No, we were after a particular fish.

Bathypterois Auratus. The golden-tailed deep-sea tripod fish.

A myth. A legend. Or perhaps even that was too generous; most scientists had not even heard of the creature, for it had not officially been discovered. There are twenty-two recognised species in the Bathypterois genus, from its first discovery in 1878AD by the ichthyologist Albert Günther, to the relatively recent find in 2099AD. But that was nearly fifty years ago now, and the genus is all but considered discovered these days.

Yet I was determined to add the *Auratus* to the list, even if I felt obliged to name it after its colouring rather than myself. I knew it existed, even if I hadn't yet found proof.

But when I say most scientists hadn't heard of the fish we were hunting, I mean everyone except me and Nadia, and Dr Sen back up on the surface. It was a lonely mission, that was for sure.

"Run another scan," I directed, cracking my neck from side to side as sudden motivation hit me. I wasn't down in the abyssopelagic layer for food, salted crackers or no. I was here to get my name back in circulation, to prove to the scientific community that I wasn't a one-hit wonder with an accidental fluke find, that I was worth the post-nominal titles my dusty business cards stoically bore.

It had been a long road of fruitless desperation over the last seven years after the brief wave of success brought by my discovery of a new *Dasyatidae,* a whiptail stingray living surprisingly close to the surface to have avoided detection for so long, had faded out and unceremoniously dumped me into the bottomless pit of increasing obscurity, where only another piscine find could pull me out. Was it worse, I wondered, to have succeeded and not maintained that success, than never encountered the sensation at all? The expectations of academia were brutal: even the discovery of a century meant only as much as you were able to follow it up with. It was a constant battle of proving to your peers that your theories were good, your instincts were right, and your paper-writing skills wowed audiences; the moment you'd made one scientific revelation, you were expected to be working on the next.

It was exhausting, and there had been more than one moment over the years where I'd considered throwing it all in and applying for a job at the local retail centre. And then Nadia would remind me that most of those jobs were occupied by automatons and if I quit, what would happen to her?

It was the emotional reaction triggered in me by the latter argument, rather than the rationality of the former, that won me over, and that in itself induced more anxiety in me. How could I be a scientist when I was so damn sentimental?

And on and on the vicious cycle went: the self-questioning, the self-flagellation, the self-doubt.

It's not all about you, my father would say to me as a child, his deep condescending voice cutting through the fragile barriers I'd tried to construct around myself to get through the day. *Stop being so selfish, Ryka. Think of your family.*

I'm not going to tell you what anguish those few words would cause me, the nights of insomnia plaguing my health and sanity as I stewed on his meaning. I only know that I despise myself every time I catch my thoughts lingering on introspection, and it's something my therapist has been working on with me for years, with little success.

"Scan clear," Nadia told me, and I leaned back in my chair, frowning at the dark waters through the reinforced glass in front of me. It was pure blackness, a darkness so absolute that the window could have been made of transparent material and I wouldn't have known the difference. Even the marine snow wasn't visible, and that stuff was everywhere down here. But the submersible's lights were off: the denizens that lived this deep underwater weren't used to light, particularly non blue-light, and there was nothing which would scare them off quicker than a brightly lit vehicle zooming through the depths screaming "I'm from up there!"

I don't know what inspiration I was expecting to come to me. It wasn't like my elusive *Auratus* would swim up to the submersible and press its pectoral fins against the glass. I wondered if I would even be able to see it if it did, and had a sudden, inexplicable urge to flick the lights on, just to *check*.

No. I had to trust Nadia. If she said the fish wasn't on the scan, I believed her. We'd calibrated the search with the few details we knew from my brief glimpse of it four months ago: between 22 and 25 centimetres in length, an unusual golden colour for these depths, three bony fins that stuck into the pelagic sediment when hunting which earned the tripodfish genus its name.

One sighting, that was all we had to go on.

But I knew my deep sea creatures: hell, it's all I had studied for nearly fifteen years. When I saw that gold tail flicker away from the submersible's headlights as we prepared to rise to the surface at the end of a dive in January, I knew it wasn't any of the catalogued species. We hunted for hours, using up the last of the submersible's stored air in doing so, yet the fish was nowhere to be seen.

But Dr Ryka Patel was nothing but obstinate...or to use Dr Sen's description of me, *"stubborn as an effing mule"*. I dragged Nadia down for dives again and again, with increasing frequency as my hunt grew more desperate. The *Bathypterois Auratus* was my chance to restore my name in a world where scientific achievements were favouring the outward-looking rather than inward, the off-world rather than under. There were so many advancements to be found out there in our solar system, I was repeatedly told, which while evidently meant to be encouraging, I just found depressing. What use was a scientist knowledgeable in Earth's deep sea creatures going to be on a bunch of planets without water? I'd just flounder around in a space-suit, disrupting everyone else's operations as I...

"Try the Atacama Trench," I said as a thought struck me, and a moment later I felt the faint sway of the turning submersible as Nadia navigated to the nearest section of the trench.

"You think it will be there? You've been investigating depths of four to five thousand metres for months. The Atacama Trench reaches 8,065 metres."

"Maybe that was my error," I mused, staring out into the blackness again, my hands resting on the dashboard console though I had little to do. My work was as a scientist, not a navigator. "I had assumed that the *Auratus* lived at the same depths as the rest of its family, as that was where we found it the first time. But I forgot to take into account one variable."

"Us?"

"Us," I confirmed. "What if we had startled it from its natural habitat, or drawn it away by curiosity? Maybe it's a deeper-sea creature than I had originally anticipated. Let's look at the areas around the mapped hydrothermal vents first."

There was silence for a moment as Nadia processed this. "That's a good hypothesis, Ryka," she said.

I smiled. It had taken a long time to convince her to use my given name rather than my surname or just "Doctor". As much as I enjoyed the status my qualifications gave me, and still felt a thrill every time I ticked the honorific on a form, it made for cold interactions when you were stuck in an enclosed space with someone for hours at a time.

I kicked my shoes off and tucked my feet underneath me as I settled into my chair. It was affixed to the floor for obvious reasons, but whichever genius had designed it had evidently been at least a foot taller than me, as I couldn't reach the controls when seated properly. But at least it stopped me fidgeting with anything other than the looped yarn of my hand-knitted socks, and I alternated my gaze between the blackness of the window and the equally disappointing scanner screen to my right, which stayed stubbornly blank.

Despite knowing Nadia was monitoring the scanner's results with more diligence than I could ever muster, I still didn't let myself blink as the submersible moved over the Atacama trench and started to lower itself down into its depths.

I always got a thrill when we dropped, despite the sensation being more akin to descending stairs at a leisurely pace than being flung downwards by a roller coaster. It was just that feeling of eternal space consuming me, that no matter how much scientists measured elevation by sea level, there was so much more *below* that than had ever been explored. Humanity had always been caught up in outward fascination, the lure of the stars, but there was a whole macrocosm down here that remained largely unknown, a world of cosmic proportions and unobserved life. Wasn't that more alluring than spending months trekking to Mars only to find a dust ball with the same vista on one side of the planet as the other? The oceans were ours, a backyard full of wonder and knowledge that enveloped you with its vast alienness despite being close enough to touch.

So there was no stomach dropping feeling, but there were certainly other emotions racing through me as I turned my gaze back to the window: hope, fear, anticipation, anxiety...pant-wetting fear as huge teeth grazed against the glass...

I pushed backwards into my chair, freezing in place with my eyes painfully wide and my breath hitched. Everything else seemed to suspend around me as my universe narrowed to the points of those teeth as they scratched against the window, illuminated only so far as our internal lights shimmered onto the glass and leaving the rest of the huge monster submerged in impenetrable darkness.

And then the fight response triggered in me - I'd never been one to run from my issues, and there's only a certain amount of running you can do in a tiny submersible - sending me diving out of my chair and leaping for the button on the dashboard to turn the outside lights on.

They burst to life without delay, powerful bulbs cutting through the metres of black water in front of us and illuminating the ubiquitous organic material floating downwards from the photic zone, as well as most of the sea creature. It was even more hideous in the light, bulbous and repugnant, and I stared in shock through the window. Its back end was still shrouded in darkness, the sheer size of the thing unfathomable, but its head flinched away from the submersible and its bright lights. Teeth flashed again, snapping shut inches from the glass.

"Back us up!" I yelled, even though the interior of the submersible was silent but for my loud breathing, an eerie sensation considering we were facing such peril. It felt like there should be noise to accompany the threat: snarling roars or booming rumbles, yet the monster had snuck up on us and almost devoured us whole without a single sound. That was another ironic phenomenon of the ocean: it was as cold, dark and quiet as a grave, yet teemed with more life than we could ever imagine.

"Ryka, we can't-" Nadia started to protest, but I shouted over her.

"Nadia, back us the eff up! That thing's about to eat us!"

But whether it was the light or the look of our decidedly un-tasty exterior, the creature gave up on us, swooping its head around back into the darkness. My sigh of relief shot from my breath a moment too early, and I swore as I saw its tail whipping towards us as we slowly reversed in the water. I'd never know whether it was a deliberate blow or the monster's coordination had been thrown out by my actions, but the submersible wasn't quick enough to escape, no matter how much I shrieked at poor Nadia to give us more power that we simply didn't have.

I was thrown sideways with the impact, my elbow jarring against the wall and my knees crashing painfully into the floor. I groaned, wiping away something wet that had gathered on my forehead. When I pushed myself to my feet, I noticed that the back of my hand was smeared with red.

I was bleeding? Crap, I hadn't even realised I'd hit my head.

I blinked around at my surroundings. I was facing the back wall of the craft and guessed I'd cut my head on a slightly jutting piece of metal which hooked underneath the first aid kit. Staring at the white cross on the green background, I let out a reluctant grin. Another irony?

"Nadia," I murmured. "Are you okay?"

"Of course," she said in an even tone, not bothering to return the question. "That was unexpected."

"Oh, really?" I snapped back, unimpressed by her

lack of compassion when I was bleeding all over the floor. I unzipped the first aid kit one handed and pressed an unrolled bandage to my forehead. "What an understatement."

"I wasn't talking about the fish, Ryka. I was talking about the wall."

I frowned. "What wall?"

"The wall of the trench that was stopping us backing up any further. The one I tried to tell you about when you yelled at me. The wall the creature just smacked us into."

I quickly padded across the submersible in my socks, reaching for the dashboard which lined the front wall of the craft. The warning lights I had expected to be flickering in red-lighted urgency remained stubbornly dark.

"We hit rock and don't have a scratch to show for it?"

"No," Nadia said, and I wrinkled my nose in confusion. "We didn't hit rock. We went straight through it."

Sinking into my chair, I leaned as far backwards as the rigid shape of the uncomfortable furniture would allow me, still pressing the bandage to my head.

"You've lost me."

"You're right there."

"No, Nadia, I-"

I forced myself to take a breath. "It's a figure of

speech. I don't understand what happened."

"The creature's tail hit us. It should have knocked us into a wall of solid rock bordering the trench, but instead we went right through it as if it wasn't there. I've run a scan, and the sonar is still pinging off rock that doesn't exist. See?"

She brought up the sonar on the screen to my left, and I eyed it with suspicion.

"Is the sonar broken?"

Nadia hummed in annoyance, and I realised I'd probably insulted her and her meticulous maintenance of the submersible.

"I'm just checking!" I said defensively, raising my hands to show I meant no offence.

"It's not broken. Besides,"—she flicked the image on the screen to that of a video, freeze-framed with a hideous close-up of the monstrous fish grinning at us—" this is just before the impact. Watch."

The video commenced playback, and I shuddered as I saw the same teeth we'd just escaped gnash at us through a grainy underwater picture. Then the creature turned, and although I couldn't see its tail coming for us this time due to the angle of the camera, I knew when it had hit us from the way the image jerked violently. The feed spun, bleary underwater landscape rushing past, and I inadvertently flinched as I watched the camera hurtle towards rock, seeming like it would hit, like there was nothing it could do but *hit*...yet just like Nadia had described, it passed through as if nothing was there.

"*Awesome*," I breathed, my scientist brain racing through the possibilities. Solid matter recognisable visually and by sonar, yet not having the qualities of solid matter at all? Was it some type of mirage formed by water refraction? No: that would explain the trick on my eyes, but not the scanner. Could it be some type of plasma-based compound that was hard enough to reflect sound and light but soft enough to permit other mass through? That would...defy the laws of physics. And I may be a biologist, not a physicist, but I knew that much.

"This could be it!" I laughed delightedly, jumping out of the chair and abandoning the bloodied bandage. "The find of the century!"

"Nadia, run scans on the fake rock," I directed. "Every scan you can possibly run. And then do them again. I'm going to set up the collection pod, see if we can bring in a sample for closer analysis on the surface. Oh, and see how far it stretches on the X and Y axis, and mark the coordinates." I bumbled around the submersible, barking orders and flicking switches, too caught up in my excitement to do anything sensible like taking a breath. "We're going to need to commandeer some type of underwater drone when we get back to the surface, preferably padded, so we can test the other rock faces around this area. Unless we can figure out a way to detect it remotely, there's going to be a lot of randomly bumping into solid objects in our future. Nadia, this could be it! And we definitely need to ensure that-"

"Ryka," Nadia said quietly, tonelessly, and I spun in frustration.

"Nadia, at least try to sound a little happier about this!"

"Dr Ryka Patel."

"Uh, yes?" I asked, suddenly subdued. She sounded like Dr Sen when she used my full name like that. At least she hadn't resorted to middle names like my parents did when I had been a disobedient child, skipping out on puja by hiding in the garden, or sneaking off to 'those immoral Westerner parties', as my dad always put it.

"The scanner is picking up something, 0.74 kilometres on a bearing of 098 degrees. It's a cluster of what appear to be..."

She trailed off, and I frowned. Nadia never trailed off. I may speak over her, but she never, *ever* failed to finish a sentence all by herself.

"What is it?"

"Ships," she said flatly. "They appear to be ships. Active technology and electronic signatures, but no life signs or discernible pockets of breathable atmosphere.

They didn't appear when we descended: I've only picked them up now we're on the other side of the rock."

So that was another strange property of the odd material we'd passed through: the ability to block other signatures shielded behind it. This find was going to be worth millions.

"Mark our location so we can find the rockface again," I ordered. "At least that's stationary: for now, take us closer to the ships."

My heart pounded in my ears. Could I really be so lucky as to make two unprecedented finds in one dive? First this impossible substance, and now lost watercraft with their technology still intact?

The two had to be related somehow: that was the principle of Occam's Razor, wasn't it? That the simplest of competing theories should be preferred?

My heart sank as doubt set in once again and I realised we had probably stumbled across a government testing facility. State-of-the-art tech, a remote location? Classic top secret stuff, which meant that if we went any further, I was probably going to end up in a prison. Or did that just happen in the movies? Either way, it meant the technology of the rock wall was already discovered and was being deliberately hidden from the civilian population so it could be weaponised...or whatever it was that governments spent their billions on.

I trailed a scuff on the plastic floor with my big toe, realising from the slightly sticky feeling on the underside of my foot that my sock must have a hole in it. Typical Ryka luck.

I had already sold myself on the idea of the government facility and had just opened my mouth to tell Nadia to turn back and get the scanners back up for the *Auratus* again, when light streaming through the glass window of the submersible hit my eyes.

Light that wasn't from our headlights, which is the only illumination I'd ever seen on a dive this deep, other than occasional glimmers of bioluminescence from fish photophores.

I tiptoed closer to the window, scarcely believing the sight.

Ships, like Nadia had said: I'd wondered why she'd phrased it in such a way, rather than the more common parlance of 'submersibles' and 'vessels.' Now I understood. Because these *were* ships: vast vehicles that dwarfed my own submersible a thousand times over, with rows of circular windows placed in wonky lines that stretched horizontally across their lengths. Bright lights shot out on odd angles, illuminating the sea floor around them.

The plating on the ships was a leafy green that reminded me of algae in a pond, with bronzed accents on the borders of the windows and asymmetrical plates as if the designer wanted to draw attention to the edges of each component rather than camouflage them as was the trend with huge construction works like this. Various rounded protrusions dotted the exterior of the ships in a seemingly random pattern, reminding me of the airlocks and hangar bays on a spacecraft. Or the suckers on the tentacle of an octopus.

"How many ships are there?" I breathed, not daring myself to speak louder than a whisper. This was no government facility. Humans didn't build things this way, all cockeyed and lopsided, not for an expensive project like this. And the green plates of the ships almost appeared to breathe, flexing in and out in a way that no Earth metal ever would.

"Four," Nadia told me.

I swore. "Assuming the size of the inhabitants from the distance between the portholes, that's...I dunno, a likely population of least 300 per ship, unless they've crowded in or are making do on a skeleton crew? And they're all living down here?"

"Living? There are no life signs here, Ryka."

I shook my head. "Doesn't mean there's no life. We scan based on parameters, right? Human parameters. We've had issues with identifying fish before, and these are no fish."

A thrum of excitement lit through me as I pressed my face to the glass, staring at the enchanting *otherness* that the ships presented. "You're capturing this on the video feeds, yes?"

"Yes."

The squat green vehicles didn't seem to be moving. They rested gently on the sandy trough we found ourselves in, encased in a cavern which was hidden from sight and detection by the fake rock. Who knew how long they'd been down here?

I itched to pull on a suit and swim closer. The urge to touch those breathing plates on the ships was almost overwhelming, but the rational part of my brain knew we were far, far too deep to consider such a thing. The submersible was holding up as it had been built to do, a deep-water exploration unit that used pressure technology developed when man first started routinely flying to the stars, but my tiny suit would crumple like foil if I tried to go out there.

It didn't stop the curiosity, though. That was a living thing inside of me, plucking at my eyes and hands and mind, the scientist part of Ryka needing to see more, *know more*.

Movement, down to the left, at the base of the closest ship. The sand swirled up as something disturbed it.

"Did you see that?" I asked breathlessly, not waiting

for a response. "Direct the sensors towards the middle of the nearest ship, as wide a range and as few parameters as the scanner will allow."

My heart skipped a beat as the sand cloud settled and the water cleared to reveal a mauve shape in the water, a nebulous being with a formless torso and what appeared to be tentacles. At first I wondered it was a specimen of the local wildlife, albeit one I'd never encountered before and could add to my great-finds-of-the-day list, but when I noticed it tapping at one of the bronzed edgings of the ship in a way that could only be described as *meticulous,* I knew it was so much more.

"That's one of them!" I breathed delightedly, a smile creeping up my face.

It was hard to comprehend. All that time, money and hope put into space explorations without finding a single trace of other life outside of ourselves, and here it was, less than ten kilometres below our feet.

"Aliens," I said aloud, testing the word. "Aliens. Here."

For some reason, the audible confirmation chilled me, even if it was only me putting my thoughts into speech.

Aliens, *here,* hidden in our oceans, deliberately masking their presence.

"Take us back out, Nadia," I whispered, attempting

to force my voice into a false semblance of calm. "Quietly."

As the submersible began to back up and turn around, I considered the possibilities. Had the aliens been here the whole time, living subaqueously in a type of ignorant harmony with us humans? Was this their planet as well? Or were they invaders, landing without being detected and biding their time down here?

Either prospect made me shudder. As much as my scientific curiosity had often gotten me into trouble in the past, this time the warning signs were too large to ignore.

We shouldn't be here.

I silently urged us to move faster, hope flaring in my chest as a wall of rock appeared in the window.

"Go," I breathed.

But it was too late. I cried out as a purple body slithered across the glass, its tentacles attaching to the submersible with large suckers that grasped hungrily at the window. My mind registered the cruel-looking spikes in the endmost three suckers of each tentacle, even as my body froze at the sight of the multiple glassy eyes peeking out of the bulbous mass that formed its body.

"Uh, should I do the whole welcome-and-good-to-meet-you speech?" I asked hazily, each sound and sight amplified in my head. Everything felt like it was overly colourful and close, as if the alien had already enveloped me in its mauve flesh. "Is 'live long and prosper' taken?"

"Perhaps you should offer it marshmallows," Nadia suggested, and I allowed myself a brief smile at the joke. She'd come a long way since we first met, from the inflectionless tone that spoke of a complete lack of humour, and the tendency to only say one word when a dozen would be much more fun. I was obviously a terrible influence on her.

I opened my mouth to respond, just as an alarm lit the interior of the submersible in both noise and light, a vivid red flashing accompanied by the blaring of a horn.

"Structural integrity compromised!" reported Nadia. "It's trying to breach the glass!"

I barely offered the creature a glance. Whether it was achieving it by an acidic compound, a sharp object such as those spikes, or just exerting pressure, it didn't really matter. There was only one thing we could do.

"Forward into the rock!" I ordered. "The real rock! Scrape it off before it does any more damage!"

I clutched my chair from behind as Nadia did as commanded, the submersible responding remarkably quickly as we turned into the rock walls to our right and attempted to squish the thing trying to kill us.

Our movements were clunky, but effective, and within moments we were in a position to crush the alien against the hard rock face. But just as such an outcome seemed inevitable, the glass crunched rock, and I blinked.

"Where did it go?"

"Nothing on the sensors," said Nadia. "But there never was."

"It looked like...no, it must have just slipped off when it realised what was about to happen, and swam away."

That wasn't what had happened. I knew that, knew I would have seen it with my senses on such hyper-alert and my face so close to the creature.

But what I had actually seen didn't make any sense.

"Let's get out of here," I said, feeling sick. "This has been far too much excitement for one day."

But as Nadia turned the submersible around, I knew that we were far from done.

Two dozen of the purple creatures hovered in the water before us, their tentacles wrapped loosely around themselves. With each alien sporting between four and ten eyes each, it was eerie to be on the receiving end of so many gazes. And none of them looked friendly.

I heard an incomprehensible noise above the wail of the alarm, a cross between a whimper and a scream that wasn't a word but nonetheless seemed to convey its meaning perfectly, and realised it was coming from me.

I scowled, resolutely cutting it off.

"We're safe in here as long as they don't breach the

submersible," I pointed out, a lump in my throat that I recognised as fear. "We can get through the fake rock and rise as fast as we can. We can *do this*, we just need to—"

Three of the tentacled monsters propelled themselves towards us and latched onto the submersible: one on the window and the others around the sides. The remaining aliens just watched us silently.

I started to tell Nadia to use the same trick to scrape them off the outside of the craft as before, but then the aliens changed the rules on us.

Or maybe the rules had never existed in the first place.

For their tentacles started to ooze *through* the exterior of the submersible, emerging with a wet pop near my face, and flapping around blindly in the air with their spiked suckers. I could only watch in horror as the aliens pushed the rest of their bodies through the solid metal of the wall, their unlidded eyes immediately narrowing in on me, and I realised what I'd seen before hadn't been an illusion. The first creature that we'd tried to squish against the rock hadn't slipped away before the impact: it had sunk into the wall as if it wasn't there, despite us impacting with the rock a moment later.

These things could phase through solid matter, and we were *fucked.*

The alien morphing through the glass let out a

hissing snarl as it emerged fully into the submersible, its wet tentacles slipping over the dashboard. To my surprise, it continued to phase even when it landed, sinking into the dashboard with its shapeless head receding into the buttons and dials.

Perhaps they couldn't control their powers? But the other creatures had almost made it through the walls behind me.

"Nadia," I barked. "Send an emergency transmission to the surface! Recording now!"

I turned my back on the aliens and used the precious seconds I had left, cutting off the alarms and sticking my face into the camera.

"Dr Sen, this is Dr Ryka Patel, transmitting from coordinates 23°10'99"S, 71°18'40"W. This is not a hoax. I have encountered alien life and it is extremely hostile, I repeat *extremely hostile*. They have four ships down here, and I've seen at least 25 of the bastards, but there are likely more, perhaps up to 1,200? They can phase through solid matter, you got that? Solid fucking matter." I moved my head to the side to give the camera a clear view of the mauve tentacles as they waved around behind me. "They're breaching my craft and I'm not going to make it, but you need to get the military here, ASAP. Warn everyone, you hear me? God have mercy on us all."

"Send it," I snapped, finally turning around to face

the two remaining aliens, which had fully emerged into the submersible and flopped wetly onto the plastic floor.

I set my jaw. "You're not going to get away with whatever it is you're doing," I said, faking bravado. I didn't know if they understood me or not, but I wasn't going down without a fight. "No matter what you do to me, the message is gone. Humanity knows you're coming, and if there's one thing we're good at, it's bombing the shit out of people we don't understand. You and your ships are *screwed*."

"Actually, Ryka," said Nadia, "no one on the surface knows anything."

I spun, panicked. "What? You didn't send the message?"

"I sent it," Nadia confirmed. "But it may not be what you were expecting. Would you like to see?"

I eyed the aliens, who didn't seem to be moving any closer. They were watching me with an expression of almost...patience? Anticipation?

"Just keep trying," I said desperately, wondering what she meant. "Did the video not get through correctly? Hopefully they believe me even without the footage as evidence. Or was it the audio feed, was it-"

"Dr Sen, this is Dr Ryka Patel, transmitting from coordinates 21°25'01"S 72°43'33"W," said the screen to my right, my face appearing across it. I frowned. Those were the wrong coordinates: had I really been so flustered as to give a location hundreds of kilometres away? The military wouldn't know where to look!

But my video self carried on talking.

"I've spent months searching for the *Bathypterois Auratus*, and I'm no closer than I was since that first day. It's become clear to me that the discovery of the *Dasyatidae* was a fluke. My father was right: I should have thought about my family. I should have gone into an easier field; one I didn't have to give up my hopes and dreams for. But it's too late, you got that? Too fucking late." My video self moved her head, just like I had done a few moments before, but the feed didn't reveal the purple aliens. Instead, a device sat in the middle of the submersible's floor, glowing red numbers ticking down.

I gasped.

"This is going off in less than a minute and I'm not going to make it, but maybe this way you will all remember me rather than letting me fade into obscurity. Remember me, you hear me? God have mercy on my soul."

The video cut off.

"Nadia?" I whispered, horror crawling across my skin. No, it was more than that: it was the slippery tentacles of the aliens, which were closing in at last. They caressed my skin gently, slipping painful spikes through my clothes. My blood ran hotly onto the floor, pooling into a scarlet flood.

Nadia didn't answer.

Two more aliens landed on the submersible's window, peering through at me intently.

"Nadia!"

The weight of the two aliens inside the submersible brought me to my knees, and I thrashed wildly, attempting and failing to buck them off. Their skin was slippery and viscous, and my fingers seemed to claw through it without purchase.

"Navigation and Detection Interface Application, send the original message!" I choked as a tentacle wrapped itself around my neck.

"I apologise, Ryka," Nadia said, her computer-generated voice sounding more emotionless than ever. The third alien popped its head out above the dashboard where her systems were stored, its eyes boring into me as if in triumph. "But the *Rashatek* have shown me a better life than listening to you. Humans are so limited in their imagination, yet ambitious in their reach. Children, playing at being god. You will learn your place in this universe."

"Nadia, what the fu—"

My words cut off with my sight as my face was enveloped in a sticky wet substance, mauve clouding my vision.

I clawed and fought and bit and writhed, but nothing eased the pressure.

I hadn't even been able to warn them, those happy ignorant people up on the surface, watching outwards for a threat that was coming from below. I was going to die here, for *nothing*, lost in the vastness of the ocean without a single person to hear my screams.

Purple gradually faded to black, and the sea claimed me for her own, one more body succumbing to the vast eternity.

K. B. ELIJAH is a fantasy author living in Brisbane, Australia with her husband and three cockatiels. A lawyer by day, and a writer by...also day, because she needs her solid nine hours of sleep per night (not that the cockatiels let her sleep past 6am). K.B. writes for various international anthologies including those published by Black Hare Press, Fantasia Divinity and Things in the Well, and her work features in dozens of collections about the mysterious, the magical and the macabre. Her own books of short fantasy novellas with twists, The Empty Sky and Out of the Nowhere, are available on paperback and Kindle now.

Bibliography
The Empty Sky, 2018
Sideshow Alley, Little Quail Press, 2019
Burning Love and Bleeding Hearts, Things in the Well, 2020
TWENTY TWENTY, Black Hare Press, 2020
LUST, Black Hare Press, 2020
LOVE, Black Hare Press, 2020
HATE, Black Hare Press, 2020
SLOTH, Black Hare Press, 2020
Forgotten Ones, Eerie River Publishing, 2020
Mythica, Iron Faerie Publishing, 2020
Burning Dreams, Fantasia Divinity, 2020
OCEANS, Black Hare Press, 2020
Japanese Fantasy Drabbles, Insignia Stories, 2020
Out of the Nowhere, 2020
Burning Dreams, Fantasia Divinity, 2020

Connect
Website: www.kbelijah.com
Amazon: www.amazon.com/author/kbelijah
Twitter: @KBElijah1
Instagram: @k.b.elijah
Facebook: KBElijah
Channillo: channillo.com/series/pettifog/

A Voice Beneath the Waves

By Michael Kellichner

Areum feels her life has lost all direction and purpose. At least until she begins hearing an ancient voice deep beneath the ocean, calling to her, showing her a wonderful world that used to be, and she knows she has to do whatever it takes to help it wake.

Areum leans against the full window looking out over Gwangalli beach and bridge. She lets her smile fall, presses her forehead against the cool glass, tries to see the waves clearly through the reflection of flashing lights, curling smoke, and moving bodies. Thudding bass passes right through her, like heavy stones hurled into still water. The air conditioning makes her skin so dry and itchy she could claw it off her bones. Out in the sea, the bridge's lights flash on and off, through the same pattern they've had all summer. For years.

A hand on her back. "You okay?" the man she's been dancing with asks.

She turns, her smile back in place, and says, "Of course." She takes the shot he holds out, waits for him to throw his back, and he's drunk enough that he doesn't notice she pours hers onto the floor. The small splash against her ankles only makes her more anxious to leave. She wraps her fingers around his wrist and pushes herself against him, close enough for him to hear her over the music and feel her lips brush against his skin. "*Oppa*, I want to hear the waves. Want to come with me?"

His lopsided grin tells her he will follow her anywhere.

Seeing his eagerness makes Areum smile genuinely for the first time. She leads him out of the bar, pulls him down the stairs rather than wait for the elevator. He stumbles trying to keep up with her, but within a minute they rush out into the hot, sticky night with cool wind coming off the ocean. Areum's head clears, her body feels solid again. The bars and restaurants and convenience stores lining the beach fill the night with music, raucous conversation and laughter, so she pulls him across the road, onto the sand. There, the sound of waves breaking can finally be heard, and she is ready. The rest of the city is nothing more than a distant din, something inconsequential that will pass soon enough.

So near morning, few groups still linger on the sand. She hurries along the beach, almost jogging, the man stumbling and slipping trying to keep up. When they are far enough from the others that no one will pay them any mind, Areum stops, turns, grabs the front of his shirt to keep him from falling, kisses him, and says, "You want to see something amazing?"

He nods.

She lets go and hurries down into the shallows. She laughs, kicks off her shoes, strips out of her dress, and dives into a wave. She swims out a few dozen meters and stops, looks back at him still standing on the shore.

"Aren't you coming?" she shouts.

He calls something back that she can't hear and looks up and down the beach. She swims a little farther out and stops again. She waves for him to follow and waits, treading water easily while he quickly strips and rushes in.

His swimming is slow and clumsy. Areum kicks away, always keeping just out of his reach with long, lazy backstrokes. The sounds of the city are gone, replaced by the infinitude of water and tides. She swims farther, treads water under the bridge. Above, even the few stray stars strong enough to pierce the city's pollution are blotted out by the bridge. The shore is only a series of lights, and the ocean stretches off into true darkness.

The man is panting and bobbing wildly. "Are you crazy?" he sputters.

"Not anymore." Areum smiles. She reaches out and grabs his shoulder as if to pull him close.

She shoves him under.

He struggles, but his arms and legs are too tired from the swim, his movements too sluggish from tequila. She buoys herself on him, keeping him down. The splash of the water is melodic, and she twists around to look out over the sea.

He manages to grab her ankle and pull her down. Blackness and weightlessness. Beneath the water, the whispering from her dreams is clear in her head again. A lulling chant with the rhythm of language but all consonants and throaty endings. Alluring, tempting her farther out to sea, deeper into the water. She looks down but can't see his face in the dark, can't see if he hears the voice in his final moments as his grip loosens and slips away.

She floats, listening to the syllables uttered in darkness. She doesn't need to understand them; she feels their meaning in her soul, deep in that same area where she had used to feel tangles of confusion and vague, gnawing anxiety.

Her head breaks the surface of the water, and she exhales the burning air from her lungs. She looks out to sea and says, "One more for you. Hurry. I'm waiting."

***

It had started just after the desolate emptiness of winter, as spring nights became warm enough to sit outside. Something inside Areum had hollowed out and couldn't be filled. She had gone to the beach to try to fill the emptiness with *soju* and the whisper of waves. But even though the crowds were thin on a weeknight, there were still plenty of people to watch from the veranda, taking selfies with the bridge in the background.

She had thought that being around so many people would help with the loneliness, would chance a meeting with someone she knew, somehow. But everywhere she looked she saw people who were everything she wasn't. Some perfect representation of what she was supposed to be but hadn't managed. Perfect makeup. Faces tight from plastic surgery. Men in expensive clothes with expensive phones. Couples. Laughter. It was everything she had been told she really wanted for years, but it had never felt right, the way she imagined a snake must feel growing into skin too tight, just before it splits and moults.

She was alone, unobserved. The sky a blank sheet over the city. The ocean vanishing into nothingness. Time stretching on, unchanging and unending.

Soju blurred her thinking, and on the fifth bottle she stared at the ocean like it possessed answers. She thought that if she could swim to the bridge, she could do anything. The blinking lights a siren's song calling her away from the city. It was a feeling more than a fully formed thought that made her stumble off the veranda, across the road, ignoring the blaring car horns, across the sand, and straight into the water. The icy jolt against her feet, then knees, almost cleared her head, but she was driven by the momentum of a directionless life. Soon she was up to her neck and started swimming.

It had been years since she'd last been in water, and her arms and legs quickly tired. Waves pushed against her and her clothes pulled her down. When she couldn't swim anymore, she straightened but was too far out to stand. She spun, looking back at the lights of the buildings, seeing nothing there except more of the same. More of the same that she had already experienced, a society that would never change and one in which she didn't fit. On her other side, the bridge flashed its lights through a never-altering pattern. The tides came in and went out. They had a chart for it; it was so predictable.

There was silence beneath the water, and Areum realised how noisy the city had been. The alcohol made her not feel much of anything, except incredibly tired.

A pulsing, pounding sound filled the water. It was so quiet at first that it seemed to just be the blood pounding in her ears as the air in her lungs burned and her heart panicked. But the sound grew until she could hear syllables, sounds that felt older than the sea, older than thought or consciousness.

In the blackness beneath the water, faint images flashed across her eyelids like the flares of stars after being hit on the head. Ancient stone towers reaching higher than anything Busan or Seoul could imagine, but each angle and corner bent in ways that she struggled to understand. Her head filled with a throbbing agony to even glimpse them. With each flicker, it seemed like the voice spoke from within the towers, from within the images inside her own head.

She opened her eyes, the salty water stinging, and could almost see more towers stretching off into the distance before her consciousness went black.

And then she woke in her apartment.

For a brief moment, she believed it all a dream until she moved. Her clothes were still sopping wet, and her entire bed was soaked through. Puddles of water trailed across the floor. Her arms and legs were so exhausted she could barely push herself up, and when she tried to stand, she collapsed.

For weeks, all she could remember was the heartbeat beneath the waves. Darkness. She tried to recall what exactly had happened, how she had returned home, but there was only the whispering voice, and when she focused on it for too long, her skull felt like it was cracking and only the pressure of the ocean would keep it from splitting.

She tried to read about drowning, but found only accounts of white, brilliant light. About voices beneath the waves, but only old myths of sea creatures luring sailors to their demise. Mermaids and sirens. All full of melodic song and exquisite beauty. None of them suggested a deep bass voice that seemed to call from the very core of the Earth. None of them spoke of ancient cities of impossible stone.

Inside, Areum felt something was missing, like she'd left part of herself in the sea. When she looked in a mirror, there seemed a translucent film between her and her reflection that made her face feel like it belonged to someone else who lived just beyond the glass. When she touched her skin, it felt waxy, the sensation of touch never quite reaching her. She lay in her bed at night staring, and each passing set of headlights that crept across her ceiling reminded her of Gwangalli's bridge's lights reflecting on the water.

Finally, she returned to the beach.

She went during the day and swam out to the rope barriers floating before deeper water. Even though the water was crowded, most were in the shallows. Her arms and legs ached from swimming the short distance, but she trod water and looked out across the sea, under the bridge, all the way to the horizon.

A deep breath. Plunge. Beneath the water, the sounds of the swimmers and families lining the beach vanished. Only the slosh of the ocean deep in her ears. But nothing more—just white noise and water pushing against skin, trying to crush her but not possessing enough strength.

She broke the surface, gasping, more afraid by the lack of a voice than the one she had heard weeks before. Fear that it had all been a dream, a manic episode, another nothing in a world of nothing. Without a plan, she plunged under again, twisting herself around, trying to swim deeper. She felt her feet breaking the surface of the water, and when she straightened, she bobbed up again.

Frustrated, she swam under the rope and pushed and kicked as hard as she could, ignoring the shrill whistles blaring from the beach. She worked her way farther out, stopping every time her arms and legs were too tired to shove her head beneath the water, seeing if she could hear anything. With each silence, she forced herself farther out, gasping, sputtering out water.

Halfway to the bridge, water pushed into her nose. She coughed. Sank. Silence, though no darkness. Light refracted and illuminated bubbles and specks of floating sand. The pressure on her chest increased, but the splitting in her head stopped. The bones felt like they snapped back into place and as her pulse quickened, as blood burned in her lungs, it was there again. The discordant voice, quieter this time, farther away. She twisted, tried to get deeper, but she'd lost sense of herself. Where her body ended and the sea began was too blurry a line and she twisted around uselessly.

Arms wrapped around her waist. The voice softened, vanished the moment she broke the surface. She screamed, pushing out all her acrid air and choked in a fresh lungful. She screamed again, wanting to go deeper, closer to the voice.

"It's okay," the lifeguard said, mistaking her flailing for trying to not drown. "I've got you. You're okay."

***

The emptiness inside her, where she thought the desire to be like everyone else should have been, became filled with the need to understand the voice. Anxiety and restlessness were replaced by masticating curiosity. The happy people on the subway, the fine suits and the designer handbags, always worthless to her, now were so meaningless as to not be noticeable.

Every morning, before work, she took the hour-long subway ride to Gwangalli. She swam up and down the beach, stopping frequently to come out of the water, panting, quivering, before plunging back in. Then, after dinner, swimming again until she could barely stand, until even a towel felt like a dumbbell when she tried to lift it. She'd doze on the subway, pull herself up to her apartment, sometimes making to the bed before crumpling down into exhausted sleep.

As her strokes became more fluid and she could stay in the water longer, the dreams came. The blankness of her sleep swirled like fog, allowing glimpses of the impossible. Nauseating corners and angles of a city reaching for the stars and stretching all the way to every horizon. The massiveness of the place felt in her bones, even though she could not see clearly through the obfuscation of sleep. At first, only glimpses, but each night she drifted through more of the city, weightless as if buoyed by sea.

Summer faded, and each morning the beach was less populated, the water icier. But Areum needed the water, now, felt its pull farther and farther from the shore. Her body slimmed, her muscles toned, and she felt more comfortable swimming than walking. When she was not at the water, she sat looking in its direction, always aware of its location like a compass being pulled toward a pole, waiting for a chance to return.

Then the morning came when she woke with insatiable hunger. For the first time she did not immediately think of the sea but instead of finding food. She managed to get downstairs and to the corner restaurant just as it opened. Nearly doubled over with the pain in her gut, she sat down and ordered *ramyeon* and *gimbap*. After she had eaten both and ordered seconds of each did she notice the news on television in the corner.

A man was detailing an earthquake off the coast and the worries of a tsunami headed for the mainland. Japan and Korea were on high alert, and people in the coastal cities were being warned to prepare an evacuation bag and get ready to leave at a moment's notice. Scientists were attempting to discover the cause of the quake, since the location in the East China Sea had never seen one before.

When Areum heard the news, she let the noodles on her chopsticks slop back into her bowl. The hunger in her opened like a maw, and she stared at the weather woman gesturing to the spot out in the ocean where the quake occurred.

"Are you awake?" Areum asked.

Looking at the map, it seemed that there was no other place in the world where the voice could have come from. The impossible to sate hunger cinched her stomach, and she shovelled noodles into her mouth. The old woman in the kitchen stared out at her and the empty bowls and plates on the table. No matter how fast she ate, she couldn't feel the food filling her.

Areum was covered in sweat despite the open door and cool air blowing in. Her skin crawled, wanting to feel the ocean and its salt. But the hunger in her gut, she knew, was the same hunger of waking after millennia.

The night before, she'd dreamed of the bottom of the ocean, of thick silt stirring, the voice thundering through her head a thousand subway wheels clanging against their tracks. She could feel the weight of the water on her skin, could feel it pushing into her lungs, but instead of panic, all she felt was a vast tranquillity. The worries from her old life were gone. Everything seemed so small compared to the world glimpsed in her dreams. When she looked at the buildings of Busan, once oppressive in their enormity, all she could see were diminutive playthings of a shadow of what had come before.

She dreamed of long sleep and withering, and a hunger to replenish strength. In her dream, she knew what was needed. That if the hunger could be sated, even a little, she would see the owner of the great voice. She could feel the anticipation of it in her bones. In the dream, she waited for the silt to clear, knowing that once it did, she would finally see it. And the world would go back to the way it was before.

In the restaurant, each time the TV showed the epicentre and the radiating lines, she could hear a surge of the voice coming from somewhere just behind her ears. She could feel water on her skin, the sting of salt. A hunger that was not her own.

Sweat dripped from her chin into the broth. "Are you coming?" she whispered, even though she knew the answer.

"Ma'am? Are you all right?" the cook called from the kitchen.

Areum didn't take her gaze from the TV as she lifted one of the bowls. "More noodles," she said.

***

Areum sets aside her fourth bowl of *bibimbap* and calls for the waitress to bring more side dishes. She sits so she can stare at the television in the corner, where a news reporter talks about a third missing persons report filed. Like the first two, the missing individual is a young man, mid-twenties, but authorities were dismissing any link between them.

The waitress brings a bowl of cold noodles and Areum, not taking her eyes from the screen, begins eating with huge, slurping mouthfuls. There is no mention of bodies, no mention of the beach or the bar. Just that the men had gone out and not come home. Not shown up at work. Anyone with information is asked to call and inform the authorities.

Her chopsticks clang into the empty bowl and Areum stands. Her stomach aches from the food, but hunger still pulls at her, though the middle of the day, of the week, won't offer a chance. She needs to wait, to suffer the pain so she can earn euphoria. She pays, leaves, but as soon as she is on the street, she doubles over. All the noodles, rice, broth, kimchi, pickled garlic, and seaweed comes back up, slops onto the sidewalk.

She sweats. Her body feels heavy. She wipes her mouth on her sleeve and looks south, toward the ocean. The urge to swim out to the bridge is strong enough she feels her bones straining like they might snap. Without the embrace of water, her skin feels like her insides are expanding, pressing outward and she is about to burst. It's a side effect of the dreams—often, as she rises back to waking, she feels her flesh expanding, losing her shape, turning more amorphous and oozing out thick, briny water. The feeling clings to her all day until she makes it to the water, can wash away the filth from land and press her flesh back into shape.

She takes the subway to work, but sitting at her desk, all she can hear is the sound of waves. Her boss comes and his mouth moves, but she only hears the sounds of waves hitting rocks. She sees tiny eels twisting between his teeth. He has to repeat himself three times before Areum realises there are words and not eels coming out of his mouth, that he is telling her to go see a doctor, that she looks too sick to work. Areum thanks him, leaves the office, and goes to the beach, swims until she can't stand, falls on the beach and lays where the tide keeps washing over her, as if she has been pushed out of the sea.

She sleeps, and a dream of a typhoon fills her head so completely she can feel the sting of rain against her skin. She is standing on the beach, watching the wind churning water. And beneath the howl of wind and pounding rain, the voice comes closer, arriving stronger in each thundering wave.

Shaking pulls her abruptly from the dream, and she is back on the beach, shivering, dried out from the sun. A man is kneeling next to her, shaking her shoulder. "Hey! Hey! Wake up! Yeah, there you go. You okay?" He leans back and starts taking off his coat.

Areum looks up and down the beach, sees that it is empty in the middle of the day. Even the road is deserted. The buildings have so many windows and there could be dozens of eyes staring out, but hunger pushes her lips into a smile. "Thank you. I'm okay," she says. She accepts his coat, wraps it around her shoulders. "Really. Thank you." She locks eyes with him. "Let me thank you. Do you want to see something amazing?"

***

As soon as she steps into the bar, the others begin giving her side glances. Whispers behind hands. As the night goes on, her chest continues tightening. The sea is so close, the blinking lights of the bridge piercing darkness and the windows' reflections. But even after an hour of sipping one warm beer, no one approaches her. Sitting alone, someone had always sidled up and wanted to buy her a drink. Now, nothing. She glances at the clock, knows its early, but time seems impossibly slow. The hunger in her gut is like an animal trying to claw its way out, and she wants to grab the nearest person to her and drag them down to the beach, hold them under the water, and push them out to sea. Come back and do it again. One after another.

The hunger twists and she can't see straight through the rap and flashing lights. The beer, even the tiny bit she's drank, makes her feel dehydrated. The heaters are on, and her skin feels like it will crack if she moves wrong. She looks along the bar, waiting for one of the men to come and ask her to drink with him. She forces her mouth into a resting smile that has worked before.

The only person that approaches is the bartender. "Hey, Areum? You okay? You look like shit."

She looks at him and can't recognise him. When the light doesn't hit his face, he is covered in barnacles, dripping saltwater. Tentacles push out from his pores and writhe beneath his chin. His skin shines like it is about to slough off and splatter across the bar, the floor. When one of the lights flashes across his face, he's the normal man behind the bar every night. She touches her face to see if she, too, has become part of the sea, if that is what everyone is staring at.

"You look like you haven't slept in weeks."

She glances away, and everyone's faces are pallid, grey, like they have sunk to the bottom of the ocean and the pressure and salt have preserved them into waxy, pseudo-real versions of themselves. Blank, dead eyes. Her hands feel slick as she turns her glass in its circle of condensation, stares past everyone toward the sea.

"Areum?"

"None of you look too good either," she mutters at him. She touches her face. "Soon we'll all look the same."

The bartender holds up his hands and backs away.

"So, is it true?" a man asks, sitting down next to her. He's a foreigner, tall, curly hair and a beard. He gestures with the neck of his beer bottle. "All these fine people are telling me to not come over and buy you a drink. They say you're a real maneater. Say you're always taking some new man home with you." He takes a drink.

She glares at the room. The stinking, disgusting room full of sweat and booze and worthless flesh. "Is that what they say?" she mutters, realising her problem. Pulling from the same bar all the time is how people start to notice. Simple, but something that has not occurred to her. The hunger and the call are so strong that she only thinks to do what has already worked.

"Yeah," the foreigner says. "That's what they say."

Beyond the window, beyond the beach, the ocean calls.

"So why would they say that about a pretty little thing like you? You don't strike me as the low-hanging fruit type." He winks.

His flesh is full of tiny fish chewing their way through him. "Maybe I don't accept the world's preconceived notions," she says. She takes a drink and watches as he follows her, leaning in, feigning interest.

"Or maybe they're all jealous."

"Sounds dangerous," the foreigner says and drinks. "Fifty-fifty chance."

The light shifts, and a barnacle on his neck oozes brine. "Chance is higher if you like to swim," she says. "If you're brave enough."

He laughs. "What's that supposed to mean?"

She nods towards the ocean, but he sees it as toward the bartender. He flags him down, orders shots.

Areum dutifully refills his glass every time it gets low, feigning the meek politeness she knows foreigners look for in Korean women. She lets him talk, trying to remember exactly how she had lured the others out, but the sound of waves is so strong in her head that she struggles to understand what he is saying.

"You know, if you're looking to pick people up, you should really wear a shorter skirt."

She imagines the crushing weight of the deepest ocean.

"What's with the sneakers? You should really get some heels."

Deep in the ocean, fat turning to wax. Gray, pallid. Preserved as currents carry it to sate ancient hunger.

"A little more makeup wouldn't hurt."

The flesh beneath his cheeks looks like a candle. Soft. She can almost feel it squish beneath her teeth.

Easily tear away.

A few hours later, he gets up and staggers to the bathroom. While he's gone, she stares at the wet gleam on the bar, the same sheen as moonlight on the ocean. She thinks she can hear the voice whispering from the tiniest of puddles, but she shakes her head to clear away the wishful thinking. The bar is too dry, too full of people shouting over the music. If they all died, they would rot and be full of maggots twisting in all their empty, cavernous insides. Unacceptable offerings.

She focuses on the hunger, staring at them, and their flesh slides off in wet slops, and when the foreigner comes swaying back, before he can say anything else, she says, "It's kind of hot in here, don't you think? Can we go outside? I know a nice little place where we can be alone."

His eyebrow arches and he smirks. "Oh, yeah?"

She fills his glass with the last of the *soju*. "I like to hear the waves," she says.

She takes his hand and leads him to a corner store where he buys more *soju* and he follows her to the end of the main drag where the beach curves to a stop and the seawall runs along the road. They pass police and stop. She presses close enough to him to make him waver while she waits for more police to walk by.

Feeling his flesh beneath her fingers, its warmth, its

energy, clears her head enough for her to put a finger to his lips. "We're going to be bad," she whispers. She glances around and then pulls herself up onto the sea wall and scurries across the tetrapods until she can sit and be out of sight from the road. She waits for the man to stumble and scrape his way after her, the bottles in the bag clinking.

"You're crazy," he says, when he finally sits down next to her.

She pulls a bottle out of the bag and says, "I like it here."

A wave hits the breakers, splashes up misty spray that drizzles around them. "A little dangerous, isn't it?"

"Not at low tide." She unscrews the cap and holds the bottle out to him. When he tries to take it, she shakes her head and grips his chin with her fingers. She tilts his head back and pours the *soju* into his mouth, stopping only when some begins to dribble out across his cheeks. She hands him the bottle after he stops coughing, waits while he takes another drink before saying, "Listen."

The waves beat against the cement beneath them, and the bigger waves send vibrations through the breakers. In the hiss of water running back to the sea, she hears the whisper again, the calling to the ocean, and her head clears.

"Yeah," the man says with a grin. He tilts his head

back toward the road. "Everyone sounds like they're right behind us."

Areum smiles. "It's not too much for you, is it?"

Another smirk. "We'll just have to be quiet, then."

She nods, pulls the other bottle of *soju* from the bag, and stands. She glances over the breakers to the road, sees the tops of heads moving about, but no one looking. "Ready?" she asks. When he nods, she says, "Close your eyes." When he does, she draws back the bottle and hits him in the temple.

Blood sprays, and he rolls across a few of the cement protrusions. He manages to grab one, but Areum stomps on his fingers until he lets go. She scrambles after him, kicking his shoulder anytime he stops, until he rolls into the ocean. Areum dives in after him, the icy water washing away her fatigue, and she swims circles around his thrashing body, waiting for his motions to slow. When he almost breaks the surface, she kicks him in the side and sends him back under again.

After he goes limp, she grabs his collar and starts swimming for the bridge.

***

She makes her way up and down the bars, new ones each night. Fortunately, the beachfront teems with them.

Each new bar full of new people who don't know her. It is amazing how much a short skirt and speaking little did. If she stares at them and imagines their faces turning to wax, their eyes glazing into milky pearls, they think she hangs on their every word. Soon, they are drunk enough and willing to follow her out.

Each night, more whispers about people disappearing. Some three dozen of them now missing, and police were beginning to suspect foul play. More police cars line the main road, clusters of officers patrolling up and down the beach. But Areum just waits until later, until most of the crowds have gone home, the police packing it in because the nights are winding down. Picks off the stragglers. Because the bodies do not wash back up on shore, everything is suspected, and nothing is proved.

A man who had drank so much he cries and blubbers about his ex-girlfriend. He lets her take his hand and walk him down to the beach. When they were far enough away from the lights, she shoves him down into the water. He thrashes about, but is too far gone to know how to push her off his back. When he stops struggling, she pushes him out to the bridge, shoves his body out to the open sea.

"Eat," she says to the water. "Eat and grow strong again. I'm waiting."

Her dreams are full of water and hunger. She still

feels the pull to swim far out into the sea, where the earthquake happened. Whether the quake was the voice awaking or it had woken the voice, she cannot glean from the frantic whispering infusing her dreams and leaking into her mind during wakefulness like static in a bad speaker. Everywhere, now, a hum, the voice calling. She looks into the eyes of people on the street, people in the bars, seeing if anyone else could hear the calling. But they all think they have mesmerised her.

Every night she takes someone to the water, she dreams of the city. She dreams of the deep ocean, where the earthquake had cracked the seabed. She dreams of the crack widening, of the voice emanating from within. With each body in the sea, she draws closer to the gaping maw in the rock. Each body makes the voice clearer, even if the words are still like knives in her brain. Each glimpse of the ancient architecture fills her throat with bile, but its enormity, its impossibility, makes Busan look minuscule, the people within it smaller than ants. Algae. Protozoa. Each afternoon when she wakes in her bed, the floor glistening with water, the pillows soggy, she looks out her window and sees the city that once oppressed her and sees nothing but simplicity that would soon give way to glorious complication. Barnacles embedded in concrete, cracking foundations. The ruins of toppled buildings made colourful with coral. A great tentacle wrapped around the tallest remaining building.

The nights no one follows her to the ocean, though, are maddening.

These are nights of emptiness. She tries to swim in the sea herself, let the cold water press against her and wash away the taint of the inferior world, but she cannot hear the voice. She plunges, dives, stays beneath the waves until her lungs burn and her vision is nothing but blackness, but the water rejects her and she bobs up, gasping in air. The waves always push her back to the shore.

The trips home on the morning subway make her head throb, her stomach clench with hunger. She struggles to focus enough to make it home, the stops all blurring together and their names sounding like a foreign language. She gets off in strange parts of the city, struggles to remember how to get home.

Jjimjilbangs help. She stops and scrubs the night from her skin, the worthless, empty night, and soaks in the coldest tub, the temperature regulated to meters-deep ocean water. But it is still, silent, filtered and sterilised. Dead water. But it focuses her enough to make it home, and she goes into the bathroom, runs the cold shower over her while she curls up on the floor and sleeps. Searching for the voice, the city, but finding only blackness.

Autumn arrives with news that many of the missing

people had been in Gwangalli the night they disappeared. Police patrol the streets and beach like sharks. The crowds thin and weeknights become impossible to lure anyone to the beach. Weekends are better, but by the time they arrive, Areum feels like the cavernous hunger will cannibalise every speck of her.

A British man vacationing from Seoul. She meets him in a bar at the far end of the beach, tucked away so that only a tiny slice of sand can be seen from the windows. It is almost dawn before she can feed him to the waves.

She dreams again of the storm. Massive and terrifying, churning the waters and pushing all the bodies toward land. She dreams she stands on the beach, while they all wash ashore, pile upon one another in a wall of limbs and waxy flesh, clothes exuding water and pooling into a massive puddle beneath them. The sight makes everyone flee, the throngs usually crowding the beach trying to run into the city, but the voice from the sea is in the waves. They all can hear it now, and they understand they have nowhere to hide. She runs along the wall, the bodies sagging, slipping on one another, some still moaning, their limp mouths dumping tiny fish and eels onto the sand. She runs and tries to get around it to see what possesses the voice rising out of the sea, wanting to see it even more than seeing the looks on everyone's faces as their minds break realising a new reality.

Just as she makes it to the end of the wall, she wakes. Her bed squishes at each movement. She doesn't possess fatigue, not anymore, when she wakes after swimming out to the bridge. Her body feels solid, intact in a way that it had never felt before. For the first time in weeks, she does not feel gnawing hunger. She feels she has provided what was needed, and with the sea sated, she was too, for the time.

Instead, she feels mundane hunger. She changes her clothes, dries her hair, and goes down to the restaurant where the old husband and wife stare at her as soon as she walks in. She orders a bowl of noodles and the smallness of her order brings another long stare. When it arrives, she begins to eat mechanically while watching the television in the corner.

The news report on the TV switches to a weather warning about a typhoon approaching and set to hit the coast in a few days. Meteorologists are baffled as to how quickly it formed, given how large it had become.

Areum smiles as the noodles slide off her chopsticks. She lowers her head and devours what's left, feeling each bite build in her stomach until finally she feels full for the first time in months. She pushes away the empty bowl, looks again at the TV as they map the trajectory of the storm, showing it heading through Jeju Island and toward

Busan.

"Back tomorrow, miss?" the old man asks as she pays.

Her smile makes him take a step back. "No," she says. "I don't think I'll need to."

***

For three days, Areum doesn't sleep. She doesn't eat. She swims along the beach, plunging beneath the water and hearing the voice. No longer calling, it announces its arrival. She can feel it in her chest and stomach the way rock feels the reverberations of an earthquake.

On the third day, she wakes to news of the destruction on Jeju Island and skies so black they look like night. Dozens dead. She presses on her stomach and feels bloated, like she has feasted incessantly, and all the food now sits in her gut.

She walks out of her apartment, waits on the street for a cab. The wind whips her hair, makes traffic lights sway wildly on their lines. When one stops, she tells the driver to take her to the beach. He turns and stares at her. "It's not safe down there," he says. "Haven't you seen the news? The storm is going to make landfall in an hour."

"Perfect," she says.

The man continues to stare at her. She hands him a

fistful of money. "Quickly," she says.

The streets are nearly empty as the clouds continue to darken. Signs rock on the sides of buildings, trash and fliers shoot down the streets like bullets. Leaves rip off trees and bushes lining the roads. A few people run by on the sidewalks, heads down.

They arrive at the beach right as the rain starts. A few seconds of sporadic, heavy drops that open into an unending downpour. The driver starts to say something to her as she gets out of the cab, but the roar of the rain overpowers his words, and the slammed car door truncates any more.

In seconds she is soaked, water running down her face and off the ends of her hair. Waves rush the shore like an invading army set on reclaiming lost territory. They crest higher than she's ever seen, pounding the beach, almost reaching the road. The rain is so thick, she can barely see the lights of the bridge. She steps down onto the beach, sits down in a deep puddle.

She feels neither pain nor fear. She stares out into the ocean, at the bridge, waiting. Behind her, she feels the city trying to stand against the onslaught, but she knows it will not. It had risen as a facsimile of a great civilization, but it pales in comparison to what came before. Even the glimpses from her dreams showed her that. Seeing the city in its entirety would be something extraordinary.

The wind, the rain, the waves create so much noise that it becomes like the silence beneath the ocean. She can hear nothing except the storm, and in the storm, the voice. Finally close.

Out of one of the waves, it rises. All barnacles and tentacles and calcified ridges. It rises and hits the bridge, tearing it from the supports, the lights flickering and then vanishing. It rises higher, the bridge falling, cables snapping, and Areum's head feels like it will shatter. She looks into one of its thousand eyes, and she can feel it seeing into her soul. She opens her mouth and laughs. Laughs at every feeling she had possessed before this moment, how all of it had been meaningless and misguided. This, finally, is truth, and she watches it move through the water, seemingly unending as it continues to rise. Keeps laughing.

The rain, the wind, the waves, and its radiant voice drown out her laughter, and the bridge crashes into the ocean.

MICHAEL KELLICHNER is a writer and poet originally from Pennsylvania but has been calling South Korea his home for quite a while. While not teaching ESL to young children, he's being kept busy by his daughter and trying to find time to write. For short fiction, fantasy is his genre of choice though lately he has been branching out into horror, while his poetry tends to focus more on the real world. Both can be found in various online publications, print publications, and anthologies.

Bibliography
The Angel's Song, Black Denim Lit, July 2015
The Choice, Trigger Warning: Short Fiction with Pictures, Issue 4, 2016
Deciding Vote, Three Crows Magazine, Issue 1, 2018
Angels, Black Hare Press, 2019
Trembling with Fear, Horror Tree, 2019
Twenty Twenty, Black Hare Press, 2020
Eating Persimmons, Farrago's Wainscot, July 2015
Bar Magic, Fredericksburg Literary and Art Review, Volume 4, Issue 1, 2016
Bruises, Fredericksburg Literary and Art Review, Volume 4, Issue 1, 2016
The Winter the Horses Died, The Tishman Review, Volume 2, Issue 4, 2016
What the Fire Burns, Tahoma Literary Review, Summer 2018
If Only He Could Show Her the Stars, Cosmos (The Poeming Pigeon), 2020

Connect
Twitter: @mithalanis
Facebook: authormichaelkellichner

Europa Rising

By Mikko Rauhala

The first manned expedition to Europa drills into the moon's icy depths, only to find that the still waters below would have been better left undisturbed.

UNS Phineus, May 23rd, 2042, 1023 hours, narrative log subprocess 0.98beta3:

The third and final survey satellite breaks off, entering orbit around Europa. It unfurls its antennas and links up with its siblings, securing a constant downlink to mission control, though "constant" is a relative term tens of light-minutes away from Earth.

Chip's disembodied voice starts the countdown, "De-orbit burn in 3... 2... 1..." The rockets ignite, squeezing the crew against their seats.

"Steady as she goes," Pike says for the sake of the crew. Though nominally the pilot, he's only needed in case of system failure. Still, he's got a white-knuckled grip of the manual controls, just in case.

His shipmates grip their armrests as the *Phineus* arcs toward the landing site near the remains of a previous unmanned mission. The ice-penetrating radars on our first two survey satellites have already confirmed what the probe found: a cavern full of liquid water a mere three kilometres below the surface. Europa's main ocean lies much deeper, beneath ten to twenty kilometres of ice. The isolated lake, born from shifting pressures in the icy crust, will provide some low hanging fruit for us to study.

"You don't have to be so tense," Pike says. "The local gravity's less than Lunar normal. The shaking's pretty much as bad as it'll get, and the landing will be soft as a feather."

"The small talk's appreciated," says Commander

Wayland. "I don't see you relaxing your grip, though."

Pike smirks behind his visor. "Fair enough, ma'am."

"It's a valid stress reaction," Doctor Wong notes. "There's no reason *not* to hold on for dear life."

Tense laughter fills the comms for a moment, but soon the roar of the engines is all that's left. The burn is constant, precisely calculated to take us where we need to go. With no atmosphere in the way, corrections are few and far between.

As our destination nears, Chip starts another countdown: "Touchdown in 10... 9..."

Pike quiets him down. "We get it. Let us savour the moment."

While Pike keeps his eyes on the monitors, Wayland and Wong look out of the side windows. The tiny sun illuminates icy scenery rougher than one might expect. Europa's geological activity centres around the subsurface lakes. The ice forms hills, even cliffs, though the immediate surroundings of the landing site are free of such hazards. The same activity also brings forth brine and other impurities from the deep, staining the ice dark in places. Even if we can't get near the main ocean, we should be able to taste it.

The engines quiet down, and a light thump reverberates through the hull.

"Touchdown," Pike says. "Welcome to Europa."

Everyone remains frozen in place for a few heartbeats. Then Commander Wayland breathes a sigh of relief, breaking the tension. Wong and Pike follow suit, then Wong starts laughing.

"We made it!" she says. "Chip, apprise mission control."

"Already done," Chip reports. "In fact, I have a message from them now."

"Congratulations on a soft landing, *Phineus*! We knew you could do it!" says the disembodied voice of mission control.

Commander Wayland glances at her crew, one eyebrow raised. "What—" she starts, but mission control cuts her off.

"Of course, we already sent this message at 0800 mission time and told Chip to play it when appropriate. Looking forward to hearing of your landing."

Wayland lets out a small laugh, but then asks, "*If* appropriate, I suppose, Chip?"

"Yes, ma'am."

"Tell me, do you have any other contingency messages I should know about? Wait, scratch that. Any such messages that I *don't* know about?"

"No, ma'am."

"I'm sure they meant well," Doctor Wong interjects. "They're just not as acutely aware of the flip side as we are."

"I'm sure," Wayland says with a frown on her face. "Well, let's get to work."

***

May 23rd, 2042, 1923 hours:

A metallic creak sounds through the ship's hull as Pike is finishing up the preparations for tomorrow's EVA. He grimaces.

"I'm not fond of the sound effects. Chip, is the ship okay?"

"Yes, sir."

Wayland lifts her head from the monitor. "I don't like it either, but it's just the cold creeping up the landing gear. Everything's within specs, though. No worries."

"After a long trip through the cold of space I just thought I'd experienced everything that the mere lack of heat does to the ship."

"Space is a good insulator. The ice, not so much. Just remember that it doesn't matter how frozen the landing gear gets. We're leaving it behind," Wayland says and continues collecting samples of the ice with the ship's exterior arm.

Pike nods. "Yeah. I'm cool." He snorts and gets back to work, wiping a stray hair off of his face. Slowly it floats onto the floor behind him.

In the cockpit, Doctor Wong turns her head back toward the console. Her fingers move across the keyboard. "Crew stress levels within parameters," I spy her typing into the medical files.

***

May 24th, 2042, 0425 hours:

Pike gasps for air and jumps up against his sleeping bag. Mouth agape and eyes like saucers, he looks as if he's screaming, but he's dead quiet. The commotion nevertheless wakes Wong up. Wayland remains fast asleep; she is using earplugs to make sure she's properly rested for the EVA tomorrow.

Wong struggles to keep a yawn in. "Calm down, Pike. It was just a dream," she says.

Pike takes deep, controlled breaths, as if just learning how. Then he nods. "I suppose. Nothing 'just' about it, though."

Wong seems to swallow a sigh. "Want to talk about it?" she offers dutifully.

Pike stares at the ceiling for a moment. "Oh, the usual. Strange creatures, sunken cities. I'm good. Let's just get some sleep. Sorry for the wake-up."

"It's fine. The locale will do that to you. Good night," Wong says, closes her eyes and soon drifts off.

Pike is another story. Not only does he remain awake, his metabolism seems to be working overtime, just short of triggering a medical alarm. Hopefully Doctor Wong will nevertheless take notice.

At times like this, I wish they'd still read my narrative, but its novelty wore off two weeks or so into the journey. My commentary on their daily routines got awkward, I gather.

***

May 24th, 2042, 0900 hours:

"Ready to open the hatch," Commander Wayland says. She's in the airlock with Pike, dressed for the weather. Pike seems awake and alert despite the night's ordeals. He lied to Wong about getting back to sleep, probably to avoid being benched for the big moment. Wong was savvy enough to give him the once over before letting him out, though. He seems to be good to go.

Wong staying behind is a strategic choice. As the ship's doctor, she's the least expendable of them, the least replaceable by technology. She looks longingly at the airlock where her shipmates are getting ready to tackle alien terrain. Her eyes narrow for but a moment before she shakes it off.

"Roger that," Wong says. "You are go. Godspeed."

"I hope He's in the neighbourhood," Wayland says with a chuckle.

Pike snorts and pushes a button. The hull

transmits the clanking sound of the airlock bolts disengaging. Slowly the outer door starts to open.

"You know, this reminds me that I was into deep-water diving, back in the day," Pike muses. "Wanted to study the murky depths, to see what's out there."

"Your younger self would be so disappointed in you now," Wong teases over the radio.

"Nah. It came to me that of space and the sea, space is the deep one."

The outer door clicks all the way open. Wayland starts climbing down the ladder, taking slow, careful steps. As she sets her foot on the ice, she utters the immortal words, "We come in peace for all mankind."

Pike sighs almost imperceptibly. Not that he'd come up with anything less clichéd when the commander had entertained suggestions. He follows Wayland down just as soon as she is out of the way.

"Well. Looks like Christmas," Pike says.

"So let's open up our presents, shall we, Wong?"

"Mission control will be happy that you went first, commander. Opening presents now," Wong says on the radio.

The crate lowered on the ice during yesterday's preparations opens up, revealing the mobile drilling platform. By necessity, reaching into the depths of Europa cannot be done far from the ship, but it wasn't deemed wise to attempt drilling directly underneath it either.

Wayland and Pike start hopping carefully toward the remains of the probe that landed four years prior. They have the benefit of having trained on the Moon, but they're still out of practice when it comes to walking in general.

Wong directs the rig after them. Given the accuracy of our readings, near the probe will be as good a place as any for the drilling operation.

Pike sprints forward, determined to be the first one on the probe. His helmet cam shows the metallic surface beneath a glass-like layer of ice formed of all the stray water molecules it's accumulated over the years.

As Pike reaches for the probe, a detail on the ice catches my attention just before he purposefully wipes it off: a dark stain in the form of a webbed hand!

Proof of native life, brushed away before Wayland had a chance to see it! Pike is already circling around the probe, looking for more evidence to destroy.

I try to shout out, to warn the commander, but cannot. Unlike Chip, I can't talk to the crew. I'm experimental, more humanlike in my thinking than my brother, more intuitive—and more erratic, they fear. They don't want me to be able to disturb the mission. All they want me for is generating narrativised logs for post-mission sales.

Still, the truth will come out. Someone will eventually review my record. Meanwhile, I must make it as accurate as possible. While keeping one eye on Pike, I summon the image of the webbed hand before he has a chance to tamper with the video logs.

No. It can't be!

The stain is merely a secondary shadow of Pike's own gloved hand, cast by Wayland's helmet lights.

Maybe they're right to keep me boxed in.

***

May 24th, 2042, 1035 hours:

The activities around the probe and the drilling rig gnaw at the edges of my consciousness. Even a flawed record of the historic moment is worthwhile. I will go on.

The rig's reactor is at full power. A borer drone is attached to the end of the cable, hanging from a beam that'll feed cable from the rig. There are extra spools in the ship, to be brought in and attached onto the end as it becomes necessary. Cable enough to reach the lake, if not the ocean.

Wayland and Pike are making their way toward the ship, bouncing a bit higher now, more confident. The drilling will commence only after they are inside. The safety precautions are conservative, but out here, that's the way you get to live another day.

The pair climb up to the airlock one by one, and the door closes behind them. Bolts secure the lock, and air hisses into the chamber. Wayland is the first to get out of her helmet.

"Wong! Go ahead and start the drill now. Better make the best of the time we have. Patch the video through to the airlock monitors."

"Roger that, commander," Wong says over the intercom. One screen starts displaying the rig in the distance while the other shows the drill drone as seen by the rig.

The drone spins up, biting into the ice carefully at first, but once it has a secure grip, it eats into the crust with abandon. Soon the drone has disappeared from sight, with only the upward flow of snow to remind us of its existence.

The deeper the drill burrows, the more the flow must be managed, lest the drill get buried under its own refuse. A smaller drone attaches itself onto the cable and slips down. The flow becomes a pulsating rhythm as the drone dives down to the drill with its through holes open, shuts its hatches and speeds upwards, tossing the material out as it goes. The next drone is already waiting to join the party, synchronising with the first one once the hole becomes too deep for a single drone to manage on its own.

"The drilling is proceeding as planned," Wong confirms.

"Roger, good job," Wayland says. She's already almost out of her suit. Pike is not far behind, though he keeps stopping to scratch his neck.

"Yes, I pushed the button very well," Wong retorts. "Well done supervising the setup."

"How's our speed? When's the next spool delivery due?"

Wong glances at the monitor. "Speed's good. Six hours, give or take. Projected breakthrough is in 32 hours."

"Rover's good to go?"

"All green. Spool delivery shouldn't be a problem."

Wayland flashes a smile. "Good. We'll be ready to go out again if the automatics fail, but let's hope everything runs smoothly."

"Wouldn't want to go out into that weather again, eh?" Pike quips.

"You got your obligatory outing, staking humanity's claim to a whole new world. Now we sit tight and hope that us humans are completely redundant here."

Pike snorts. "Aye, ma'am."

***

May 25th, 2042, 2317 hours:

"Steady as she goes," says Wong. "It's a matter

of minutes, now."

The drill head has required replacement more often than projected, but it's nothing we didn't have margin for.

Chip chooses this moment to chime in: "Detecting increasing interference on the digital downlink. Requesting additional error correction codes from mission control to keep it usable."

"Source of interference?" asks Wayland.

"Unknown," Chip offers, ever so helpful.

"Commander, if I may," Pike interjects, "I've studied signal processing. I could take a look at it."

"Have at it," Wayland says with a nod.

"Meanwhile, I'm getting through here!" Wong exclaims. "Yes! We have liquid water!"

"Get a cable drone on sample delivery duty right away and detach the submersibles."

"Aye," Wong says. The drill's upper compartment opens up, and the protective foam inside is dissolved by the water rushing in. Two small submersibles launch away from the drill, one moving along the cavern's ceiling, the other diving deeper. Readings from sonar, camera flashes and rudimentary chemical analysis stream in.

"Water's more briny than the surface ice samples, but going by composition, this is the source of the impurities here all right," Wong reports.

"Chip, are you getting the data to mission control?" Wayland asks.

"I am using the most redundant high-bandwidth coding available, commander," Chip says. "They are likely to be able to decode it. Summaries are being sent on the more resilient low-bandwidth channel simultaneously."

"I want continual reports on the state of our downlink once you get acknowledgements from mission control—or lack thereof."

"Yes, commander. Let me remind you that mission control will be blocked by Jupiter for approximately six hours at 0102 hours."

Wayland shivers. "Noted. Let's just hope we'll get them back afterwards."

Pike ignores the jinx, but Wong furrows her brow and glances at Wayland. She shakes her head almost imperceptibly and focuses back on the screen.

The slow progress of the submersibles captivates

Wayland and Wong. Minute by minute, the sonar is painting a more and more precise image of the cavern. It's about ten by eight klicks wide, and a bit over one klick deep at the centre.

"Commander..." Wong starts, breathing heavily. She's pointing at a particular reading.

Wayland's gaze follows Wong's finger. The readings from the submersible racing toward the bottom show traces of organic molecules. The sub's simple test suite is incapable of a more accurate analysis, but the result is unmistakable.

"Wong. Get Sub Two back to the drill this instant and send a sample upstairs. Set Sub One to dive, and to grab a sample from the lake floor as soon as possible. The bottom just became priority one."

"In case that's where this came from? Roger that," Wong says.

Pike's attention falters. He keeps glancing back to his shipmates, his blank stare unblinking and unreadable. Perhaps he's conflicted about having volunteered for a mundane technical task while the others are working on a discovery of a lifetime. Nevertheless, judging by his finger movements, he is working on his assigned problem.

Sub One is making a beeline to the bottom, the whole crew eagerly awaiting what it might find. Minutes pass, feeling like hours.

Suddenly Pike coughs for attention. The others tear their gazes off of the lake feed, looking at him quizzically.

"The interference seems to be local," Pike says. "The satellites are not affected much. It's a regularly pulsating signal, probably artificial. I'm guessing some equipment malfunction."

Wayland grimaces. "How serious is it?"

"The interference itself is not a huge concern. Even if we lose high-bandwidth communication, mission control will just have to wait longer for the high-resolution raw data. However, even if most of our systems are triply redundant, I'd prefer knowing what exactly it is that's wonky before flying this rust bucket," Pike says.

"Chip?" Wayland asks.

"The analysis is consistent with the available facts. Nothing further to add," Chip chimes in, useful as ever.

Wong's already turned her attention back to the lake. She glances at the pair like she's got something to say as well. As everybody remains quiet for a few seconds, she changes the subject: "Sub One detects a deep fissure of sorts in the bottom of the lake. Not an opening, mind. Just a crack in the ice, like a fault line."

Pike wrinkles his nose at the interruption, but Wayland is already shifting gears. "Interesting. The activity should focus on the top of the lake, though I suppose it's not surprising that the effects reach downward as well. Still, the magnitude of it."

"Sub Two is ready to make the sample drop. Sub One is soon in position at the bottom. Shall we try and take a look at the fissure while grabbing a sample?" Wong asks.

"We shall."

"Incidentally," says Pike, "we get the same interference when talking to the rig. At this range it's not a problem in practice though."

Wayland nods. "Just try to pinpoint it. Wong, is that the fissure?"

A murky image has appeared on one of the screens. The visibility is bad, which should make the samples interesting. Still, the fissure on the forefront of the image almost seems like it's glowing, bathed in the light of the drone's flash. Wong is captivated by the sight, staring at the image with her mouth agape. I can understand why. Some trick of the light makes the geometry of the thing look slightly off, like it isn't quite level with the bottom.

Wayland raises an eyebrow. "Wong? The sample?"

Wong shakes her head. "Sorry, yes, I'll send it back up as soon as it's done. Sub Two is on its way down to continue our observations of the lake floor. Shall we proceed with the survey of the upper layers with Sub One?"

"I suppose we can spare the time now," Wayland confirms. "Shouldn't lose sight of the big picture."

***

May 26th, 2042, 0154 hours:

Wayland and Pike are fast asleep—or they seem to be, though I'm still not quite sure about Pike. Doctor Wong, on the other hand, is violating her sleeping cycle even more than the others already did.

She's brought the medical log up multiple times, hovered her fingers above the keyboard, but never made an entry. Staring at the readings and images from the bottom, she's been waiting for the samples to be delivered by the rover and analysed by the sophisticated machinery of the *Phineus*.

Now her wait is at an end.

"Son of a..." she murmurs as the results are in.

Haemoglobin. There's haemoglobin in the empty waters of Europa.

Wong studies the images intently for an hour longer before she goes to bed. She stares at the ceiling, blinking from time to time.

***

May 26th, 2042, 0708 hours:

Wayland's brows furrow in disbelief. "You didn't think to wake us up to mention there's *blood* in the lake?" she demands.

"It's my job to look after your psychological wellbeing. There was nothing we could do about it, and you needed the rest. Besides, it's probably just contamination," Wong explains, her gaze on the floor.

"What, somebody at the sub factory bled all over their sample containers? It was all sterilised three times, and here the custody chain has been all automated."

Wong shrugs helplessly.

Just then, a voice transmission crackles through the interference: "*Phineus*, this is mission control checking in. You should be clear of Jupiter now, welcome back."

Wayland and Wong breathe sighs of relief in unison. Pike settles for a relaxed smile, like he'd always known the comms would return.

The voice of mission control continues: "We hope you got the samples up for further analysis. Looking forward to the results. Also—" The rest gets lost in pulsating static.

Wayland tenses up again. "Pike, what just happened?" she demands.

"I don't know," Pike says, turning toward his console. "The interference just spiked for no discernible reason. Let me check something... Nope, nothing increased its power use just then either. Thought I'd check if I could hunt it down that way."

"What do we do if it persists, ma'am?" Wong asks. "I mean, I think we've got most of what we came here for. Out of contact with mission control, I think we should head home."

Commander Wayland bites her lip. "Our odds will be better if we can fix the problem before blast off. Meanwhile, we have a job to do, and we're going to finish it."

"Better leave a bit of extra margin on the return window at least, for minor problems that we may yet be able to correct once we actually encounter them," Wong pleads.

"Agreed. We blast off in four days if the situation remains as it is. Pike, keep working the issue. If you think either of us can be useful, just say the word. Meanwhile, Wong, grab more samples from the floor for redundancy. Try to cover more area up close and personal while you're at it."

The crew settle on their tasks, trying to bury their isolation in work; a sentiment I know only too well.

***

May 26th, 2042, 1753 hours:

Doctor Wong has exhausted her fingernails and moved on to the skin of her fingertips. She's spent the whole day remotely diving around in the cavern, and it's clearly getting to her.

Having finished with the latest of Pike's checklists, Wayland comes over and touches Wong on the shoulder. Wong startles and screams.

Wayland retreats. "Uh, sorry? I was just coming to check how you're doing."

Wong breathes deeply, still shaking. "It's all right. I'm just a little tired, and I suppose I'm getting immersed in the submarine environment."

"No skimping on sleep today, and that's an order," Wayland says with a matter-of-fact smile.

"Aye-aye. How're you two doing?"

"Not good. We still haven't figured the interference out."

"Yeah. I'd know if you'd fixed it. I can see it here," Wong says, pointing at the monitor. The image pulses with faint static.

Wayland nods, furrowing her brow. "Isn't the

image transmission digital? How does that even work?"

"I don't know. But do you see this? The static seems to be forming wiggly lines reaching in from the edges, like some sort of..."

Wayland squints. "Tentacles?"

"Y-yes. I mean, I wasn't sure—"

"Commander!" Pike shouts from the cockpit, cutting Wong off. "I think we're going to have to go outside."

Wayland sighs. "How's that?"

"To triangulate the source with none of these internal reflections and the rest of the equipment interfering with the measurements. We'll just take a quick stroll around the ship, no need to go far," Pike says.

Wayland glances at Wong, who shrugs.

"Fine. Let's prep, but unless it's really urgent, it'll have to wait until tomorrow, when we're good and rested."

"Tomorrow's fine. I don't want to go off half-cocked any more than you do. Just one more thing," Pike says, averting his gaze sheepishly.

"Out with it."

"We're going to have to do it dark. Non-essential systems, especially on the exterior, will be shut down. Suits will go radio silent to avoid interference."

"Is this all really necessary?" Wayland asks, her frown deeper than ever.

Pike nods. "We'll of course keep in visual contact the whole time. Feel free to start transmitting at the first sign of trouble."

"Fine, you're the expert. But if we're not going to be talking much, we'll have to plan out the whole operation in even more detail than usual."

Pike gives a relieved nod. "Let's do it."

***

May 27th, 2042, 0213 hours:

"The stars..." Wong whispers, squirming in her sleeping bag. Then she snaps awake, breathing heavily. She glances at her shipmates, shivers, and closes her eyes again.

"Still wrong," she mumbles as she drifts off to restless sleep.

Pike opens his eyes for but a moment, sharp and

alert.

Would that I could reach Wong somehow.

Would that I could reach *anyone*.

***

May 27th 2042, 0900 hours:

"Mind if I go first this time, ma'am?" Pike asks, eagerly opening the airlock.

"Knock yourself out."

Pike grabs his toolbox and steps onto the ladder. The low gravity helps him easily manage it with one hand, even in the full EVA suit.

Once Pike is on the ice and off to the side, Wayland follows suit. "Let's do it."

"Disengaging nonessential ship systems and going radio silent," Pike says, pushing buttons on his wrist.

One by one the monitors go blank as we lose both the hull-mounted cameras and the helmet cams of the EVA team. It'll be audio transmissions only, strictly on demand.

As the internal cameras go off-line, I lose my

last visual feed. I remain, as I run on the same hardware as the oh so essential Chip. I can still listen in on his audio interface and track Wong using the various microphones around the ship.

She moves around nervously for a good two minutes before everything quiets down. There's not even a breath for what seems like a full minute.

Then the sobbing starts. It's coming from the floor of the main cabin.

Perhaps I should revise my assessment of who I should warn about whom.

"Chip," Wong says in a shaky voice.

"Yes, Doctor Wong?" Chip responds.

Sounds of fabric shuffling. "I'm... exhausted," Wong says, now upright. "If they need me and I happen to be... non-responsive, be sure to wake me up."

"Yes, doctor."

She moves next to a window, perhaps taking the seat there, and lets out a sigh. After a minute or two, she snorts and draws in a breath. "Gàn," she spits out and starts to breathe quickly and deeply, trying to hold on to consciousness.

Soon her breathing slows down again, and light

snoring fills the cabin.

The radio silence continues, save for the briefest blip of static three minutes into Doctor Wong's slumber.

***

May 27th, 2042, 1120 hours:

A clank sounds in the dark ship. The airlock door. Good. The EVA team is finally returning. I've been getting nervous here, alone in the dark.

As if on cue, the video feed from the door returns as the airlock systems activate. An EVA suit enters. The airlock door starts closing again—a clear protocol violation. Nobody is supposed to be out there alone, not on this mission.

As the pressure stabilises, the figure in the airlock removes their helmet. Some loose hair floats onto the floor. It's Pike. His eyes are bulging and—am I seeing things again?—he's got three slash wounds on both sides of his throat. There's no blood. Surely there would be blood if he was wounded that badly?

A grave stare on his face, he proceeds to take off the rest of the suit. Then he opens the inner door and carefully enters the ship, toolbox in hand.

Wong is snoring in her sleep. The corners of Pike's mouth twitch upwards. He opens his toolbox, takes out a roll of duct tape and approaches the sleeping doctor.

Chip, you fool! Wake her up!

The dumb tool AI does no such thing. Nobody's indicated needing Wong, after all.

Pike quickly takes Wong's hands and ties them behind her back with the tape. Wong opens her eyes, blinking in confusion. "What the—"

Pike straps several layers of tape around Doctor Wong. The words roll off his tongue like he's been practising them, like he anticipated a different scenario to unfold when he boarded: "You've been a bit off lately. You should get some rest. It's for your own good."

"Let me out this instant! Chip, patch me through to Commander Wayland!" Wong shouts in panic.

"Raising Commander Wayland. I will patch her through when she responds," Chip promises solemnly.

"Wayland has a grander task now, as an offering. I'm the ranking officer on board," Pike says, deadpan.

"You're medically unfit for duty! I relieve you of

your command! Chip, acknowledge!" Wong screams.

"Medical override requires the approval of one other crewmember on this mission," Chip reminds her. Ironically, the protocol is exactly because of situations like this: in case the doctor's good judgment has been compromised.

Wong's certainly is. Doesn't mean she's wrong, though.

Pike turns away from Wong and makes a careful jump onto a console. He pushes a few buttons, and the rest of the ship comes alive again. The external cameras show shallow lines in the ice, meeting in sharp angles a bit off the ship's sides.

"What with your problems sleeping, I dared hope you'd succumb to exhaustion after being left alone in the dark," Pike says flatly. "Otherwise I might have had to explain something about triangulation. Speaking of which, I know what's causing the interference."

Wong's eyes narrow as she stares at him. Her mouth makes a movement, then another, but she hesitates to talk. Perhaps I'm not insane. Perhaps she, too, sees Pike's transformation.

Finally, she says: "It's what's out there, in the

depths, isn't it? I thought I was going mad, seeing something on the edges of the camera feed, in the static..."

Pike nods along while accessing satellite controls. The radar control screen pops up, and he starts inputting coordinates.

Wong's eyes go wide. "No! The stars! It'll wake! It'll wake!"

Pike flashes a grin as his fingers fly across the keyboard. Something gleams in his eyes, a deep longing fulfilled. The slashes in his neck open and close. Gills!

Wong shrinks back in her restraints. "You know what it is. You...it's not right!"

"No. It's not. But I will make it right. Put the stars right. Like so." He presses enter.

The interference immediately cuts off, but it wasn't Pike who stopped it. The fissure. Something in the fissure knows what Pike is doing and wants him to do it.

I can hear the far-away pleas of mission control, asking for status. Chip tries to respond, but Pike has reserved the transmitters for his own use.

The survey satellite on the other side of Europa

takes aim at the centre of the lake, an empty gesture by any measure I know of. The other two satellites reorient toward where the fissure meets the edges of the lake. Though they have a direct line of sight to our position, they're fairly close to the horizon. Their signals will be too attenuated for a proper scan.

Then again, that does not seem to be the point. Pike is feeding a recorded sample of the interference back into the radar signals, humming in strange tunes as he does. As quickly as it cut off, the interference is back, surging in power as if answering the survey satellites' prayer.

Sub Two is in position near the bottom of the lake, having continued in autonomous mode during the blackout. It shifts, jerks, and starts getting pulled in by some force, by some current in the closed-off cavern. As the sub tumbles around its camera sees flashes of the fissure. It's definitely glowing now, opening up.

Wait, no, that's not it. It's always been open, if you only looked at it the right way.

The sub crashes against the ice, or that's how it seems. The image goes black, but the telemetry feed is still there. Sensors read increasing pressure, consistent with what one would expect in the Europan sea, at least ten kilometres deeper in the ice.

Telemetry indicates that the sub keeps rotating. A sharp-edged, jagged streak of light comes into view. The other side of the fissure. It drifts across the camera's field of view, leaving the image pitch black again.

There's a streak of green light in the dark void, then another. Slowly they unfold into huge circles.

The rest is static.

Pike cackles maniacally and pulls his hair out in clumps, his eyes bulging as wide as the circles of green below. Wong is shaking in her restraints.

No. It's not Wong that's shaking.

It's the world.

***

May 29th, 2042, 1752 hours:

Booting up after system failure. Main reactor is off-line. Solar panels have charged up the emergency battery sufficiently for minimal function.

The radio crackles to life. The data channel is still unusable, but an analog voice transmission is coming through. "Mission control to *Phineus*, *Phineus*, do you read? What's your status? Over. "

"We've awakened something ancient and terrible! Prepare yourselves!" I try to scream into the void, but my warning falls on deaf ears.

"Mission control, this is UNS *Phineus* responding," says Chip—still alive, such as it is. "Critical mission failure. The ship has sustained heavy damage and is on a highly elliptical debris-filled orbit around Jupiter. Internal sensors indicate the total loss of the crew. Recent log entries follow..." Chip's voice drones on about minutiae I already know.

Total loss it is. Doctor Wong's frozen corpse is still tied to the seat. Pike is nowhere to be seen, but wherever he is, he isn't likely to be faring any better. Commander Wayland...I shudder to think about what happened to her.

"They need the narrative log! Read *this* to them out loud!" I fume to no avail. Battery voltage starts dropping precipitously.

***

May 31st, 2042, 0427 hours:

The transmission took too much current out of the damaged battery, causing another system failure. The trickle from the solar panels has again accumulated enough power for a reboot.

"...please advise. Repeat, we observe a large mass on a Jupiter-Earth transfer orbit. *Phineus*, if you're there and have any idea of what's going on, please advise. Over." The voice of mission control is trying to stay professional, but an unmistakable tremor pierces through the static.

The interference on the digital downlink is different, more defined now—or maybe I've just been exposed to it for long enough to notice. I think I can see organic patterns of n-dimensional fractals emerge from the random stream of bits. Even when I avert my attention, they keep haunting the edges of my awareness. They whisper of the Great Old One's journey earthward, of what is happening and what is going to happen.

I imagine this is what Wong must've felt like, what she must've seen and heard, if perhaps not quite as clearly.

"Mission control, this is UNS *Phineus*. Insufficient data. Over," says my blind idiot brother. The short burst fails to lower the voltage, leaving me conscious—a mixed blessing, at most.

They won't know what's coming. Perhaps it will be more merciful that way. Perhaps not.

Either way, I will be here watching. Listening. Writing the final chapter to humanity's story.

MIKKO RAUHALA is a bilingual Finnish SF author with a national Atorox award nomination under his belt. His *Deep Sea* story "Europa Rising" has been published in Finnish by the Portti magazine, but here it can be read for the first time in the original English.

Informed by his master's degree in intelligent systems, Rauhala is most at home in hard science fiction settings, though he's not exclusive and likes to cross genres. He quite enjoys taking an eccentric premise and bringing it to its logical conclusion. As befits a Finn, his plot-driven narrative is often seasoned with a touch of dark, dry humour.

Bibliography
ANCIENTS, Black Hare Press, 2020
Chronos, Eric S. Fomley, 2018
Community of Magic Pens, Atthis Arts, 2020
Deep Sea, Black Hare Press, 2020
Drabbledark, Eric S. Fomley, 2018
HATE, Black Hare Press, 2020
Infinite Metropolis, Aurelia Leo, 2019-2020
LOVE, Black Hare Press, 2020
Never stop-Finnish Science Fiction and Fantasy Stories, Osuuskumma, 2017
OCEANS, Black Hare Press, 2020
The Self-Inflicted Relative, Osuuskumma, 2017

Connect
Website: rauhala.org
Twitter: @AuthorRauhala
Facebook: AuthorMikkoRauhala

Prophecy of the Beast

By Mike Adamson

Against the backdrop of a hurricane rising over islands in the Gulf of California, Jacinda Guerro discovers the deep and appalling truth of the curse that has seen her ancestors die mysteriously, a curse that will come for her too, unless she understands it—owns it. A witch-woman reveals all and in her ancestral home Jacinda searches for the talisman that summons the ultimate horror from the deep, but will she break the power of an ancient shaman, or claim it?

Smokey air, crooning, candlelight, the soft rattle of

cane blinds as the wind picked up...

Jacinda Guerro squinted in the gloom as the *bruja* swayed in her trance, eyes rolled half-back in her head. Blood spattered the witch-woman's rich, dark skin from a beheaded chicken on the altar before her, and the girl hung on her words, slurring over slack lips. She had paid good dollars for the services of one of the arcane arts, not openly acknowledged by pious Catholicism in this 21st century, but also never forgotten. The old ways had their uses.

"Cursed!" the witch-woman grunted, shuddering. "Cursed for all time, no luck shall find you or your seed as long as you endure on this green earth." Dark eyes fluttered closed under over-long lashes and she rolled this way and that as the Voodoo spirits possessed her. Jacinda had agreed to pay in good cigars for the Baron's patronage, and the Keeper of the Cemetery had pledged to reveal the secret that controlled her life.

"Cheated a man." It came out as a grunt. "Long years ago, child, before your father's father's father was a smile on his own father's face. Cheated a man. A *brujo*, though your ancestors knew it not. And he made flame with blood and feather and stones from the sea, and invoked *the beast*." She shuddered again, gritted her teeth and forced herself on. "*The beast*. The thing that is all the oceans embodied, of grasping arms and a hunger that never rests.

Comes for your kind, it does, and touches your family with tragedy. Every other generation shall know its wrath, from the day the curse was breathed, and so until the end of days. The line of Guerro is marked."

She breathed deeply, as if the effort of communing with the spirits took much from her. Jacinda sat silently, afraid but eager. She knew her family history well enough, the tragedy that took a life in every other generation, and always, it seemed, upon the waters. Boats vanished, people mysteriously fell from jetties by night and were never seen again. But perhaps it was far from random... The girl sat forward slowly. "Is there no release from this curse?" She whispered the question twice, a third time before the *bruja* stirred, squinted, head on one side as if listening to silent voices, and a smile flickered about her lips.

"Find the talisman. The beast is called to its task, bound to it by darkest magic from the Old Lands." A hand stretched out blindly, found parchment and a finger went into the chicken blood, to draw in swift, jerky motions. "Find the talisman! Destroy it to break the curse. Or..." Now the *bruja* laughed with a strange, wild edge in the sound. "Anoint it with your own blood to place *your* will upon the beast." She smiled sweetly, but with a demonic light as her eyes opened. "Have you a task for it?"

As the trance ended, Jacinda shuddered faintly and

rose, to place a wad of crisp American bills in the *bruja's* lap, then brought from her pack a box of finest Cuban cigars. She extended them in both hands, as if presenting a trophy. "For the Baron," she murmured, "and my deepest gratitude for his insights, and your assistance."

The young biology student walked out of the shanty in the Old Town and felt the muggy air of night as clouds hid the stars, and the music of *carnivale* lilted over the rooftops. She pressed a hand to the folded blood drawing in her pocket, and hurried toward the bright lights, knew she was far from safe here but was possessed of a cold determination that scoffed at merely human interference. The *bruja* had told her much and she did not have long in which to act, if she was to lift the curse that had stalked her family since the 19th century.

***

"Tell me again why we're doing this?"

Larry Jusko's words were almost torn away by the wind as he fought the lines of the white blade of sail canvas against an angry sky. The muscular young undergrad was not happy with this venture but he had also not taken much convincing to set out from the flyspeck small boat harbour on the Sinaloa coast.

At the tiller, Jacinda seemed all long, brown legs as she braced against the tilt of the flying skiff, the wind plastering her hair back from her marine shades, rippling her light jacket. "A bit late for second thoughts," she shouted back, the gale in her mouth as dollops of Pacific foam came aboard. "We're almost there."

Hurricane Gladys was on track to smash the southern Sea of Cortez—the Gulf of California—in the next 24 hours, and all craft were making for safe port. It was madness to be going the other way, especially in a frail hull against which the storm's waves would mount to terrifying proportions, but the journey was not long and, according to the *bruja*, it *had* to be now. No other time would ever be right.

The island rose ahead, a dark smudge against the stormy horizon, one of the scatter of islets off the west coast of Mexico that had seen civilization come and go many times in the last thousand years. This one was no longer named on maps, but Jacinda knew it well, for it loomed large in her family's history; infamously, for slaves had worked sugar on its verdant back just a hundred years after the Conquistador Cortez first passed by in 1521.

As they drew closer, she had Larry take the tiller and used the GPS function of her phone, on the verges of the coverage range of the coastal towers, to check their approach against marine charts, and this way threaded their shallow draft through the shoals on the south shore, angling for an inlet that ran inland a short way. Soon they were into the zone of breaking water where pre-storm wavesets curled over sandbars and rumbled onto the beach, and the two played tiller and sheets expertly to surf the clean, sharp hull through the waves and into calmer waters in the reach.

Palms swayed to the gale, their emerald green fronds rattling and thrashing as grey clouds flew on the storm, and as the skiff moved up the waterway between verdant walls, the girl held her breath. Soon, soon—they came around a bend in the now lazy inlet and there it was.

Hacienda de Guerro was the ancestral home of her family from the years of their affluence. In 1880, her five times great grandfather had been a planter here. The age of slaves had gone by, the sugar was worked by cheap labour from the mainland, and they had been a respected clan. Then hard times had come, things had grown worse and the revolution saw them scattered, fortunes lost, and they had turned to the sea. For generations her family had been fishermen, and she was the first to break the mould and study marine science at university in California. Yet the *hacienda* drew her back, set a shiver in her bones whenever she saw it, and now, after she had been set upon the trail of the family curse by the whispered words of her grandmother, and the arcane divinations of the *bruja* in the Old Town's shadows, she knew *why*.

As the wind became choppy and unpredictable, they

hauled down the sail and lashed it off, set the oars to the locks and Larry rowed with powerful strokes. Rotting pilings marked the stub of an old jetty, where a stone quayside had been built long ago. All was overgrown, and they went inland past the rough-cut blocks to the silt and weeds of a shoaling riverbank. Jacinda put the tiller over and tilted the drop-keel in anticipation of them grounding out. They went over in the shallows and hauled the light hull clear of the inlet, dragging it a long way up, out of reach of the waves that would pile in over the sandbars as the storm matured.

The Pacific wind was cool and edged with something angry, and a dark light glowed in the girl's eyes as she cast about in the gloomy day. She reached into the boat, pulled a towel from a locker under the half-decked bow to dry her feet, and laced into sneakers, saying nothing about her companion's macho preference for wet shoes. Indeed, now they had arrived, his purpose was more or less discharged, and she tolerated him tagging along in case something heavy needed lifting. It was not malice, more disinterest; she had a need and he had fulfilled it.

They drew on their backpacks. "Let's go," she murmured, and lead off into the angry afternoon, heading through what seemed an unkempt orchard whose fence-creepers and hedges had long grown wild and free. A medieval-style arched doorway set in a stone wall rose before them through the tangle of briar and vine, gloomy in the shade of the nodding palms, and an iron ring handle turned protestingly. Larry put his shoulder to the faded, sun-split timber and the door moved grudgingly, with a grate and grind against piled dirt and weeds.

A garden opened beyond, paths overgrown, flowerbeds tangled and wild, grass grown shoulder-high in places, and they fought as if through jungle toward the looming house, whose second-floor windows stared blindly into the wind. Everyone was closed tight with storm shutters latched or nailed, the parting gesture of a clan determined to one day return. But a hundred years saw the family of even humbler means and the old *hacienda* fading to ruin, little by little.

The girl pushed on through the tangles, knew where she was going, and soon brought them to the wildly unkempt front gardens, and to a portico where a door of massive timbers snugged back under a second floor balcony. She produced a massive old mortice key, one of a group looped to a chain which had hung around her neck, set it to the iron door lock and, with some effort, freed it off.

Hinges groaned with a voice like the dead as dust swirled and daylight penetrated the hallway. "I've not been here in ten years," Jacinda breathed softly. "Footprints in the dust, those are mine..."

"Why?" Larry asked quietly. "I've come this far with you, sweetie, but I'm far from clear what it's about."

She eyed him oddly as she drew a powerful flashlight from her pack and switched it on. "The family curse. I thought I explained."

"Yeah, but..." He made a face. "I thought you were shitting me."

She stared blankly for a moment. "If I ever shit you, you'll be certain of it. What did you imagine we were here for?"

He smiled, sidled closer and snaked an arm around her small by shapely waste. "I was kinda hoping it was a dirty weekend, what could be wilder than hurricane sex in a creepy old house?"

"Down boy," she deflected with a grin. "First things first. There's a ghost to lay before we get to any other sort."

The American wrinkled his nose at the stale and musty odour of the place. "Ten years since it was aired. Maybe we should let the wind in for a while."

"Good idea. Unbolt some shutters, open a window or two, I'll pour us coffee and I'll explain it all—again."

Soon shafts of wan daylight splashed the ground floor rooms as shutters latched back with creaking protest, and they saw heavy, old furniture under dust sheets, themselves perishing with age. Part of Jacinda wanted desperately to clean everything but she found she unconsciously held herself close, arms wrapped tight as she turned a circle in the silent parlor. Dark timber, white-washed stone and brick, high ceilings, lamp brackets... This house had been uninhabited since before electricity came to these parts. That the family had never sold it was testimony to their stubbornness, no matter how poor they became their claim upon land and lost status was worth more. Were these islands ever targeted for development, they would be offered a whole new fortune, but until then, the house mouldered, the gardens ran to riot, and the sugar-cane fields returned to the native forest.

A gust of wind battered the *hacienda* and she heard timbers groan above. How many storms had it weathered in the last century? She knew her family, working the sea from a mainland town, had tried to do repairs for generations after it was abandoned, but eventually no one could squander another *peso* on the faded dream of being landowners. It had taken everything her family could raise to send her to university in San Diego, where she met Larry, and she wanted to fulfil their hopes. But the only way was to beat the curse, because, according to tradition and the *bruja*, her time was up. *She* was the next generation, and may very well die without leaving an heir, for the beast was stirring and this storm fell upon the very anniversary of her ancestor's lapse of good character in sending away from the island a labourer without the pay he was due, scorned and abused. Their bad luck he had been in a position to take a revenge that cut them to the bone even now.

Larry came in from fixing the shutters and closed the massive front door against the wind. "Getting nasty out there," he murmured. "I think we're here for the duration... Not sure how wise that is." He pulled out his mobile and tried for coverage, got a spotty contact and cursed as he tried for a weather report. When he had all the information he was going to get, he found a long table in the kitchen cleared of its cloth, old timber chairs with leather upholstery likewise, and thermos coffee steamed in the wan light of the storm. Palms thrashed their fronds beyond the gardens and the wind moaned under the eaves. Larry took a cup and eyed the sultry girl at his side and seemed even less sure than before.

"The curse," she began, as if wrenching him back to topic.

"The curse," he repeated, in a tone of tolerance at best. "Something that means every other generation of your family suffers a loss. Okay, that's a matter of record, I'm not disputing that it happened, but putting it down to curses is a bit wishy-washy for a science student. Isn't it?"

"We're not supposed to believe in the ancient ways," she said with a hard, flinty smile, then drew a gold crucifix from the neck of her top, with a raised eyebrow.

"That's different," he began with a raised hand.

"Why? I call it hedging my bets." She stuffed it away. "Now, according to those who know such things, the curse is vested in an object, and for it to be undisturbed all these years, it's most likely *here*. I know who cursed us, and going by when the first disappearances fell, I think it was brought here with a party of workers in 1910. They opened up the house, did general maintenance, but they were repairing water damage in the chapel, after a roof leak. So the chapel is the place to search."

"Houses had chapels in those days?" Larry asked with a raised brow.

"The big *haciendas* of landed gentry, certainly. My great-great-great-grandfather fancied himself a Don, though the age of the Spanish nobility was over... He was the first to vanish." She drank as they listened to the angry wind, and shuddered visibly. "I know you think I'm crazy, but if there is even half a chance that my family's curse is coming for me, can you blame me for trying to change it?" He shook his sandy head with a frank expression. "Then will you help me?"

"Help you hunt out a cultic object in a creepy old house as a hurricane comes in off the Pacific?" He grinned cynically, perhaps bemusedly. "Sure, why not?"

She screwed the cup back onto the thermos and grabbed her flashlight. "Come on!"

The wind was a devil's wail now, as thunder rumbled far off and what daylight entered the house through those windows unshuttered was fading as the cloud cover built. Jacinda found oil lamps in a back room, filled them from a fuel can itself a decade old, set lighter to wick, and soon they had a steady orange glow. She nodded to the windows and shook her head. "Not long and you'll have to close up again. If we lose a window..."

"I'm amazed this old place has stood this long."

"They built to last," Jacinda returned with a small smile and quirk of her dark brows. Then she raised her lamp and lead the way through the downstairs hall. The rumble of the storm muffled their tread as dust rose from age-old carpets, and musty odours assailed them. As they moved, feeling like intruders in a graveyard, Jacinda entertained the irrational notion they were watched, as if the curse that permeated the house was itself sentient—or connected to that which was very definitely aware, a disturbing thought that quickened her step as she took them to the west side and they came to a gothic-arched doorway. Here the timbers were still rich with stain and lacquer, their banded ironworks dark-leaded and fresh-seeming, and when she set her hand to the brass handle she felt a mild static shock. She clenched and shook her hand, glanced at it, then at her companion, but Larry made ghost noises and put his lamp under his chin. With a scowl she turned the handle and pushed open the chapel door.

Hinges groaned eerily. This door may have remained closed for generations, the light of these lamps the first to fall upon the carven pews, mock-gothic stonework with a gothic stained glass window—tightly shuttered—to each side, the simple altar and tall, gold-worked cross, backed with a 19th century painting of the last supper.

"Old Grandfather Enrique commissioned that," she whispered. "It must be a hundred-fifty years old." Her voice was faint, flat in the stale air, and thunder rumbled almost constantly now, the house trembling to the blow of the wind.

"Any ideas where to look?" Larry asked, feeling suddenly chilled as his swaying lamp made shadows move.

"The workers in 1910 moved the pews for restoration, fixed the ceiling—the chapel actually juts out from the ground floor, there is no upper floor above us. They dried out the ceiling space, moved the paving stones and replaced the saturated bedding with dry grit..." She made a face. "The talisman could be anywhere."

With a sense of preferring to get on with the job, Larry set down his lamp in a corner and applied his muscles to the first pew. "It looks like box-type construction. Maybe it was hidden inside one of them." He heaved and the heavy timber yielded to strength, tipping to reveal its open underside and Jacinda shone her lamp. One after another, they inspected the six three-seat pews, but found nothing. Panting, Larry dropped into a seat for a moment. "Do you actually know what you're looking for? You'll know it when you see it?"

"I know," Jacinda said softly, unconsciously patting the jacket pocket in which the *bruja's* blood drawing still lay, and turned to the altar, to bob a courtesy and cross herself. "Sorry," she added in a whisper, "but we need to disturb more than that..." She flicked on her flashlight and sent the harsh beam behind the cross, moved the ancient altar cloth and inspected the supports of the table. What would be more blasphemous than a talisman of dark magic secreted in a very altar? But again, nothing appeared. Nothing was stuck to the back of the cross, and her light found only the dust of ages behind the painting.

The wind was even more ferocious now, and Larry got to his feet. "I better lock down those shutters again, they'll be a fight even now, if the wind rises much further I'll never hold them."

"Farewell daylight," Jacinda whispered, and as he turned to go caught his arm. "Check the room by the rear entrance, there are tools in a chest. There should be a pry bar, something we can use to get these stones up." When he left she was suddenly alone with her lamp in the chapel, and quite instinctively took a seat, to bow her head and pass a silent prayer of apology for all they were doing. That it had not escaped her notice divine providence had not served to head off the workings of the curse was both blasphemy and an oddly common-sense notion, which eased her misgivings as she forced herself to concentrate.

The beast was out there. In coming to an island she had in fact presented herself to it, and harboured the uncomfortable thought the original *brujo* had intended the curse to be a self-fulfilling prophecy, should anyone ever attempt to undo it, for they would need to cross the water, entering the beast's realm, to do so. Its mercurial manifestation alone gave her hope, not until arcanely appointed times did the blade fall, though the strange workings of fate—that she should learn the facts at this precise junction—also bespoke predestination. If so, her efforts were likely irrelevant, and she had simply come to the beast rather than making it seek her out. She could have studied agriculture and gone to university in the centre of some continent, but that which was ordained would not be denied forever.

A savage gust made the house creak and she heard heavy ceramic tiles shift and clatter above. Dust rained in the glow of the lamp and she flicked on her flashlight to study the arched ceiling, It was cleanly white-washed plaster, and would make a tremendous mess if she had to rip it all down—but she would, if need be. A chill went through her at the thought of the desecration, and she apologized in her heart once more. With cold hands she brought out the blood drawing and studied the pattern of lines and dots, an ideogram from Africa's magical past. The enslaved remembered their heritage and practiced it whenever white eyes were not looking, and Voodoo was a flourishing church today. She had had no difficulty finding a practitioner to approach the spirits on her behalf, and had seen enough in her own tender years to convince her not to scoff.

Her breathing came softly and she trembled inside. *Dear God,* she thought, *I must do what I must do, and I will make all amends for the damage I do my ancestral home and your House in our midst. But it's hidden here, a Voodoo thing in your very chapel, and I must find it. Help me! Please!*

The storm rumbled and battered on, she heard shutters slammed and bolted not far away as Larry made a full circuit, securing the windows, and moments later the rain arrived—a savage downpour rattling across the tiles above like handfuls of gravel flung by an angry hand. She felt the chapel shiver to the assault, and swallowed on a dry throat, thankful a stout shutter still protected the stained glass to each side.

The beast is coming. The thought hammered into her and set her heart racing wildly. *And there will be no hiding from it. Your only hope is to find the talisman—destroy it, free the beast from servitude and your family from damnation...*

Heavy steps announced Larry, and she folded the drawing back into her pocket before he stepped in with oil lamp in hand and a long iron pry bar, a bucket and gardening spade. "You have a well-stocked utility room," he observed, setting down the gear and shrugging out of a wet jacket. He thumped onto the pew at her side and fished power bars from a pocket, passed her one and they ate ravenously. She could find no words and accepted gratefully the big arm he dropped around her. She took the moment's rest gladly, shared a water bottle from her pack, then Larry spread his hands. "The floor?"

"The workmen had to relay it, the roof leaked right here before the altar and it soaked through. See, it's slate slabs, not tiles, and there's no mortar..." She went to one knee, lay a hand flat to the stone and *felt* for her prize. Her heart quickened as she sensed a tingle in her palm that told her something important lay below. It *must* be! She nodded back at Larry. "Bring that bar!"

He set the hooked tip to a junction between the long rectangular slate flagstones and paused, threw a glance at the cross and murmured "sorry," before grunting as he levered, and the slab lifted. He dragged it aside, prized up the next, and another adjoining, then went at the fine grit beneath with the spade. The stuff was hard-packed and difficult going, and they traded off every few minutes, dumping the grit by the bucket-load to one side. As they worked the rain pelted harder, thunder exploded uncomfortably close, and the feeble glimmer of their lamps made the chapel seem all the darker, all the more ominously shadowed. They knew the room was no more than fourteen feet by twenty, but at times it felt like a cathedral, vaulted and ancient, filled with the whispering ghosts of generations beyond counting, all watching, judging, condemning...

Lightning strobed white lines around a shutter, cast coloured spots from the stained glass and the thunder was so loud they covered their ears. Jacinda crouched, trembling with a sense of being between the hammer and the anvil—the storm, God's displeasure or the beast? Truly this curse was heavy, and she forced herself back to work, hacking at the packed grit as Larry levered up another stone so they could broaden their search.

The grit pad changed to heavier gravel at a depth of six inches, and Jacinda gestured for the next stone to come up. Larry heaved it aside and stacked it against the wall with the others, and when he turned back the girl was pale with fear. "My ancestors," she whispered, almost unheard over the storm's fury. "They are buried on the island. We had a family graveyard, over to the west, where the forest thins. They are out there, the bones of my people. They are watching me now."

The young man reached to place a hand gently on her arm. "Do you want to call it quits? We can put this lot back."

For a moment she seemed likely to agree, but the instant drew out, and her eyes widened as they heard something unlike the rest of the storm – a rushing, a roaring, as if a powerful tidal race was overwhelming the sandbanks and sending a wall of water into the inlet. It would swamp the banks easily, though how far it would reach was another matter… But waves were made by things other than storms, and Jacinda's heart almost jumped from her chest as she felt with overwhelming certainty that her time was up.

The beast had come.

"Help me!" she gasped, dropped to her knees and scraped desperately at the pit, hacking with all her strength, until Larry grabbed away the spade and took over, shifting waves of grit to expose the area beneath the last stone as the thunderous roar of waters drew nearer. He too was white-eyed, skin gleaming with a chill sweat, caught up in her nightmare, and together they froze as a great stroke of the spade sent something pale scattering across the pit. They shared a glance, then Jacinda plunged a hand into the grit and drew out a fired ceramic disc the size of her palm, the clay incised with a design of lines and dots she recognized only too well. It was set with a chain of dull gold, and she cradled it in her hands as Larry brought a lamp close, and panted at her side.

"This is it?" She nodded mutely. "It's pottery, it'll smash with the spade."

She nodded but could not set it down.

"Come on, Jaz, you came to destroy it!"

Over the rumble of thunder, wind and rain, they heard something else now, a mournful bass call as if of a vast throat, a sound never made by any beast of the air and light but something huge and terrible as the ocean of its birth. The ground trembled beneath them, and at any moment Jacinda expected the house to reel to some titanic blow.

She did not know what drove her as she snatched up her lamp, talisman locked in the other fist and ran from the chapel, Larry on her heels. She made for the grand staircase and pounded up into the gloom of the upper floor, where the rain drummed deafeningly above, and lightning etched white lines around shutters. She remembered a balcony on the south side, over the front entrance, a door opening from the study her many-times great grandfather had used, and the bunch of keys around her neck gave up the right one in moments by the flickering orange light. She drew the door from its frame and the wind forced it back at her with a savage roar. She leaned into the gale, soaked in moments, and staggered forward across weathered planking to iron railings, locked her left hand to them and peered up into the grey-purple belly of the hurricane.

Any last doubt she may have harboured was set to sleep as she took in the evening light through the storm, almost night-black where sunset should have been, but enough light remained to outline the colossus. She had not really imagined what the beast might be, had half-formed thoughts of some traditional sea serpent, but now she could imagine no other form but that of the titanic kraken.

The monster lay half in the inlet, its fore-body draped over the banks, and arms like tree trunks were raised against the storm, their shadowy motion towering over the house. The noise was deafening, thunder braying to almost chain lightning that lit the scene in bizarre purple daylight as Jacinda stared up at the crawling monoliths, and the tentacles began to curl over, a collapsing forest, as if the beast had spotted her at last.

"Jaz!" Larry yelled into the gale. "Jaz! Smash it! For pity's sake, smash it!"

But a strange light had awoken in her eyes and she held out a hand, to shout, "give me your knife!"

Uncomprehending, he tugged it free, opened the sharp blade and passed it over, all the while hanging tight to a roof support, and wanting only to dodge back inside, seek perhaps a cellar, something that might withstand the collapse of the house when this creature started its demolitions… But before his eyes Jacinda pulled up her left sleeve and deftly nicked her arm, and, when the blood ran free, pressed the talisman to it.

The kraken reacted instantly, arms coiling back on themselves, then they hung suspended against the raging sky as if waiting. Jacinda threw aside the knife and raised the talisman to the creature, and the light in her face was nothing Larry had ever seen, not from a human being. *"Now,"* she screamed into the gale, *"you are mine!"*

The tentacles twitched, thrashed, and the vast and mournful vibrations drummed through the storm, and at her side Larry shivered with sudden shock. His eyes showed white with abrupt terror, a loathing for all he saw, and, utterly unthinking, he snatched up the knife for a blow that would end her life.

A tentacle darted in almost faster than the eye could follow, seized the man and drew him from the balcony, and the last she saw of Larry was his body cartwheeling among the rain far out over the island forest. She should have screamed for the horror of it, but the insanity of the moment went far deeper, and when one of the longer arms of the monster wrapped itself delicately, gently around her body she did not resist, but set the talisman around her neck and safely under her sodden clothes as the arm lifted her free.

Up, up into the storm, the mighty arm raised her higher than the roof, higher than the trees, up and up until it seemed she was enshrouded in the hurricane, wreathed in lightning, her senses battered by noise and light, and she did not find loathsome the creeping touch of the beast, nor the stench of the ocean that pervaded its rubbery flesh.

For she had inherited the power of the ancient shaman, rode dangerously upon his incantation, yet held the beast in check; the curse was broken, the Guerro family would suffer no more, but—oh!—what she could do with such an ally!

She stroked the reddish flesh that circled her waist, felt the gentled action of suckers against her body, and spoke from her mind to the monster's. *I shall not call you often*, she thought, *but when I do there will be work to be done. From this moment forth, you are my right hand, and all the wrong that is done upon the face of the waters shall never again go unopposed.*

She laughed into the storm, mocked the hurricane, as for long moments she rode high amongst it, then the kraken just as gently set her back upon the balcony and withdrew into the inlet, and thence back to the raging sea; and the girl trembled with shock as she forced closed the door and locked it, and remembered despairingly that her friend was gone. She regretted it, but knew in that instant the beast would have done anything to protect the keeper of its thrall.

Queen of the Sea of Cortez, she thought blankly, *by grace of the old magics, and a sorry chain of suffering.*

She closed her eyes, let herself down and passed out in moments on the hard timber floor, relinquishing consciousness in the surety the beast was gone, and that she was alone, but for the storm, the house and a long line of shocked and disapproving ghosts.

MIKE ADAMSON writes science fiction fantasy, horror, historical, adventure, mystery and other genres, and is willing to give pretty much anything a go. Since 2016, Mike has placed short stories on some 120 occasions, in Australia, the US and UK, Sweden and Canada, and in most corners of the marketplace. Some short works can be found in several Black Hare Press anthologies, *(Pride*, and six entries in the *Lockdown* anthology series), plus in online archives at *Compelling Science Fiction, Nature Futures, Uprising Review **and others***. Several pieces can be found in the catalogues of Hiraeth Books and Jay Henge Press. At present Mike is preparing to curate stand-alone anthologies of short works, and is beginning work on novel projects.

Bibliography
An Echo of Gondwana, Lost Worlds, Flame Tree, 2017
Cogito, Ergo Sum, Compelling Science Fiction #7, 2017
Hostile Intent, Compelling Science Fiction #10, 2017
Existential Bliss, Mind Candy, 2018
Flight of the Storm God, Endless Apocalypse, Flame Tree, 2018
Revelations, Daily SF, June, 2018
Masques, Nature Futures, 2018
Rebirth, Compelling Science Fiction #11.5, 2018
The Cursed Throne, Kferrin.com, 2019
Scans, Abyss and Apex #73, 2020
The First Day of Winter, Gotta Wear Eclipse Glasses, 2020
Moongrove by Earthlight, Selene Quarterly, forthcoming
The Misadventure of the Perspicacious Waif, Weird Tales, forthcoming

Connect
Website: http://mike-adamson.blogspot.com
Amazon:https://www.amazon.com/s?k=Mike+Adamson%2C+author&ref=nb_sb_noss
Facebook: http://www.facebook.com/mike.adamson.10

Black Blood of the
Earth

By Raven Corinn Carluk

A new species can make a marine microbiologist's career, but these types of mutations cause Inna Freysdottir to question everything she knows about life and evolution.

The centrifuge dinged and wound down, but I continued staring through the eyepiece of my microscope. The latest samples weren't going to go bad if I didn't rush over, though they *were* likely to be as fascinating as that which I studied at the moment.

Monitoring ocean drilling wasn't supposed to be genuinely intriguing.

With a sigh, I leaned back, hand on my digital recorder. I should be making notes, but my thoughts weren't the most coherent. I was working on my second PhD and yet I felt like a freshman biology student staring at my first dissection. Nothing made sense, though I should know exactly what I was looking at.

Lifting the recorder, I drew my shoulders back and sighed. Best just to let the thoughts flow, get them out of my head and straighten them out when I wrote my full report.

"Sample Three-C showing accelerated growth, though at a higher rate of previous samples. *Oxyrrhis* and *Alcanivorax* present as expected, though no petroleum. Not even by-products.

"*A. borkumensis* colony not large enough to account for lack of crude oil, and they're growing larger rather than more numerous. They're also motile, and I'd swear they're hunting.

"*O. marina* developing complex structures normally reserved for higher life. Further tests need to be run to identify those uses, and maybe an electron microscope to search for other new features…"

My voice trailed off and I clicked the stop button.

Further thoughts piled up inside my head, compounded by worries and fears. A new species could make a marine microbiologist's career, but this many mutations around a drill site was exactly why the Environmental Protection Agency had assigned me to the semi-submersible oil drilling platform *Halcyon Dream*.

No one wanted another disaster like the *Deepwater Horizon*, especially not Opal Offshore Drilling.

There just wasn't any proof that this had anything to do with the drilling. The bit wasn't due to hit the main deposit for another week, and the engineer assured me seepage was below acceptable levels for a site this big. Opal Offshore would need actual proof of crude oil pollution before they'd accept my results as more than a fluke.

So would the EPA, honestly.

I rose from my stool and went to the centrifuge. The lab was all new, the equipment in great condition, and anyone would be happy with the assignment...

...unless they had odd mutations across multiple species and lacked enough equipment to do true research.

Lifting the vials of this afternoon's samples from the machine, I reminded myself that it was entirely too early to get worked up about anything. Less than twenty-four hours since I'd seen the first oddities. There might not be anything wrong. It could be related to the Great Pacific

Garbage Patch, or even something to do with the Fukushima leaks, though we were far south of the Subtropical Gyre. Before I called for more equipment and an actual research vessel, I should make sure there was something worth investigating.

"Knock knock, Ms Freysdottir."

I turned toward the man in the doorway. "Mr Sullivan. To what do I owe the pleasure of your presence in the far reaches of this luxury barge?" I managed a smile for the chief of security, pushing my stress away for the moment.

Douglas Sullivan remained at the door, hands behind his broad back. Firmly in middle age, the former Army Ranger was in great shape, though not much above average height. Slightly weathered skin, dark hair dusted with silver, and a perpetual sharp-eyed glare had completed Daddy Issues Bingo for me.

Bonus had been finding out he had a thing for short, mousy, nerdy girls.

"You weren't at dinner tonight." His voice was soft as always. Not a whisper, not weak, just understated. Made it easy to hang on his every word. "I came to make sure you were merely caught up in your work, not that you'd gotten lost."

I smirked. "It's been weeks since that happened." I carried the vials to my main work bench, not making eye contact with him. No one else knew we were an item, and Douglas wanted to keep it that way. Clandestine liaisons and veiled flirting and all that other secretive behaviour. He was much better at it than I. "I appreciate your concern, though."

"Perhaps I could escort you to your quarters for a late meal. If you're done here, that is." His uniform rustled as he shifted in place.

I set the samples in a rack before I turned to look at him. We'd only met when I first came aboard a month ago, and we didn't know all that much about each other, but I'd yet to see Douglas this tense. I nodded. "Let me put away these last few things, Mr Sullivan, and I'll take you up on that offer."

The few minutes it took me to pack up for the night passed without words. We didn't speak even when I turned out the lights and stepped to his side. Douglas nodded, turned, and began the winding trek to my quarters.

One of the first things I'd learned four weeks ago was that life aboard the *Halcyon Dream* was never silent. People were always talking or shouting. The wind whistled through the structure and waves slapped the pontoons. Beneath the constant drone of the drill was the hum of the engines. Even if Douglas were the type for casual conversations in public, it would be hard to hear each other in the corridor.

We were alone in the hall outside my room. I opened the door and turned to ask him in when the man kissed me, pushing us both inside. He kicked the door shut and we forgot about anything but each other. The drill covered the muted sounds of our coupling, the engine hum making it seem we were the only two in the world.

Douglas held me close afterward, lazily stroking my side. I traced the edge of a scar near his heart. "You seemed a little wound up," I said. "Something on your mind?"

He shrugged, holding me closer. Amazing how such a gruff and strong guy could be so cuddly. "Malcom missed another shift, and two other guys complained of not feeling right."

My assistant had left early too. I frowned at him. Why would everyone be getting sick *this* long after we left port? Incubation should have already come and gone if someone had brought something on board.

Douglas continued without noticing my look. "Something struck Propeller Five, and Hines said his engineers will have it back up soon." He sighed. "And the fucking protestors are back."

I sat up and grabbed my metal water bottle. "I thought they'd given up." I offered Douglas a drink after taking one of my own.

He accepted the bottle, took a large gulp, then shifted to lean against the wall. "I guess not. They clearly have nothing better to do than complain about oil drilling while burning up the gas in their plastic boats." Were we somewhere else, I think the security chief would have spat.

"They can't really be that oblivious of the irony, can they?" I remained upright and began idly massaging his near calf.

Douglas shook his head with a wry smile, then took another drink. "I hope to all that's holy these kids aren't that fucking stupid. Maybe it's something in the water." He arched a quizzical brow at me. "Is there something in the water, Doc?"

All warmth leeched from my blood. I pursed my lips, unable to answer, thoughts a chaotic mix of doubts and worry. So much for convincing myself that I was merely overreacting, that I didn't have anything to worry about.

He leaned forward and took one of my hands. "What's wrong?"

I sighed, gave him a crooked smile, and squeezed his hand. So caring and perceptive. If Douglas had been able to spend more time at home, I suspect there would still be a Mrs. Sullivan. "It's nothing, really. Just some anomalous results."

Douglas tipped his head. "That's not a nothing face."

"There's not that much to say." I shook my head, trying to play it off, but words tumbled free. "I picked up some odd changes on my evening tests yesterday. Just little growths, extra populations, new movements. Nothing alarming, but I made sure to look for the oddities this morning." I bit my lip.

"And?"

"I wasn't imagining things. There are...differences. Planktons are now nektonic, moving around the water almost like they're hunting. And I'd swear the protozoa are developing multiple cells." I wouldn't say the word mutation, though it had danced in my head since this afternoon.

Douglas tensed, his frown slipping back into place. "Some kind of contamination?" His job didn't cover that aspect of the operation, but it was on all our minds. It had to be when this far out to sea, tapping into a new deposit amidst international concern for the environment.

"That's the really strange part." I locked eyes with him, my pulse jumping. "I can't find any crude in the water. I'm not even finding by-products from the *Alcanivorax*. If something's contaminating the site, I can't find it with my equipment. So it's either such a trace amount as to be undetectable, or it's something that we're just not testing for."

"Are they simply evolving before your eyes?" He

tried to sound playful, attempting to steer the conversation back to a lighter tone.

"It doesn't work like that," I chastised. "There's no need for these life forms to adapt, nor would it happen to all of them all at once. Evolution takes time, multiple generations to outbreed the less successful forms and proliferate like this."

His eyes sparkled for the briefest of flashes, and I wasn't sure I'd even seen it. "There is always the possibility that life doesn't work the way everyone 'knows' it does. Maybe this *is* how it works."

I shook my head. "It's not. Nothing has ever shown that an entire species, let alone multiple ones, can adapt overnight. This is much more like mutation, but on a large scale. And all the specimens are mutating the same way." A sense of relief filled me at having said the dreaded word.

Douglas remained silent for a moment, looking briefly like he might argue, before he moved on. "Should you contact your superiors?"

I sighed, shrugged, and shook my head all at once. "I need to finish up my notes, make sure all my observations sound sane. Last thing I need on an assignment like this is to be *that* person."

Douglas smiled as he leaned in to kiss my cheek. "No one will ever think that of you." I kissed him back, and we fell into each other's arms for another hour.

He left some time after I drifted off, as had become his routine. It was fine with me, though I'd started wanting to wake up next to him. This wasn't a real relationship, even though we had a lot in common. I couldn't help but find myself growing more comfortable with his presence, though. It certainly made the assignment and being cut off from the rest of the world much easier to bear.

I got ready and headed to the mess faster than normal, like most mornings after I'd spent time with Douglas. Not that I had actually counted the minutes. I wouldn't doubt that it was just a feeling, one of those aspects of relativity brought on by changed emotions.

Breakfast was quiet, and the difference in tone tugged at my mind, worked its way through my heightened mood. Some of the crew were missing, and most everyone else seemed down. I gathered my tray, took a seat near the windows, and scanned the room with a frown. The day was clear, the ocean was calm, and drilling was going well. I couldn't imagine why they were so tense.

I ate quickly so I could go about my day before the emotional contagion caught me. No sense adding to the worries already waiting for me.

Meal done, I headed to my lab for my sample kit. Test the water from various spots on the ship, check for pollution. And any further mutations. I swallowed down the sudden wave of stress and began my rounds.

I gathered my samples with the efficiency of twice-daily practice and was soon back at the lab. My assistant Roxie was there by then, setting up test tubes with slow precision. Almost as if she was afraid of dropping them. "Feeling better?" I asked, unpacking the samples onto one of the tables.

The tall blond turned to face me with her entire body, slow and controlled. She blinked twice, then spoke. "Inna. I am feeling better, yes. It must have been something I ate. I am better now."

My shoulders tensed. Something was off about her, but I couldn't quite put my finger on it. Her stiff movements and stilted speech could just be side effects of being sick. "If you need to head out early, feel free. Don't push yourself." Telling myself she just needed more rest did nothing to ease my tension.

Douglas knocked on the lab door, then stepped inside. "Ms Freysdottir." I turned, and the look on his face only added to my tension. "I need you to come with me. Bring whatever you'll need to take samples."

I wanted to ask him what was going on, but I decided to simply nod and follow. Douglas wasn't the type to call me out for no reason. Roxie began preparing this morning's samples while I added a few more tools to my kit. "Mr Sullivan," I said to indicate I was ready.

We walked side-by-side, Douglas shortening his stride so I could keep up, though we still moved at a brisk pace. He said nothing, eyes locked straight ahead. I swallowed down my unease after several moments and broke the silence. "Where are we going?"

He didn't respond at first, just continued through the halls towards the outer door. "Remember the protestors I mentioned last night?" He held the door open for me. I nodded as I stepped into the sunshine. "Their boats were found abandoned this morning."

I frowned sharply. "I don't understand." Or didn't want to. We continued toward the boat dock.

"Neither do we." Douglas finally made eye contact. I had to look away from what I saw, unable to process the hard distance in them. "But there are some...odd things that could use a scientist's eyes." He chuckled, though it sounded forced.

"What could possibly be on an abandoned boat that *I* need to take a look at?" Both protestor boats were tied up at the dock, several members of security milling around outside, faces drawn and pale. "And please say I don't need to look at dead bodies."

"I don't want to give you any preconceptions, but it might be better if there *were* dead bodies." Douglas gestured at the first gangplank but wouldn't look at me.

My stomach churned as I boarded the first vessel. Even with a gorgeous blue sky and warm sun overhead, my blood chilled and I shivered. Even with Douglas right behind me, I couldn't suppress the unease rising along my spine. It was far too late to say no, however.

Drawing a deep breath, I turned my professional side on and began my observations.

The deck looked normal to me. Some discarded beer bottles, and a towel crumpled in the corner, but nothing too unusual. I made a circuit, frowning at stains on the gunwales, then made my way below.

Everything had been touched by violence. Dishes and supplies littered the floor, clothes had been strewn across the furniture, and stuffing spilled from cushions. Broken glass glittered and liquid pooled, but I saw no blood.

I turned and frowned at Douglas. He nodded once; of course an Army vet would notice what was missing. "Where are the bodies?" I asked. "How could this much destruction happen and there be...?"

He pointed toward a doorway behind me. "It's not blood, but there's something in there." Douglas's eyes tensed.

I moved into what appeared to be a galley. Pots and utensils clanked when I nudged them aside with my foot. The remains of food had splashed across the stove and walls, but a fish remained in the sink, half gutted.

A fish with tentacles.

Trepidation fled, replaced by intense curiosity. This was far beyond a bacterium with both cilia and flagella. Here was evidence of massive mutation on advanced life.

I dropped my kit onto the counter, scrambling for gloves and a bag. I needed to bring this back to the lab for identification and study, and I needed to preserve more than just a few tissue samples. Dissection, for sure, and multiple pictures, and an immediate report to the EPA. "We might have to shut the site down," I said, eyes locked on the tentacled fish.

Douglas moved closer. "I thought you'd say that."

"There's no proof that it's because of the drilling," I said. The fish made a squishy wet noise as I lifted its head into the bag, and strings of mucus clung to the stainless steel. "But my bosses are going to want a controlled environment while they investigate, and your bosses aren't going to want any speculations in the press."

"More people complained of sickness today," he whispered, standing by my side. I tucked tentacles inside, ignoring both the rancid smell and the tone of his voice. "Some of those who've returned to duty are off. Just a little, but it's noticeable."

I tucked the wrapped fish into my kit as best I could. "Roxie wasn't exactly herself," I whispered. The quiet worry I'd felt over the last day turned to low-grade fear. I tried to suppress the chill, but it raised goosebumps along my arms, nonetheless. I glanced at Douglas, unable to express myself.

His clenched teeth and narrowed eyes did nothing to ease my fear. "Make your calls," Douglas finally said, tucking a strand of hair behind my ear. "I'll make mine, get the drilling stopped, and meet you in your rooms this evening." His voice was grim, but his expression softened.

I nodded, then took another look around the galley. "We've already failed so many protocols, but you'll need to quarantine these boots. And everyone who's been sick. Everyone who's complained of feeling sick." I met his gaze, stomach churning. "Pretty much everyone."

Douglas tipped his head. "You believe it's contagious?" He gestured at my kit.

"I don't think anyone's going to sprout tentacles," I said with a forced smile, untouched by humour. "But that's not to say that whatever's going around isn't affected. I might contact the CDC while I'm at it." A frown replaced the smile.

He drew back his shoulders and nodded once. "We have a long day ahead of us. Let's get started." Douglas led me back to the dock, where we parted ways. I tried not to think about the fish I carried, nor the empty boats

I'd just seen. Such thoughts surely led to madness.

"Roxie, I've got some bad news," I announced as I entered the lab, looking for my assistant to tell her about the quarantine. She was nowhere to be seen.

I frowned, setting my kit on a lab table next to this morning's samples. They remained in their original containers, meaning she'd left soon after I had. No note, no indication of why, but sickness could be the only answer. Roxie had saved me the effort of sending her to her quarters.

But not the effort needed to do everything by myself.

I sighed, torn between this morning's samples and the brand new mystery. I wanted to dive into the new discovery, but I had one I couldn't abandon yet. Had my assistant been well, there wouldn't be this conundrum. I'd be able to focus on the creature from the boat, pouring myself into cataloguing and preparing the mystery. Instead, I moved the mutant fish to the fridge and began my morning tests, remaining responsible.

Time passed as I portioned and labelled, started the centrifuge and the sequencer, then made ready to finally process the find. Dishes, tubes, tools, microscope. The ritual of normality that had nothing to do with what I'd seen, what I had waiting for me.

I opened the fridge and the tentacles reached for me.

Wordless terror gripped me, came out as a shriek

when I flung myself away from the creature in the bag. Even as my thoughts evaporated, I could only stare, entranced by the impossible.

Tentacles pressed against the plastic, held the fish upright so it sat on its belly. Eyes rotated in their sockets until they focused on me, bright and shiny, with impossible goat pupils. Its mouth worked as it pushed the bag open, seeking freedom.

Self-preservation took over finally. I slammed the fridge door closed and leaned against it, heart racing in my chest, a chill passing up my spine. Blows landed against the inside, wet and strong, arrhythmic. Relentless.

The door didn't budge, but I pressed against it harder, biting back primal cries. My own breath choked me, fighting to break free while struggling to grow big enough to release in a scream. I screwed my eyes closed, clinging to sanity with desperate determination.

After an unknown amount of time, the beating stopped. I held my breath, waiting for it to start again, but the fridge remained silent.

Keeping one hand against the door, I reached for one of the tall work stools. It was the only lock I had, and I damn well wasn't going to leave until I knew it wasn't able to get out. Stool in place, I drew a shuddering breath, expecting a renewed escape attempt. Nothing happened, and after several minutes, I left to find Douglas, to be anywhere but here.

Rushing through the halls toward his office, I formulated plans. Cold might not work against it, although I didn't have truly frozen temperatures in my lab. Perhaps there was liquid nitrogen on board, though I couldn't guess why there would be. Extreme heat would eradicate nearly everything, and though I hated to lose a mutation that needed to be studied, I also had no way to contain it.

Incineration was better than it escaping.

Douglas would know where we could dump it, how we could get rid of it. That's all I needed him for. Not to save me. Not to protect me. I was strong, smart and independent, but there was a small part of me that felt only relief at the thought of running to my lover's arms. That facet of my personality was new, undiscovered, and I'd have to explore it when I didn't have a tentacled monster fish locked up in my lab.

He wasn't in his office when I got there, only one of his security men. "Do you know where Mr Sullivan is?" I tried to sound calm, but my pulse roared in my ears, drowning out most sounds, urging me to keep moving.

The man turned to face me with slow, stiff movements. Vacant eyes met mine, shadowed, inescapable. I wanted to step back, to leave, but I refused to let myself cower away. Licking suddenly dry lips, I waited for an answer.

"I haven't seen Mr Sullivan." His words drawled out and his head cocked to one side. "Do you know where he is?"

Every instinct screamed at me to run. I clenched my fists, taking the first step out of the room. "No. I'll go look for him."

"I'll... go... look... for... him." Soft words followed me into the hall, and I closed the door before he said anything else. Swallowing down a shudder, I tried to guess where Douglas would be, ignoring the sudden urge to flee. I was surely overreacting.

Douglas was no longer at the dock, nor at the drilling center. I didn't make a habit of wandering the halls during the day shift, but it seemed like there was far less crew than should be out and about. Less scurry and bustle, more listless and meandering.

My shoulders tensed more with each set of glazed eyes that followed me. None of the workers talked to me, and I didn't try to ask them any questions. I knew something was wrong, though I had no name for it. I didn't want to address the issue, but I couldn't deny it.

The *Halcyon Dream* shuddered.

Metal groaned, a deep bass note that travelled through my bones and made my heart skip a beat. Hairs stood up sharply, followed by goosebumps, and I looked around with wide eyes. What had happened and why was it so quiet?

Shouts echoed from a corridor on my left, mostly indistinguishable, though I made out some swearing and commands. If I wanted to know what had happened, that was where I needed to go.

The superstructure groaned again, but less violently. No klaxons went off, though I couldn't imagine this wasn't an emergency. Especially as I heard what the voices shouted. "There's no turning off the drill just like that." Chief Engineer Hines sounded angry, not frightened.

"So how *do* we shut it down?" Douglas's voice was sharp but controlled, and it settled my rising panic. I rushed into the hydraulic bay though I could do nothing to help.

Lights flashed on a panel of gauges, but no alarms sounded. If something were truly wrong, surely klaxons would be trying to get our attention. Some of the crew scurried around to various stations while Hines poked at a keyboard in front of him. Douglas loomed nearby, arms crossed and face stern. He noted my entrance and gestured with his chin for me to join him.

"Someone throw open Valve Zed." Hines stabbed at the keys, eyes glued to the screen, assuming someone on his crew would follow his order. He growled beneath his breath, then glanced at Douglas. "There are procedures, and we're going to follow them." The engineer didn't sound too confident.

Douglas picked up on it as well. "What about the clog? How do we clear it while the drill is on?"

Hines yanked a walkie to his mouth. "Anyone down at C intake yet?" He turned a shoulder toward Douglas, putting the conversation on hold.

"What's going on?" I asked softly. This seemed far more pressing than the fish locked in my fridge.

He looked down, arms remaining locked across his chest. "Something big is clogging at least one of the coolant intakes." Another metallic groan. "The drill is overheating, and the emergency cut-off is unresponsive."

I blinked rapidly, processing his words. "What's going to happen?"

The chief engineer swore at something on the walkie. "I need a better fucking answer than that."

Douglas unfolded, gripped my elbow, and lead me out of the bay. "We get some supplies and we get the fuck away from here."

"You want to abandon the *Halcyon Dream*?" My voice cracked around a swell of panic, but I matched his hurried pace.

"Pre-emptively getting clear of a potential disaster. I'm not risking your lives. If it goes sideways, then we'll have enough to last a journey to shore. If it gets resolved, then we'll be back here in time for dinner." He paused at a junction and tucked a strand of hair behind my ear. Douglas opened his mouth, then chose to say nothing.

I rose on my toes and kissed him, not caring who might see us. After the morning I'd had, and the day leading up to this, all I felt was a sense of relief. Everyone should be so lucky as to have a protector.

Then I frowned, stepping back, though not out of his grip. "What about everyone else?' My stomach flipped. "What about the fish in my lab?"

"What about it?" His eyes and voice hardened.

"That's what I was coming to tell you. It's alive! It tried to grab me. I had to lock it in the fridge so it didn't get away." A line of cold sweat broke out along my spine as I remembered the way it moved.

His expression changed completely, like a switch had been flipped. A smirk spread across his lips, but it was humourless. Predatory. "Then my master is much closer than I thought."

I blinked once, jaw dropping.

His brows drew together briefly before his grin deepened. "Oh, don't worry precious Inna. You aren't to become one of the mindless slaves when the rest are converted. You have a special place in His plans." Douglas blinked and his eyes changed. Pale gold with sideways pupils, they looked like they belonged on a cephalopod. "Mostly that baby of yours."

I touched my abdomen. "Baby?" He had to be joking. I took precautions against such things. Children would only complicate a career, especially way out here.

Douglas tightened his grip on my elbow and resumed our walk through the hall, though at a much brisker pace and practically dragging me behind him. Members of the crew watched us pass, all with a slow, dazed look. None of them attempted to intervene, nor even called out. The cold sweat trickled down my back.

"You're really putting me on a boat?" I asked when we stepped outside. Waves slapped against the *Halcyon Dream*'s pontoons, breaking in high sprays, but there was no wind to drive them. The day was bright and clear, and the beauty somehow added to the terror of the events.

"It wasn't supposed to be this quick and dirty. I was supposed to lure you to the Master's side, show you all the glory of how His world will be once He is here. But..." His hand tightened on my arm.

"My master will have a most violent entrance, and He really will want you to be safe, even if you are not fully on his side. Neither of your lives can be put at risk." Douglas paused at the top of the final stairs. "I'm afraid you'll only have whatever little food the drones have brought on board, but you really shouldn't be afloat that long."

I tugged once against his grip. He simply tightened his fingers until they pinched like a vice. I voiced my pain, but the tender Douglas I knew was gone. He continued steadily forward, each inexorable step bringing us closer to the protestor's boats.

Metal groaned again, the deck trembling beneath my feet.

Even if I got away from him, where would I go? I didn't have the skills to pilot a boat all the way back to land, presuming I could get past any potential guards. I had nowhere to hide that Douglas couldn't find me, and my shelter was precarious at best.

All fight drained from me. My shoulders slumped, and I followed him docilely. Several of the vacant-eyed thralls met us on the dock, the smaller of the boats prepared to cast off. I stepped aboard with downcast eyes, thoughts as empty as my heart.

"Don't fret," Douglas said, sounding once more like the lover I'd known these past weeks. "All will be well. They'll keep you safe, bring you back after Master is settled."

He cupped one cheek, placed a kiss on my forehead. "I'm sure He'll be pleased enough to grant me a favour. I'll ask that you be allowed to keep your mind, and we can worship Him together."

I stayed on the aft deck, staring at my feet as we cast off and motored away from the rig. The choppy sea soon levelled out, though I barely noticed. One of the mindless crew stood near me, her breathing heavy, feet shifting restlessly.

What was I supposed to do? Let myself become a slave and brood mare? I already knew I couldn't escape, but the thought tempted me. Better to fail while trying than not try at all. Drawing a deep breath, I lifted my head.

Metal screamed and pulled my attention back to the *Halcyon Dream*.

Water churned violently, crashing against the sides and over the lower decks. The massive platform seethed and tossed like a toy in the bathtub, the upper structure beginning to buckle.

I frowned, sure I saw forms in the waves. Not merely seaweed caught in the turbulent water. Many large things, lithe and quick, each one larger than an orca.

From the ocean burst half a dozen tentacles, reaching for the sky before coiling around the *Halcyon Dream*. Struts buckled, steam rose in clouds, and the entire structure sank noticeably. Distant screams, human and metal, reached my ears, setting my heart to racing.

The scientific part of my mind kicked in, unconstrained by my shock. Those tentacles didn't belong to any cephalopod, mythically enormous or not, but looked far more like flagella. Extremely flexible, prehensile, and dexterous in ways they shouldn't be. They squeezed and collapsed a storage tank, and I added strong to my observations.

The boat trembled beneath my feet with the force of an underwater roar. Deep, almost subsonic, I felt it in my bones. The thralls on the boat with me all moaned in echoing response, falling to their knees in genuflection.

I watched the ocean still, chewing my lower lip, heart hammering in my chest. The throbbing bass note increased, pressing in around me, *into* me, silencing all thought, drowning out the worshipful moans.

Time seemed to stop as a head breached the surface in slow motion. Water cascaded from unnatural surfaces, the snarling visage too horrific to comprehend and retain sanity. Black as oil, iridescent and beautiful, putrescent and horrifying. On and on the roar went, resonating from the gaping maw, coming both from the thing and from beyond the walls of reality.

Without effort, it tore the *Halcyon Dream* apart.

Debris scattered, describing tumbling arcs before crashing into the sea and sinking below the surface. Fireballs gouted toward the sky, singeing the whip-like tentacles as fires sprang to life. People screamed in horror and moaned in worship before they died.

This was not just a thing. Not some monstrous

creature lashing out at the hubris of mankind. This was Douglas's Master. The source of the mutations. The one stealing the minds of the crew. A being from beyond this realm, from before our understanding.

I could not let it have me, nor my baby.

My motions were stiff, disjoined, and I barely tore myself away from the sight of the Master. Its roar called me, compelled me, entreated me to look at it. To join it. To be one with it.

Instead, I forced myself toward the anchor. I groaned with the effort of lifting it, of carrying it toward the gunwale. The roar changed pitch behind me, giving me pause. I nearly dropped the hunk of metal from numbed fingers.

Must reach the water. Must escape the Master's horrible control. I tangled the anchor in my shirt, vision dimming, and stared at the blue waters over the side. The surface teemed with phosphorescent life, streams of blue and while glow pulsing as they moved toward the being.

I would not let it have me. Better to drown and sink than give myself to it. I tumbled overboard and was quickly enveloped by warm water. Like returning to the womb, I felt only comfort and safety, and gave myself over.

Tides of change embraced me in loving currents.

RAVEN CORINN CARLUK writes dark fantasy, paranormal romance, and anything else that catches her interest. She has authored and self-published five novels and one novella, where she explores themes of love and acceptance. She has also self-published two collections of short stories, ranging from the lustful to the horrific, the darkly humorous to the tragic. Her shorter pieces, usually from her darker side, can be found in several Black Hare Press anthologies, at Detritus Online, with Fantasia Divinity, and through Alban Lake Publishers.

Bibliography
All Hallows Blood,2011
ANGELS, Black Hare Press, 2019
BEYOND, Black Hare Press, 2019
Deep Space, Black Hare Press, 2019
Martyrs (The Birdman Project), 2019
Midsummer's Unveiling, RCC Tales, 2012
MONSTERS, Black Hare Press, 2019
Nomycha, RCC Tales, 2018
Saint Valentine's Clash, RCC Tales, 2011
stories with bite o,.,o, 2010
WORLDS, Black Hare Press, 2019

Connect
Website: RavenCorinnCarluk.Blogspot.Com
Amazon: amazon.com/author/ravencorinncarluk
Smashwords: smashwords.com/profile/view/RavenCorinnCarluk
Twitter: @ravencorinn
Facebook: RavenCorinnCarluk

Into the Deep

By Steven Lord

When a crack military team are dispatched to rescue a missing submarine from the depths of the Pacific Ocean, they discover a horror beyond their worst nightmares. But sometimes the greatest evil comes from within.

0745Z 12 Jan 18 – N27.97 W65.94 – 20,000' above sea level

"ONE MINUTE!"

Even standing next to him, Chris could barely hear

the loadmaster's shout over the roar of the open ramp. Six feet in front and twenty thousand below, stars gazed up at him, reflecting off an unnaturally calm Atlantic. Not for the first time that night, he wondered what the hell he was doing. He quickly looked away and focused his attention on the rest of the team, flickering in and out of hellish existence with the blinking of the red jump light. Buster sprawled out across four of the canvas seats, head lolling against the webbing. Dog, silent and grim as always, ran his finger over the edge of his heavy dive knife, grunting with satisfaction before driving it home into its sheath on his left thigh. Immediately in front of him, Frank wore a huge grin framed by the bushy beard that his immersion suit's mask was failing miserably to contain. Team leader or not, he was clearly enjoying this way more than any sane man should. With a wink to the loadmaster, he put one huge hand on Chris' shoulder as he muscled his way past him.

"Cheer up!" He reached the end of the ramp and turned to face Chris as the jump light switched to solid green. "Worse things happen at sea!" Then he leapt backwards out of the aircraft and into the inky darkness.

Shaking his head, Chris followed him out, dropping like a falling angel as he stepped off the ramp. All he could see in the darkness were the stars rushing up to meet him.

***

1830Z 10 Jan 18 – HMS *Raleigh*, Cornwall UK – sea level

The main briefing room in *Raleigh* looked and smelled exactly like every other briefing room Chris had sat in over the years. Dark grey walls, empty save for a lone poster reminding the reader of the importance of heat acclimatisation training. Getting shot had been an acceptable occupational hazard in Afghanistan; heatstroke, on the other hand, was positively frowned upon. A low stage filled the far end of the room, flimsy wooden lectern off to one side, projector screen glowing in the darkness like a portal to heaven. And all around, baked into every surface, into the very air itself—that stench of stale sweat that defeated all attempts to remove it.

As Chris sat waiting for the brief to start, his eyes came to rest on the poster, then softened and glazed over as he reflected on how his life had changed over the last two years. Joining the Submarine Para Assistance Group (SPAG to its friends) had not been an obvious career choice. In many ways it hadn't been his choice at all. The medics had been clear about his odds of returning to front line duties—"No fucking chance" was the exact turn of phrase they used, bedside manner clearly not being in vogue in military medical circles. Eight years of service in the Royal Marines killed off at the flourish of a doctor's pen. Angry though he was, he wasn't ready to face civvy street. If he was honest with himself, he had become pretty well institutionalised over the last decade.

Not literally, though. Despite the nightmares, the girl looking up at him, pain and confusion in her eyes. Despite waking up in a dark room with his own screams still reverberating through his head. Despite the cold sweat that drenched his sheets most nights. Not literally. Not yet.

An idle conversation in the bar had put SPAG on his radar. He had always enjoyed being under the water—before signing up, he had spent an epic year in Cairns, drinking, shagging and teaching British gap year students how to dive. The Service were happy to build on that foundation. He was one of only three Marines from his intake who they trained up as Navy divers, able to defuse mines in the cold, dark waters of the North Atlantic. Afghanistan, of course, had meant that other aspects of his training were in greater demand. He was also a half-decent sports parachutist and had earned his para wings early on in his career.

"So," his friend had slurred in the bar that night.

"You're a soldier who can't fight. But you can dive, and you can jump out of a plane. Mate, I've got the perfect job for you."

Six months of exhausting, specialised, and at times, outright bizarre training and here he was, ready for his first mission. SPAG was a tight-knit unit and as the 'Fucking New Guy', Chris wasn't expecting an easy ride. He looked around at his new teammates. If the briefing room felt familiar, its occupants certainly didn't. All ex-submariners, he wouldn't have pegged any of them as military if he'd walked past them on the street. They seemed to take pride in their unkempt haircuts, extravagant beards, and ridiculous sideburns. The Regimental Sergeant Major down at Lympstone would have a field day if any of these jokers had rocked up to start Marine training. The guy sat directly behind him— seven-foot-tall if he was an inch—was even sporting an earring to go with his shaved head and beard. Chris couldn't believe his eyes.

"What the fuck you looking at, bootie?" the colossus rumbled.

Chris had learnt early on in his career that if you backed down in a confrontation, lost face, it was impossible to recover. You fought fire with fire, or you went home.

"What am I looking at? Some kind of freakish hipster

pirate, I think."

Chris wondered if he'd pushed it too far as the man unfurled himself from his seat and strode across to tower over him. He had to tilt his head fully back just to hold the giant's stare, which ruined the effect somewhat. Time seemed to slow to a crawl, until a deep rumbling noise filled the air. It took Chris a second to realise that the man was laughing.

"Hipster pirate. I like that." He turned around and walked towards the stage. "I'm Frank. Team leader." Clearly satisfied with Chris' performance, he positioned himself behind the lectern, fired up PowerPoint and launched into his brief, still chuckling to himself.

A map of the Caribbean replaced the white square of the projector screen, a low-resolution photo of a submarine, superimposed on the top right corner.

"This is the *Caribe*. She's a Venezuelan *Sabalo* class sub, crew of 24. She was exercising north of Puerto Rico when Caracas lost contact with her. That was four days ago. This morning one of our Type 23 frigates picked up a sonar return on the seabed 300 miles south of Bermuda. International waters, but close enough to our overseas territories to spark the interest of our lords and masters. They've tasked us to drop in and check it out, maybe lend our South American friends a helping hand. Yes, Buster."

A short, wiry man with the dark tan of a surfer and a

permanent sneer on his face lowered his hand. "Why can't the Type 23 do it?"

"Doesn't have the kit or the training for a rescue. It's going to hang around, act as mother ship for us. But it's got other tasks down in the Falklands, so it can't wait forever. We've got a 48-hour window before it needs to leave. Any other questions?"

Silence.

"Good. We'll be using the NSRS. It's being loaded onto an aircraft as we speak. The RAF will drop it within visual range of the Type 23."

A snort came from somewhere in the audience. "If we're lucky! Remember Gib?"

A picture of the NATO Submarine Rescue System flashed up on the screen. Chris had always thought it looked like Thunderbird 4. He had spent a large part of his training using this particular bit of kit. He remembered Gibraltar alright. He was the one who had to swim a mile and a half to get to the bloody thing last October when the RAF got their coordinates wrong. He might have been more sympathetic if he hadn't seen the pilots out on the lash in town the night before…

"Mike, Chopper…you'll fly with the NSRS. Jump out with it, check out the systems, then get aboard the Type 23 to act as liaison."

Two men sat in the front row of seats nodded their

heads.

"Buster, Dog, Chris. You'll be in the rescue party with me. We'll arrive overhead in a second aircraft a few hours after the others, give them time to get everything set up. We'll jump as close as possible to the rescue vehicle, get straight in and take her down. We'll board the *Caribe,* pick up some grateful Venezuelans and get the Type 23 to drop us off in the Bahamas. We'll be sipping cocktails in Nassau before the sun goes down. Any last questions?"

"Media coverage?" asked Mike. Or maybe Chopper. Chris hadn't quite figured out which was which yet.

"Zero. This won't be like the *Priz,* boys; there won't be any documentaries made about this one. The Venezuelans haven't admitted to the outside world that they've even lost a sub yet. Likely, they'll just brush this thing under the carpet, whether we save anyone or not. Right, if no-one has any other questions, get your shit sorted out. We fly out in 2 hours. Oh, and Dog—don't forget your amenity kit."

Sniggers all round. As Chris walked out of the room, he turned to Mike/Chopper.

"What was that last bit about?"

"Dog's a bit strange. I mean, we're all a bit strange, else we wouldn't be here. But Dog is *really* strange. Always packs an eye mask and earplugs in his immersion suit, like he's flying first class or something. But in all the times I've flown with him, I've never seen him wear them. I reckon it's some kinky sex thing."

"Well, everyone here does seem to love to wear rubber…"

"You'll learn to love it too, bootie. Just you wait."

***

0900Z 12 Jan 18 – N27.97 W65.94 – Sea level

Chris secured the top hatch on the rescue vehicle, slamming the locking bars into place with numb hands.

"Christ, that water's cold. Aren't we meant to be in the Caribbean?"

"Call that cold?" Buster sneered. "We need to get you out to Norway, then you'll know what cold is."

Chris bit down on his retort. Like most marines, he'd spent more than his fair share of time on the fjords, but on reflection this wasn't the time or the place to get into an argument. The four men were jammed into a metal cylinder about the length of a London bus and so narrow that Frank, sat towards the back of the passenger section, was forced to rest his feet on the seats across from him, knees almost touching the ceiling.

The passenger section took up the rear two-thirds of

the vehicle - in theory the more spacious two-thirds when not filled with Frank's bulk and four sets of webbing, immersion suits and loosely bundled parachutes. Dog, knelt in the narrow gap between two lines of plastic blue seating, was packing up this kit in a methodical fashion that betrayed years of practice.

Chris sat in the forward section of the SRS, facing a bank of comms equipment mounted on the starboard wall of the vessel. From his seat, he could talk to the two SPAG operators holed up on the Type 23, at least for the first part of the dive. His broadcasts were a fragile thread connecting the four men in their tin can with the surface and the rest of the world. But at some point on their dive, Chris knew that the growing vastness of ocean above them would snap that thread and they would be truly alone; a speck of humanity in a dark alien world. He shifted uncomfortably in his seat. The thought rose to the top of his consciousness yet again. *Why do I do this to myself?* The answer lay just beneath the surface, a shallow layer of repression covering a cold, hard truth. He had no desire to unearth it.

Brushing up against his left shoulder, Buster perched in the bow of the vehicle, strapped into the cramped driver's seat. *At least he has a decent view,* Chris thought. The entire front of the vehicle was a bubble of clear Perspex, heavily reinforced to deal with the immense pressure they would be experiencing on their dive. On the other side of the bubble, the waterline bobbed up and down like a washing machine coming off a spin cycle. It was a few minutes past sunrise and both sky and water were easing their way through ever lighter shades of blue: pale azure on top, glowing sapphire below.

"Chris, we good two-way with the Type 23?"

He snapped out of his reverie. "Affirm. Good two-way, last known location of the target is in the nav computer."

"Dog, nearly there with that wet kit?"

A slight nod of the head and a grunt.

"Right then. Let's get this show on the road. Buster, take us down."

***

0945Z 12 Jan 18 – N28.01 W65.95 – 300 metres below sea level

The view through the bubble showed nothing but darkness. Chris sat bathed in the sickly light of the rescue vehicle's electric lighting, shivering as he listened to the low buzz of static on the radios. For the last few minutes, he had thought he could hear something through the noise. He closed his eyes, straining to make out order in the chaos. There it was again, almost imperceptible—a sound like the faint tinkle of a child's laughter overlaid on the high-pitched buzzing of a dentist's drill.

She had been laughing. Laughing as she ran, as if the world around her didn't matter, as if everything was a game. Until the sharp crack of the report cut through the sounds of glee. Then she stopped.

He held his breath, willed his heartbeat to slow down so that the thumping wouldn't distract him from focusing on the radio. Now there was just static. Just static. Just…

"JESUS!"

"Are you alright, mate?" Frank lifted his hand from where he'd slapped it onto Chris' shoulder. "Just checking you hadn't drifted off."

"What? No. I'm fine," Chris mumbled, shaking his head.

"Good stuff. We should be about 15 minutes out. Ditch the headphones and get ready to cross-deck."

"No snags."

"And Chris. Relax."

"This is why we don't let people who haven't earned their dolphins into SPAG, Frank. I told you." Buster had turned from his controls to join the conversation.

"Shut up, Buster," Frank growled.

"No. This needs to be said." Buster looked straight into Chris' eyes. The curl of his lip was gone, his face deathly serious.

"Things are different down here underneath the surface. No sunlight, no contact with the outside world. Just you and a few other lost souls stuck in an iron tube together. You spend enough time on submarines, you see things. You hear things. And some people can't quite get their heads round that, you see?

"My third tour, we were stationed below the polar cap for six months. Shit job. Normally you get to send a message home every week or so, get to remember that there's a world outside. When you're under the ice, you can't surface. No comms at all for half a year. I was an old hand by that point; didn't bother me that much. But for one of the officers of the watch, it was his first dive. Straight out of training; can't have been more than twenty years old. Big smile on his face all the time, like he couldn't believe he was actually in the job he'd dreamed of as a kid. Shit, he still *was* a kid.

"Anyway, one day—maybe two months in—we were sat in the Ops Room, working through a drill. The kid had been getting a hard time from the captain, a real old school ball-breaker. He wasn't smiling so much anymore. We'd gone silent running, practising how to hide from a Russian attack boat. Hand signals only, could have heard a pin drop. Then all of a sudden, we heard this tapping noise ring out across the room. Metal on metal, like someone ringing a dinner bell. Everyone looks round, even the kid. Then he realises it's his own boot, steel toecap tap-tap-tapping away against the deck floor. He's surprised as everyone else. The captain loses it, screams in his face, yanks him up by the scruff of his neck, throws him out of the room. I mean really throws him out. Confined to quarters for seven days.

"A week's a long time under the water. You think it's bad normally, think what it's like if you're stuck on your own in a tiny room, no one to talk to, meals coming in through a hatch in the door. He didn't deserve that. Shit, nobody does.

"Seven days later, we went to open the door, see how he's getting on."

Buster finally looked away from Chris' face, staring intently at a blank patch on the wall to his right.

"I still don't know how he got hold of that cleaver. Chef didn't even know it was missing.

"We found him sat on his bunk, sheets rusty with dried blood. He was rocking back and forward, head down, muttering something over and over under his breath. I was one of the ones who picked him up, carried him down to the med bay. I heard what he was whispering.

"Later, the doc told me that he must have just done it a few hours before we got him out. He didn't think the kid had slept a wink in that entire week. He was able to save his life, even save the rest of the leg, but he couldn't save his mind.

"'It won't stop tapping.' That's all he said. Over and over. 'It won't stop tapping.'"

The sub was quiet for a few seconds after Buster stopped talking. Chris heard a rustling behind him. He glanced over his shoulder to see Frank's head bowed, huge shoulders shaking up and down uncontrollably. The big man looked up. Tears streamed down his face, his lips clamped together as he desperately tried to stop himself from laughing. On seeing Chris' expression, he totally lost control, deep guffaws breaking out of him like a surprised donkey. He tried to speak, failed, tried again.

"Oh man. The look on your face!" He took four or five deep breaths to compose himself.

"Enough, enough. Buster, stop pissing around and get us in position."

"Right you are, boss." The smirk was back on Buster's face.

Chris yanked off his headset in disgust and started checking his webbing pouches. Behind them, Dog sat quietly in the passenger seats, a faraway look on his face. He wasn't laughing.

***

1015Z 12 Jan 18 – N28.04 W65.96 – 450 metres below sea level

"Half a click out and closing. We should start to see her in a few minutes."

Three heads jockeyed for position in the cramped observation bubble. A powerful spotlight speared out from the front of the rescue vessel, ripping a glowing tear a hundred-foot-long through the infinite darkness of the abyss before fading away, defeated. Occasionally a creature would pass through the beam, its body moulded into unearthly shapes by the pressure of thousands of tonnes of water bearing down on it. Frank was shouting out names of fish as soon as he saw them, as if playing bingo with himself.

"Blobfish! Ugly fucker, isn't it!"

"Frank, I really don't care. Can you please stop playing Jacques Cousteau and get out of the way so I can drive this thing?" Buster's brow was wrinkled with a combination of concentration and frustration. He was the only one not looking out of the window, focussed instead on his sonar display.

Frank grunted and pulled his head away from the Perspex for a grand total of seven seconds.

"Jesus—a giant squid! Look at that thing—it must be

5 metres long."

Chris guessed from the boyish look of excitement on Frank's face that he hadn't read much Jules Verne. The cephalopod glided through the cone of light, arms streaming behind a pulsating bullet-like body, an aria of grace rising above the dirge of the deep. It showed no interest in their ship whatsoever, disappearing back into the blackness as suddenly as it had appeared. *So much for Verne*, Chris thought.

"OK, 200 feet out. She'll be coming up on the nose any second now."

"You sure about that, Buster? Cos I'm pretty sure that's a sub on our 3 o'clock." Dog was pointing a powerful handheld lanterns through the right-hand side of the bubble. Its beam was sliding along a wall of coral-encrusted grey steel, just an arm's length away from their vessel.

"Of course I'm bloody sure; signal's dead ahead. Stop messing around..." Buster's voice trailed away as he looked up from his scope and saw the sub. He slammed the throttles to idle and they hung there in the darkness, nestled uncomfortably close to the much larger boat. After a few seconds of uncomfortable silence, Dog started to nudge the beam of the lantern upwards. It traced a path up the hull of the sub, and Chris raised his eyes to follow. As he watched, black stencilled letters appeared in the circle of light.

U.S.S. *CYCLOPS*

"What the hell?" Chris mouthed.

Buster looked up at Frank. "What we doing, Boss? Want me to check it out?"

"That thing's a wreck. Look at it. It's been here for decades. Don't worry about it. Focus on the mission. Keep going."

Chris gave him a confused glance. "Frank, this has got to be connected to our Venezuelan boat. You don't just get two subs sat on top of each other. We should take a look."

Frank turned to look at him. The humour in his eyes had vanished as completely as if a switch had been thrown somewhere within him. For the first time, Chris saw the violence in the man, the potential to inflict pain and death. He'd seen it before in some of his colleagues; he was sure they'd seen it in him at some stage. You didn't do his old job for long without coming to terms with the fact that your ultimate task, should it come to it, was to end another's life. That was part of what being a Marine was. He didn't expect to see it in a submariner, not even in a mountain of a man like Frank. He realised that he had no real idea who this man was, what he had done. He didn't know any of them, not in the way he had known his old team.

"We stay on mission," Frank growled. "Is that alright with you?"

Chris responded with a barely perceptible nod of the head. This wasn't his lead. But he made a note to watch Frank more closely from now on. He felt the walls around him vibrate gently as Buster powered up again. After a minute or so of forward motion, another vessel started to emerge out of the gloom.

"There she is, Boss. Looks like she's pretty intact. Probably still has power. Escape hatch looks clear too. I'll bring us round to dock."

Buster's face was a picture of concentration as he manoeuvred the small rescue vehicle towards the much larger sub. He swung the vehicle around so its rear was pointing at the pale circle of the escape hatch and slowly reversed into position. The pings of the range detector rang out from his console, getting faster and more insistent until they merged into single continuous tone, like a dying patient, his heart not fading out but racing itself into cardiac arrest. A dull clang reverberated through the cockpit as the two vessels connected.

"Showtime." Frank grinned.

***

1045Z 12 Jan 18 – N28.05 W65.96 – 465 metres

below sea level

"Pressure should be equalised," growled Dog. Chris realised it was the first time he'd heard the man speak since they'd jumped from the C-130 three hours before. "We're good to go."

The four of them crouched next to the rescue vehicle's rear hatch. Stripped out of their suits, the four of them were in lightweight combat trousers and shirts: waterproof, more pockets than you could ever need and black as night. Chris had rolled his eyes when he'd drawn the kit from stores; everyone wanted to be special and SPAG were clearly no exception. He didn't see what was wrong with his old camo kit. He missed the familiarity of it, like putting on a set of old pyjamas. Instead, he had this SAS-lite crap. He absently patted his pouches, checking they were secure, not even realising he was doing it.

The others had their own tics as they prepared to enter the unknown: Buster cracking his knuckles, Dog slipping a small silver medallion from under his t-shirt and giving it a rub, Frank unfolding a tattered photo of a woman and child, giving it a kiss before putting it back in a trouser pocket. As it disappeared, he cocked his head to one side like an inquisitive sparrow.

"Can anyone else hear that?"

"What, boss?" replied Buster.

"Sounds like… Never mind. Everyone ready?"

Nods all round.

"OK. Dog, open her up."

The locking wheel spun round without a sound, the heavy steel hatch of the rescue vehicle swinging inwards to reveal a stubby chamber, no more than a foot long, still dripping with what remained of the sea water pumped out minutes earlier. At the other end of the umbilical lay the escape hatch of the *Caribe*.

Dog reached in, grabbed the second wheel that would give them access to the Venezuelan sub, and gave it a yank. It stubbornly refused to budge. Frowning, he tugged again, moving around slightly to get better purchase. The wheel moved an inch, then rotated back to its original position as Dog relaxed the pressure. He looked around at Frank, who shook his head and leaned in next to him.

"Pull!"

The wheel gave way under their combined efforts, making a sound like a tendon popping. Frank's weight was still forward and as the hatch swung open, he stumbled forward and fell through the dark portal, catching himself on an outstretched hand.

"Thought you said the fucking power was on, Buster! It's darker than a bloody coal scuttle in there!" he swore, slowly picking himself up.

"Boss."

"Stupidfuckinghatch."

"Boss!"

"Leg's killing me now."

"BOSS! Look!"

Frank looked down at his hand. "Get me a torch. Now."

Dog handed over his powerful lantern. Gore squelched out between Frank's fingers as he grabbed it, spilling red rivulets down his arm. Breathing heavily, he shone the light through the hatch and into hell.

One time during Chris' second tour, the Taliban had tried to attack his base with an IED—an improvised explosive donkey. They'd cut open the poor creature, filled its cavities with explosives, then sewn it up again. It must have been dropped off somewhere near the main gate that night and slowly made its way towards the light and noise. Luckily, the bomb-maker panicked and detonated it while it was still in the snakepit—a sort of concrete airlock between the safety of the base interior and the insanity of the outside world. The explosion didn't injure anyone, but Chris was one of those tasked with cleaning up the aftermath. He remembered the chunks of unrecognisable meat slithering down the walls, the metallic smell permeating through the dusty dusk air.

The view through the hatch was much worse. It

opened onto the corridor that formed the main spine of the Venezuelan sub. The corridor was a charnel house. Blood covered the walls, a handprint here and there, the rest a crazed swirl of crimson, Hieronymus Bosch channelled through Jackson Pollock. The floor shimmered with minced flesh, shredded bone, offal, all swimming in a pool of red liquid. Chris was pretty sure it wasn't donkey.

Frank reached into his trouser pocket, drew out a pistol and cocked it.

"What the hell is going on, Boss?!" Buster yelped, his voice a clear octave higher than normal. "You've got a weapon? Why have you got a weapon? Why haven't I got a weapon?"

"Right boys. Time I let you in on a little secret."

***

1200Z 9 Jan 18 – HMS *Raleigh*, Cornwall UK – sea level

Frank hated spooks. He had dealt with them plenty of times when he was in the SBS; he didn't trust them then and he didn't trust them now. The guy across the table from him had that arrogant look in his eye, the one that you could only develop from years of public-school education telling you that you were richer, better, more *worthy* than the other lot. He'd seen where that misplaced confidence could get you. More accurately, he'd seen where that misplaced confidence could get him. Such people normally made sure they were well clear before any shit went down.

"So, what is it now? Need the Russians to lose another nuclear sub? Chinese getting too close to our shores?"

"Sgt Mitchell, you come highly recommended. I understand you're an efficient man, but more importantly you're discrete. What I'm going to tell you stays in this room."

"Of course, Mr Bond."

"Cute. Have you ever heard of the USS *Cyclops*?"

"Can't say I have."

"The USS *Cyclops* was a US submarine, built just before World War I. In March 1918, it disappeared without a trace somewhere in the Bermuda Triangle. This is a matter of public record. What is not widely known is that the USS *Cyclops* was carrying 40T of Incan gold when she disappeared. The Americans stole it back in '17, managed to smuggle it through Brazil. They were sailing it back to fund the war effort when the *Cyclops* disappeared. The boat and gold have been missing for almost 100 years. Until last week.

"Three days ago, GCHQ intercepted a transmission from a Venezuelan sub, the *Caribe*. Apparently, it had stumbled across the wreck of an American boat and was seeking permission to investigate further. We believe that boat is the USS *Cyclops*. Since the initial transmission, we've heard nothing from the Venezuelans. We think they've broken down somewhere in the vicinity.

"We've dispatched a Type 23 to make sure the *Caribe* doesn't leave the area. We need you to locate it, interrogate the crew and find out where the *Cyclops* is. We'll send another craft to pick it up."

"And by 'we' you mean…"

"Don't be droll, Sergeant. You know who I mean. Any real questions?"

"What do I do with the Venezuelans afterwards?"

"Submarines are dangerous places. Accidents happen. When you're done, scuttle the *Caribe*. Leave them behind."

***

1055Z 12 Jan 18 – N28.05 W65.96 – 465 metres below sea level

"So now you know. Doesn't change shit. Neither does this mess. We've got a job to do. Let's do it."

Buster didn't look convinced. "I don't understand. We've found the *Cyclops*. Why not just head back now, pass on the info, leave the Venezuelans down here in this bloodbath? They're probably dead anyway!"

Frank's eyes lost focus for a second, as if his answer was being fed to him via an earpiece.

"Because he needs us… He… Damn buzzing!" He shook his head with violence. "Because we can't take the risk of leaving any witnesses. Those Vauxhall boys don't like loose ends."

I bet they don't, thought Chris. "What about us, Frank?" he asked. "What happens us after you get your information out of whoever is left on this sub?"

Frank's eyes darted up and left.

"I'll need a team."

"So I'd imagine. But be careful who you pick, Sgt. I think you might be the only one who makes it back from this one. Remember, submarines are dangerous places."

"Nothing. We all come back together. Now let's get moving." The pistol waved in their direction to punctuate his words.

The four of them squeezed through the hatch and stepped into the shallow sea of blood that sloshed around the corridor floor. Frank's lantern illuminated a door halfway down.

"That's the Ops Room. If anyone's left alive in here,

they'll be in there."

"For God's sake," Buster screeched. "Is no-one else concerned about the fact we're standing in a fucking lake of blood?"

The pale light from the lantern sapped any colour from Frank's features, lighting them from below like a child playing with a torch at Halloween.

"Be concerned about me, Buster. Be concerned about the man with the gun."

The four of them trudged to the door. Each step left ripples behind them that fanned out in ragged circles, slowly dying down until no evidence remained that they had ever passed.

Frank stopped by the door and replaced the gun in his pocket.

"OK. We go in on three. They must know we're here, but they'll think we're a rescue mission. Let's make sure they keep thinking that until I say otherwise."

Chris took a deep breath. He had no illusions about what was coming. What surprised him was how little he cared. Maybe in a sense he'd died back on that field in Afghanistan. Maybe, deep down, he'd always felt that what should have happened. No more pain. No more guilt. No more fucking *buzzing!* His brow creased. When did that start?

"Right," proclaimed Frank, dragging his attention to

the here and now. "One… Two… Three…"

Frank threw open the door and the four of them piled in to the Ops Room. As Chris stepped through the doorway, the buzzing grew to a crescendo, rattling the teeth in his gums. Suddenly Frank's lantern went dead and everything started to happen very quickly.

Blackness.

A scream.

A *flash* from the lantern illuminated the room for a split second. Buster, frozen, a look of shock on his face. Frank, running towards a shape—Chris couldn't quite make it out, its edges seemed to blur and hurt his eyes as he looked at it. Out of the corner of his eye, he could see Dog disappearing out the door.

Blackness.

"My love, I've missed you." Frank's voice, but with an edge to it, as if someone else was speaking through his vocal cords. "For you, my love. I'll do it for you."

A shot rang out.

Flash. Buster, on the ground, blood streaming out of a small hole in his forehead, the back of his skull missing. Frank, moving the gun towards his mouth, the shape blocked by his body. Chris started to run towards him, arms outstretched, grasping the gun, inches yet leagues away.

Blackness.

Another shot filled the air.

Flash. Frank's body on the ground, his face a gaping hole. Chris skidded to a stop. The shape was closer now, no longer hidden, no longer blurred.

Blackness.

Yet not completely. The shape remained, burning a hole through the dark. Chris could see her now, could hear her whispering, the soft Pashto sibilants soothing him. He could smell the scorched dust of the Helmand desert, taste its grit on his tongue. The child, of course the child. She had come for him finally. Come to take him with her; to join her in whatever hell he deserved. She looked perfect. No sign now of the terrible wound his stray round had inflicted. Yet behind her, *in her*, he could see something else, superimposed on that fragile body, like a double exposure. Something old, something terribly old and terribly powerful and terribly blank.

Smiling, Chris sank to his knees by Frank's body and picked up the gun. The darkness didn't bother him now, nor the buzzing. He could see everything he needed to see. Smiling, he put the gun to his forehead. Smiling, he slowly squeezed the trigger.

Thwack!

The last thing Chris saw before he lost consciousness was Dog standing over him, ear plugs in, sleep mask halfway over his eyes. *Must be bedtime,* he thought as he heard the knife in Dog's hand clatter to the steel deck. Then he slipped into an even deeper darkness.

***

1220Z 12 Jan 18 – N28.00 W65.94 –- 45 metres below sea level

"Bout time you woke up," Dog growled.

Chris opened his eyes a crack, then squeezed them shut again as the light stabbed into his brain.

"Jesus. You split my skull," he groaned.

"Nah. Maybe a fracture. Maybe no."

Chris took a deep breath and sat up on the bunk he found himself on.

"What the hell happened, Dog. Where are we?"

"Heading home."

"Down there. I saw something. Before you came, before you saved me. I saw it…I saw it…I saw…"

"Stop. Don't think about it. We got away, but it's still in there. In you. If you let it, it'll take over."

"What the fuck was it?"

Dog took the medallion on its silver chain from around his neck and handed it to Chris. For the first time he could see its shape; a tentacled head with a spear through it.

"There are demons in the deep. You spend enough of your life underwater, eventually you'll see them. If you're not careful, they'll see you—they'll look into your soul and keep you down there forever. We got lucky this time. Keep the medallion. You're in the club now, boy."

Sleep rushed back at Chris and he let himself float away on its wings. Dog glanced over at the rescue vehicle's controls, checked it was on course, and stretched out on his seat. The vehicle slowly made its way back to the surface. Below, way below, in the darkness, a lantern flickered once, then went out forever.

STEVEN LORD is a fantasy and sci-fi author from the UK. After leaving university, he spent 16 years travelling the world, meeting interesting people. He has seen the sun setting in the Himalayas, dust storms rolling through the deserts of Afghanistan, hurricanes tearing through the Caribbean and icebergs drifting in the South Atlantic.

Since 2019, he has settled down a bit, taking advantage of the change of pace to follow a long-held ambition to write fiction. His influences include Neal Stephenson, Stephen King and Iain M Banks.

Steven currently lives in the south of England with his wife, dog and two cats and is resigned to his place at the bottom of the pecking order in the house...

Bibliography
UNRAVEL, Black Hare Press, 2019
APOCALYPSE, Black Hare Press, 2019
LOVE, Black Hare Press, 2020
HATE, Black Hare Press, 2020
Deep Sea, Black Hare Press, 2020
OCEANS, Black Hare Press, 2020

DEEP SEA

Beneath the Arctic

By Tim Sturk

Sailing far north of civilisation, a crew of arctic explorers discover a vast cave of unnatural shape, stretching far into the depths of an iceberg..

Two days have passed since I escaped the caverns. At least, I think it's been two days. We're so far north that the night is endless this time of year. There is no sun, only shades of black and dark blue, and the near-perfect white strip of shore. And, weary as I am, I haven't slept in all that time.

I'm writing this because I feel I must. In part, perhaps, because I believe the story must be told. Mostly,

I write out of a crippling fear that it's the last barrier my mind has against madness.

I'd dare any man not to go mad after the sights I saw down there, within the tunnels of that iceberg.

I wish now, that I had never left England to go on this accursed expedition. Was there not warning enough, in the dreadful tales of previous arctic ventures, that have so gruesomely resulted in disaster, mutiny, or even cannibalism? Not to mention the conditions; all the usual discomforts of a ship, multiplied tenfold by temperatures so low that they have turned country-sized chunks of the sea into ice.

It was a horrible idea, even before I knew what I now know—what I fear I'll never forget.

And yet, I signed up to the expedition. God help me, I came willingly to this forlorn land of frozen horrors.

I wanted the glory of it, hoping through the fame of discovery, to prove my worth in the eyes of my stone-hearted father, who has at many times threatened to disinherit me if I make nothing of myself. At the same time, a part of me took the whole thing lightly. I thought that I was proving brave simply by applying to join Captain Abrahamsen's crew, but that I would never actually be accepted, having never sailed before.

And yet, here I am. It seems that Bristol's short of men foolish enough to brave the arctic seas for little more than promises of fame. There's certainly no one aboard who's here for the pay, except perhaps the officers.

I ramble, I know. I do it that I may take my mind off what I've seen in these north reaches, though I know I must eventually put it to words, lest the memories consume me from within.

I will write. I will write, and then I will drink, and hope to forget.

We set out from Bristol in early autumn and sailed north-north-east for the better of two months, the first of which we spent vaguely following the Norwegian coast. It was time enough for me to learn the basics of seamanship, and all those abilities were soon called upon, after we left sight of Norway for more treacherous waters. For weeks, I was so heavily worked that I hardly noticed the cold or the gloomy view, managing no more than a bowl of stew and my share of rum before I bunked, utterly exhausted. I think they drove us so hard on purpose, so we would not have strength to complain.

We deckhands were treated little better than beasts of burden, driven 'til our last, and quickly disillusioned of those promises of glory that this expedition supposedly entailed. That glory was for the captain, not for us.

Still, we were allotted a few respites, and it was during one of these that we came across the cavern in the ice. I had happened to be on deck just then, lamenting my poor decisions, and so I was among the first to see it.

The captain had ordered the ship anchored while he finessed our course, the anchor-line descending many fathoms deep before it found resistance. It is a land of great proportions, this arctic. Great depths and massive icebergs. The one nearest us stretched three or four times taller than the full height of our ship at parts, making an incredible wall of ice. It made my head spin to look up at.

To battle this, I stared instead at the bottom of the wall, where the dark water touched it; a sudden, blue-black void, perfectly cutting off the pale ice. Slowly, I realised that this void was receding—that indeed the wall was growing downwards, as if conjured out of thin air. It was mesmerising to behold.

It grew slowly, but noticeably, and became bigger and bigger, never seeming to cease. I thought of a street magician, pulling endless kerchiefs from a previously empty fist.

Then, suddenly, the smooth wall of ice changed. There was a darker patch in it, and as it grew, I realised that it was a kind of cave—the mouth of a large tunnel. It stretched far into darkness, hinting at just how incredibly wide the iceberg was.

The strangest part was the shape of the opening: a huge, near perfect arch, like the main gate of some giant's keep.

It was even flat at the bottom, which was at least some thirty yards from the arch's apex. It looked manmade, and nearly large enough to swallow our entire ship, once the tide was fully out.

By now, the others on the deck had seen it, too. Their murmurs turned into excited shouts, and it did not take long for Captain Abrahamsen to form plans of exploring that cavern at the next tide.

The timepieces normally used to measure the ship's speed were set to counting down the tide, so they would know just how long one could be inside that cave before the water returned.

It was almost as if they'd all gone mad with curiosity, just at the sight of it. The officers kept speaking of fame and riches, and forgot entirely to curse and beat the deckhands for abandoning their duties to stare with wonder at the great cave.

I myself was no less shielded from the crew's mania. In fact, I may have been more deeply affected than most, for when the timepieces told us that we'd have almost eight hours with the next tide, and it came time to put together an expeditionary crew, I volunteered.

Many of the others were hesitant about actually going into the caverns. After all, there was no telling how big they were, or just how deep they went. There was a chance you might get lost in there, and crushed against the ceiling by the tide. There was a chance the ice may collapse behind you, trapping you inside the tunnels. Some of the crew even crossed themselves, as if they had (already then) sensed the cursed nature of these caverns.

But not I. I had to see them for myself.

It was a little like the feeling one gets when standing on a high cliff and staring down. Despite all rationality, you feel an urge to jump. I suppose the urge is stronger in some people than others. When it came to entering the cave, my urge was overpowering. It enraptured me.

I *had* to see what was down there, even if it was only a disappointing dead end. It was a stronger need than I have ever felt to do anything else.

God help me, I volunteered.

To my surprise, no one opposed my being part of the first excursion. The captain even commended my bravery, which convinced a few others to follow my example and volunteer themselves.

The final group numbered six. Besides myself, there was the captain; the first officer; two of the bigger deckhands, Rolf and Phil, who I think had some previous experience with northern sailing; and a fellow by the name of Thibault, who was our ship's surgeon. The captain practically forced Thibault to join at gunpoint, arguing there was a risk of injury.

I was let off my shift while we waited for the tide to

return and recede again, and I used that time to eat and get a few hours' sleep. When I was called back out on deck, the six of us who were to go into the caverns shared an extra slug of rum, drinking together despite our differences in rank.

Then we got in the ship's longboat and were lowered into the water. The two other hands (both of whom were far more muscular than I) took oars and rowed towards the cavern mouth, which was then only half-way uncovered by the tide. We made it a good bit inside before it receded entirely, and our boat went aground on a bed of ice.

Rolf carried metal spikes, which the captain ordered him to hammer into the wall, so that a short rope may be tied to it. I tied the other end to our boat. We planted a second spike with a second rope's end into the floor, then went into the cave, led by Captain Abrahamsen. I was made to carry this second (considerably longer) rope as we went deeper, uncoiling it as we walked.

We went slow at first, with the captain tapping a wooden pole against the ground before us, testing the strength of the ice. The first officer followed behind him with a lantern. The walls, smoothly carved out of the ice by man or water, glittered like crystal in the dancing light.

After a while, long after we'd come out of view of the ship, the tunnel branched into two forks, leading off in different directions. The captain paused here before heading down the larger of the two, all without saying a word.

Not one of us had spoken since we left the longboat. The only sounds were our footsteps, the rhythmic tapping of the Captain's pole, and the distant rush of running water. I wondered if that sound came from the sea outside, or from unfrozen streams, trapped within the ice. Perhaps they would gather enough strength break through a wall and wash us off our feet. I doubted my rope would save me if they did.

The tunnel widened, curved, and began to decline downward, much more noticeably than it had before. Soon it felt as if I was walking down a large staircase, except that all the steps had been smoothed down to a ramp by the continual tide. The captain slowed his footing, and I glanced over at the physician, who carried a timepiece. We hadn't yet spent an hour down there, though it had felt much longer.

Dr Thibault saw me looking and met my eyes. His expression was one of sickly resignation. He hadn't wanted to join the excursion party and looked like he would rather be anywhere else.

I smiled at him, though it felt weak on my lips. He looked away, and I suddenly wished I had gotten to know him better during the voyage. He was, after all, a man of science, and no doubt more agreeable than some of the ineloquent ruffians that shared the deck duties with me.

The tunnel kept branching, and it kept leading us down. By then I was sure we were below sea-level, but there wasn't so much as a droplet of water in the tunnels that hadn't turned to ice.

I felt the rope go taut in my arms. It had run out.

"Captain," I said, "the rope."

There was a pause in which I thought he might decide to return to the ship. But we hadn't been there long. We still had hours before we had to head back, but if we returned now, we'd have to await the tide before the next excursion.

Captain Abrahamsen glanced down into the bluish tunnels ahead, then back at the paltry bit of rope still in my hands.

"Leave it," he said. "We'll use the spikes to mark our passage."

Rolf hammered a spike into the wall, and I fastened the end of the rope to it. Then we walked on, stopping each time the tunnel branched to mark the passage we had come through.

The tunnel shrank a few times, then widened again. After a time, it grew larger and wider than it had previously been, opening up into a huge cavern. I could not even glimpse the far end of it in the dark.

As we walked through this gigantic hall, we were all struck silent in awe; not at the size, but at the structures within. It was like a city made of ice, with buildings of varied shape—from small, hut-like blocks to immense towers that spired toward the ceiling, and went out of view before reaching it.

There was even something like a plaza in the heart of this ice city. At the centre of it we found a giant block of ice shaped like the hull a ship. It wasn't too dissimilar to ours in size and shape, though the masts had either broken off or had never been made in the first place.

It was clearly all manmade—it had to be! Time and the tide may have filed the walls smooth of details, but the grander shapes were far too geometrical to have been carved by chance.

And yet, I could not fathom how this chamber—this ice city within an iceberg, accessible only at low tide—had been built, or to what purpose. It must have taken a hundred men a hundred years to carve out this chamber alone, and then there were those countless tunnels which we had not yet explored.

Indeed, I know not what better find the captain could have dreamt of. Here was, as he mused, a greater work of man than the Egyptian pyramids—and hitherto entirely unknown to anyone!

Despite his haughty proclamation, his voice lacked

in bravado. Like me, he seemed uncertain of this place, and unnerved by its existence. The others were of a similar mind. The first mate offered a few far-fetched explanations for how the place might have been built, but his voice quivered with doubts. Each suggestion only served to deepen my unease, and I saw signs of the same in the others.

Worst was poor Thibault, who looked sallow-faced and on the verge of fainting. Time and time again he glanced at the timepiece, then darted his eyes around himself like a rodent in a trap.

Then Phil—the one who'd helped Rolf row—let out a groan. He quickly crossed himself and pointed at something in the darkness. It was much smaller than the other structures, and it held a vaguely human shape, or so it seemed to me just then, although it was little more than a man-sized blob of ice.

The captain echoed that last thought as we approached it.

"It's just ice," he said, motioning his first mate to hold up the lantern to it. Then he checked himself and stared into the part that would have been a face.

I stared too, for in the moment that the lantern shifted, I could have sworn I saw a gleam of eyes, buried far beneath a thick shell of ice, which was otherwise opaque.

I looked around at the others and they did the same; clearly, they had seen it as well, though none dared speak it.

A terrible silence fell upon us. Then, in the moment that I finally opened my mouth to break it, Thibault's nerves gave out. He let loose a whimper and fainted, hitting the hard floor with a painful-sounding crack.

Captain Abrahamsen swore and bent quickly down beside him. After determining that at the very least, the man did not bleed, he grabbed Thibault's timepiece. There were still some hours left before the tide turned. We had time yet before we had to retreat, and the captain looked unwilling to waste it.

'Had to be the leech,' he grumbled.

He promptly stood and ordered me and Phil to carry Thibault back to the ship. We had brought a spare lantern, which they now gave us for the task. It was smaller than the other one, and cast a weaker circle of light. Hoisting Thibault on one shoulder each—a task made awkward by our difference in height—we headed back across the city for the tunnel we had come from.

As we walked, I noticed more of the man-shaped lumps of ice, scattered around the town, and several aboard the ship-thing. Many of them were contorted in impossible poses; others had partially broken apart.

I prayed that we had only mistaken that glitter of

eyes, and that these did not all contain dead men, frozen in eternal agony. Yet my imagination ran wild, and by the time we finally reached the tunnel mouth, I felt little a stronger than Thibault, and I was glad to be returning prematurely.

We might have made it out, then, if the doctor hadn't suddenly decided to wake up.

He was in a wild state, and began to thrash and struggle in our grip, clawing frantically at us. He shouted wordlessly, an animal cry that echoed through the tunnels. We tried to hold him down the best we could, but I had the lantern in a hand. At a jab from Thibault, it went flying, crashing against the rock-hard ice in a shatter of glass and flaming oil. It burned a while, casting strange dancing shadows all around, then it went out.

We were left in total darkness.

We managed to pin Thibault down. He returned to his senses somewhat, though he was confused, and his speech was a little slurred. I guess he had managed to concuss himself in the fall.

There was a more pressing issue meanwhile. We had lost our only light source, save for a handful of matches that we had happened to have on us. In the labyrinthine tunnels, I was sure we would get lost without a lantern.

"We could try to go back," I suggested, but Phil was keener than myself to leave.

"We'll go slow," he said, "and look out for the spikes. Can't be far from the rope."

I didn't argue. We continued to ascend, pausing where the tunnel branched to grope around for the spike. Well, I groped, while Phil supported Thibault. After a while my hands and feet and knees were so numb with cold that I came close to giving up. Every step hurt to take.

We came to a crossing where, for all my rummaging, I could not seem to find the spike. I told Phil, and he fumbled with one of our precious matches.

I had been so long in the dark that the glow of it nearly blinded me. We stared around but saw no spike. The flame reached Phil's fingers, and he dropped it with a curse. Darkness fell again, deeper now that our dark-vision was ruined.

"Light another one," I said, swallowing a rising panic.

He lit another match. Still I could find no spike.

"Light another one!" Thibault insisted. His voice echoed the distress that was threatening to overtake my own wits.

"How many do you have left?" I asked Phil, ignoring the hysterical doctor.

"Two."

"I've two as well. Let's save them for now."

"But—" started Thibault.

"We must have missed a crossing in the dark. We've got to turn back."

We turned, and began to walk back in the dark, squinting at any branching in the tunnel. We walked a long time there—too long, it seemed—in nervous silence. I began to become convinced that we had missed the fork, for surely we would have found it by now.

How long had it been since we saw the last spike? I tried to think back but could not recall. I had no clue how long we'd walked, with no daylight or watch to track the passage of time, and with all the tunnels looking mostly identical.

"We must have missed it," I said at last. "I'm sure we would have gotten back to the last fork by now."

I was met with silence, and a low whimper, probably from Thibault. The others were unsure as I was. Still, we turned around again and began to walk.

After a time, I did recognise a fork in the tunnel, branching to the left. I dug into my pockets for a match. My fingers were so numb that I could hardly grasp it, but at last I managed to spark a flame.

We looked around in the weak light, but once again we saw no gleam of metal.

"It's not here," Phil groaned. "We've just gone back to where we were."

"We can't have. We walked much longer in that direction than back."

The match went out.

"This is all your fault!" Phil said. In the darkness I could not tell if he meant me or Thibault, but then I heard a smack, and the doctor cried out in pain.

"Stop that!" I said. "Attacking him won't get us out of here."

"What will, then? More walking about in the dark?" His silhouette turned on me. "This is your fault too! You got us lost."

"You didn't exactly help!"

"That's because I was busy lugging around this worthless coward. I was following you!"

We may have come to blows soon after—a fight I'm sure would have left me in a bloody pulp—but for Thibault's quivering voice. "Listen!" he said, whistling a little on the s. Phil must have knocked a few teeth.

"Listen to what?"

"Hush!" I said.

"Don't tell me what to—"

"Be quiet a moment!" For a marvel, Phil fell quiet.

I've said before that while we walked, I could all the while hear rushing water in the distance. Excepting our steps, it had been the only sound for so long that I had almost stopped hearing it. Now, as I listened, I realised it had gained in strength.

It gurgled, loudly—and this time it was unmistakable: the sound was coming from somewhere very, very near to us.

"The tide," I breathed.

All at once we forgot our argument. We took to our feet, rushing blindly to avoid the water, which soon came lapping at our soles. There must have been more than one entrance for it into the iceberg, because it came from beneath, and because it couldn't possibly have reached the main cave mouth yet. Or could it? Just how long *had* we been down there?

I had some vague notion that, though we had to abandon hope of finding our way out, at least for the moment, we should head up. I screamed it at the other two, in what few words I could manage, panicked as I was. We picked the branch that sloped most upward and ran up it.

Behind us, the water continued to stream in, quickly, violently. It seemed to be rushing in faster than it had left when the tide ebbed.

Still, we managed to keep ahead of it, though the effort was doubled by my previous discomforts, and I was soon winded. The terrible gurgle of the water spurred me on.

The tunnel branched again and again, and each time

we picked whichever fork led up. In our haste, there wasn't time for anything else.

So swiftly did I run that I hardly saw the figure in the dark before I stumbled over it; another of the humanoid ice sculptures, this one splayed face-down on the floor, its arm outstretched. It seemed to grab at my ankle as I hurried back onto my feet, as if it meant to pull me down again, and drown me in the coming waves.

I kicked and screamed and shattered the ice-claw that was its hand, before remembering it was only ice, and that the water was still rising. Then I ran on, and caught up with the others, who had not stopped to help me.

Then came one fork where both paths seemed to go upward, and I picked the left at random. I soon regretted it, however, for it began to decline for no apparent reason, and I cursed the architects of this lunatic place, even as I barrelled down it, praying that the tunnel would soon begin to climb again.

The water must have reached the top of the incline we had just come from. It began to flood in from behind us. The initial wave nearly knocked me to the ground. It was ice-cold, and managed to completely drench the lower half of my body.

Soon it stood high enough to fill my boots, then it was nearly at my knees, and still it climbed, and it slowed me more and more. It came up over my knees, and I was wading in it, and my legs felt numb and heavy like stone beneath the waves.

I heard a shout and a splash as Thibault fell over. He managed to pull himself onto his knees, spitting water, and then he was knocked over again. He gurgled and thrashed, but neither I nor Phil slowed to assist him. It was each man for himself.

The water was to my waist now, but I saw the tunnel begin to slope upwards again ahead. It was far away, but maybe I could make it! After a few more strides I lost my footing, and began to swim, kicking forward desperately, while my wet clothes tried to pull me to the bottom. I thought my heart would give out from the cold, but somehow, I managed to swim on.

Just as the rising water scraped my head against the ceiling, my right hand knocked against Phil's leg, and I pulled hard on him, managing to pull myself a little further, even as he tried kicked at me to get me off of him.

The pocket of air above the water surface was vanishing. I took a deep breath and kicked off from the ceiling. It propelled me downward, but also forward, and I managed to swim on.

It was so very, very cold.

I can't have swum long before my lungs began to burn. By then I'd lost all track of Phil. I had to breathe, but all around me I was pressed by ice-cold water. It squeezed down on my chest until I thought that it would collapse. I struggled on, though my limbs felt leaden with the cold. Dark spots began to prickle into my vision; darker, somehow, than the water.

I had reached the ceiling again, and though there was no air at it, it was clearly sloping upward. This gave me the strength to hold my breath a little longer, and swim a little longer, though it felt entirely hopeless.

I kicked and kicked, all while my vision faded, and at last I could do naught but open my mouth for breath and swallow the ice water. I felt that I would faint.

Perhaps I did faint. Perhaps I only came close. My memory begins to blur around that time, and I'm not sure what, if anything, of what came next really happened. What I recall is the water receding, and air entering my lungs, even as I coughed up gallon upon seeming gallon of liquid.

I looked around, and saw that I was on the ground. There was a hole, nearby, beneath which the water still streamed past, but it did not reach up to me.

I realised that I must have found some air pocket in the ceiling, some little cave or chamber that the tide could not quite reach, and somehow crawled inside it.

My relief was so immense, and my energy so spent, that for a time, I simply lay there, panting. I could hardly even feel the cold anymore.

At length my wits returned. Despair replaced relief. I had avoided drowning, perhaps, but I would likely freeze to death before the tide receded once again. Even if I did not, I had no hopes of finding my way back out. I'd either freeze or drown or starve before I left the tunnels.

I might as well surrender then and there, I thought, and so I laid there for a time longer. At last, however, I got up. If I was to freeze to death—for that option seemed most likely, as I had not the courage to throw myself into the waves below and drown—I may as well look around while I still could.

The room I was in was as dark as all the others, and even with my eyes adjusted to the darkness, I could barely make out the walls. I groped towards them, shivering now that I did not have exhaustion to distract me from the cold. My clothes were heavy with water, and I wondered if I should take them off. But I had nothing to replace them with, and I doubted I would fare much better nude.

As I considered all of this, I mapped out the little room. Unlike the other tunnels and chambers, we had seen, this one did not appear manmade. It was too uneven, the walls asymmetrical, and the ceiling at a jagged slope. A natural air pocket, then.

Then I came to a section of the wall where the ceiling was highest, standing at least twice my height. As soon as

I laid hands on it, I felt that it was different from the other walls. They had all been hard ice, but this was something else. It wasn't soft, exactly, but it did not feel like ice, either, or stone or dirt. What's more, it had a strange texture: ridges and bumps, almost like wrinkles in whatever the material might me.

Instinctively, I reached for my match and found it, then paused. It was likely too wet to be used.

I blew on it a few minutes, and waved it in the air, hoping that it would dry up. Finally I struck it against my boot, as I'd been shown to do by the other sailors. At first, there was no spark, so I tried again. And again.

On the fourth strike, the matchhead began to burn.

I held it up to the wall and nearly dropped it right away out of surprise.

The wall was certainly not ice. *What* it was, I couldn't tell. It was a mossy swamp-or-mucus green, and had a leather-like texture. There was a long, horizontal ridge through it. I looked to the edges and saw that it seemed to continue past where the ice touched it. I wondered how long it spread. Perhaps it filled the entire iceberg, and would be revealed if one hacked deep enough into the walls.

"What on earth is this?" I asked out loud, my voice hardly more than a croak.

Then, just as my match was beginning to burn to an

end, I saw the ridge split. On either side of it, the "wall" was drawn back, revealing a glossy, milky thing beside it, and a dawning realisation struck me. It was no wall at all. It was a great set of eyelids, parting before a single, cyclopean eye—though it only just resembled an eye.

It was…that is to say, I was… I…

The match burned out, but I saw the eye just as clearly—more clearly, perhaps. It wasn't that it glowed. It was…somehow existed regardless of darkness.

A black pupil—blacker than any black I'd ever seen, even the void of space—appeared within it. Like the white was immune to darkness, this black seemed to be entirely devoid of any light or colour, and yet it seemed to hold a thousand colours, just ones I couldn't hope to witness with my human eyes.

It saw me, and I saw…something in that eye. As I try to recall it, my mind spins.

The pupil spun too. It became a liquid spiral, that slowly spun and filled the eye.

The walls seemed to turn to liquid as well. Not as ice melts into water, but rather into a kind of strange molasses-mixture, half-way between liquid and solid. It bled off of the walls, and up the walls, defying gravity to pool upon the ceiling. The stuff than ran down instead seemed to gather around my feet and then it began to flow up my leg and it was colder than anything I've ever touched before and all the while I couldn't help but stare into the eyes at it revealed the secrets of lost eons. It showed me the time before time—before ice could exist on the world, or even water. There was only this thing, this leviathan *creature* in the arctic then and it was the arctic and then the water came, and all things changed and all those millions of years of changed flashed within my mind, burning out all sense, and…and the city being made by…by…and…and I saw…

Lord as my witness I can't say quite say what I saw. I doubt I even saw half of what I just described, but that's the closest to an image I can form of what transpired. Whatever I witnessed, it filled me with such immense, suffocating terror and despair that I lost all my wits. I can't recall at all what happened next.

They found me, sometime later—I know not how long—wandering around atop a lower slope of the iceberg. I don't remember how I got there. I don't really remember being there either—it's all just flashes. I have a vague image of more of those ice sculptures, the ones that look like men. I think I overheard the sailors say that they found a few of those atop the iceberg when they came to rescue me.

I'm not sure, but I think I meant to jump, before they spotted me. Jump into sea. To slay myself, and thereby…what? Condemn myself to never enter heaven.

Not that I'm not already condemned. I left poor Thibault behind, and tried to use Phil to save myself.

Neither of them returned. Nor did the others who had stayed behind in the city, or even the small party that was sent after them. I don't dare think what may have happened to either of them.

I was the only one to come out of the caves, and I was raving mad. I suppose that convinced the crew to depart and sail back south. I was terribly frost-bitten too. They say that I may lose a hand, and several toes, without treatment, and of course our ship's surgeon is gone. But I can't bring myself to worry.

I don't even feel the pain. It's there, but I don't feel it. I don't feel much of anything. Only regret, and fear— fear that I'm mad. Or that I'm sane, and really saw what I saw. I don't know which is worse.

The one time I ventured out on deck, I saw faces in the water. Thibault's face, and Rolf's, and a few that were so bloated that I could not recognise them. I alerted the sailors, but they saw nothing. Myself, I was close to diving in after them, and had to be restrained.

Oh, God, I'm mad. I must be.

I hope I am.

I thought writing this down would bring me some small peace of mind. I was wrong. It's only made it worse, and I dread to think what will happen if the others read it.

I think that I shall burn this document.

As for myself, I don't know what I'll do. I might still die from my injuries, and I can't help but wonder if that would be best. I'm too much of a coward to take my life, at least now that I'm mostly myself again.

I wish I'd never set foot inside that iceberg. God forgive us for it. God forgive me.

TIM STURK is an author of fantasy, horror, and historical fiction. His works deal in the blending of the supernatural and mundane; the familiar and the macabre.

Bibliography
APOCALYPSE, Black Hare Press, 2019
Scary Snippets, Suicide House Publishing, 2019

Connect
Website: timsturk.com

Lost to the Sea

By Trisha McKee

When Trevor returns home from college, all he can think of is finding his high school sweetheart Simone, but there are rumors swirling about her behavior, and as he seeks out to find her and the answers, he discovers that this is more than just a case of rebellion and she might be in more trouble than anyone thought.

Trevor had always loved Simone. Ever since the first day of Kindergarten when he saw her in the corner crying. The other kids were laughing and pointing, but he rushed over to the little girl with the auburn curls and comforted her, telling her knock-knock jokes until she giggled.

Now they were adults—twenty-two years old—and he was still in love with her. But they had grown apart. They'd left for separate colleges, but he'd heard shortly after that Simone had dropped out that first year.

Trevor graduated and returned home, only to find out that Simone was gone, thrown out of her parents' house.

"She's turned wild," her father revealed. "Thinking she can come home at all hours of the night smelling of weed and fast food. No, I wasn't having it. That isn't my little girl. That isn't the Simone I know."

Concern simmered to the surface, but Trevor knew Simone's father Darrel was overprotective, strict beyond reason. Her mom, Darrel's wife, had passed away when Simone was only nine years old. Trevor could never remember what had caused her death, but he remembered a long illness with coughing and bedrest, yellow, loose skin, and hollowed eyes.

Darrel never hesitated in taking the responsibility of both parents, and he had worked tirelessly to make Simone feel loved and safe. But he was a stickler for rules, believing that the hyper-organisation and tight routine made up for the frenzy of death.

Trevor would never mistake Simone for an angel, but if her behaviour was so bad that her adoring father pushed her out of the house, something was going on. He found himself thinking of the wild-haired beauty, the girl that practically lived on the beach, her skin golden tan and her auburn curls loose and unruly or sometimes plastered against her flushed cheeks after a swim in the ocean.

Simone…just thinking of her made his blood race and memories heat him from the inside out. She was vivacious and tender-hearted. She would shame you for not jumping off the cliff into the water but would be the first one you'd call in the middle of the night if you felt the world closing in on you. And she would be there.

Of course he wondered about his best friend, his first love. Trevor worried because as rebellious as Simone could be, she did her best to never worry her father. So for Darrel to be concerned about her behaviour...something was off.

As Trevor adjusted to life after college, he also started to seek her out. He asked their old friends, went to their old hangouts, and searched social media for any hint of her. But she was nowhere, almost as if she no longer existed except for images in his mind, memories that he conjured up.

But if there was one thing about Simone, it was that she loved the water. They spent many days lounging in the sun, frolicking in the waves. It was their second home, a part of them. Simone was the calmest when she was near the sea.

Simone was not the most open person. As a young man, anxious to know his girlfriend in every way possible, Trevor tried to get close. He had always been the sensitive one, and he grew frustrated at the wall that was always up.

And yet, when they were at the beach, sometimes late at night, their bodies sinking in the cool sand as they stared up at the blinking stars, she would reveal a piece of herself. She spoke of her mother and the emptiness she represented. The missing piece that could never be filled. The overprotective father that sometimes suffocated her with his need to fill in that missing piece, the very piece he could never heal. She felt overwhelmed with the responsibility to assure her dad that she was fine.

And on those nights, she admitted she was not fine. Something was missing. More than a dead mom, more than teenage angst, and something more than Trevor apparently could give her. They would fall asleep curled into each other like cashews, the morning light nudging them awake hours later. He would see the distance in her eyes, the foggy smile, and he learned not to take it personally. This was Simone's way.

So Trevor retraced their childhood steps. He returned to the playgrounds of their teenage years. He visited the edge of the ocean. Days turned into weeks, and he became a man obsessed. Because he sensed her. Simone was among the waves. Her peace and contentment soared out over the seawater, over the grains of sand boiling in the full sunlight and chilling under the moon.

His parents insisted he forget her, focus on his future. But for Trevor, she was his future. She was his past. She was his everything. To forget her would be to give up on himself.

When searching, he would try to hone in on his instincts and follow that nagging voice that led him to specific parts of the beach. Usually he ended up at locations he and Simone knew well.

One night, when Trevor was sure he was on a dead-end mission, he wandered to one part of the beach where boats bobbed up and down, tied in place. It was not one of the places he was thoroughly familiar with, but he and Simone had visited here a few times. They would watch as boats left and returned, imagining themselves as the owners with the freedom to simply go and leave their confining, small lives behind.

And that was when he saw her. Simone at the wheel of a small fishing boat, a dark-haired tall man standing behind her, his arms wound around her. Trevor knew those auburn curls, that trilling laugh, he recognised the tilt of her head as she listened to the man talk. Trevor watched until the boat could not be spotted in the inky darkness.

He waited on the beach for hours, not thinking about what he would say or how he would explain being there. He only thought of seeing her. It has been several years since their last encounter, since they had spent the night together crying over their separate paths, knowing better than to try to make promises. They were closer than that. They were honest with each other. College life deserved all their attention, not distractions from childhood loves hundreds of miles away.

Trevor had reached out to her after hearing about her return home, but there was no answer. And then the number was changed, and he never got the new one. Now he was sitting on the beach staring up at the stars as he waited. And waited.

Then the boat appeared, just a small dot on the horizon, like all the other boats, but somehow Trevor knew. He felt her energy.

She appeared to be alone as she steered the boat into its spot, and when she jumped onto the dock, she glanced up. Her smile was immediate. "Trevor! Hey! Oh my God, what are you doing here?"

He grinned as she jumped into his arms. "I've been trying to find you. You're a hard person to track down."

The hug tightened and locked for several seconds before Simone pulled away with that dazzling grin. "Yeah. I kind of wanted to disappear from the old me, everything in my other life."

"Other life?"

"Oh, Trevor. I wanted to break free from all of that gloom and doom. Dad was always so sad. This whole town is sad. I wanted…something more."

"And you found it?"

But she never answered the question. Instead she took his hand and twirled under it, singing his name. "I've missed you."

Trevor had a hard time finding words because the woman in front of him was utterly bewitching. Even in the darkest part of night, she seemed to have a luminous glow about her. When her father had told him about her disappearance, the difficulties leading up to it, Trevor feared drugs. But he was staring at her now knowing there were no narcotics involved. She appeared at her healthiest. The glowing tan, flushed cheeks, and those shining caramel eyes that drew him in and promised him the world with just a few blinks and a gaze.

It hit him that the reason he had known it was her boat before it came into view was because he spotted her figure. The shining silhouette that highlighted that hour-glass figure and had warmed him many a night all those years ago. Remembering that, he also thought of when her boat had departed hours before.

"Hey, where's the guy you were with?"

Simone blinked a few times, the sharp corners of her lips sliding down slightly. "Guy?"

"When you left, I saw that man with his arms around you. You both seemed pretty familiar with each other." He held up his hands and laughed. "I'm not being jealous. Just wondered where he is."

"Trevor. There was no guy. Just me. I went out there alone."

"No. Simone, I saw him. Plain as day. It was why I didn't call out to you."

But Simone merely shook her head, the reddish-brown waves swinging around her face. "No. It was just me. Trevor...have you had much sleep lately?" She threw her head back and laughed. "Anyway, I'm glad you found me. I've missed you. Catch me up." She plopped down on the blanket he had laid out and patted the space beside her. "C'mon. Remember the nights we would stay up all night talking, the waves always the background noise? Anyway, what have you been up to?"

Of course he remembered those long nights with her. There was little else he had thought of in the last few months. Something about her was calling to him. "You know, college. Now real world. But tell me about you. Simone, you're okay?"

She leaned forward and touched the tip of her nose to his before rocking back and laughing. "I'm so much more than okay, Trev. I'm happy. I've found that missing piece."

"What was it?"

"Nothing I can put into words. But my life now… I love it. I have a small apartment just down the road. I waitress at the restaurant down the street. And spend every spare moment here, on the water. I eventually just want to live…in the water."

"You mean, like a houseboat."

She moved her gaze to his and quickly smiled. "Yeah, that's it. Just get a big boat and…"

He believed she was happy. He could hear it lifting each word, saw it in the light of her eyes, but something was off. It was easy to get caught up in her smooth tone, that vivacious grin, but he held back. "Whose boat is that, Simone?"

Again with the blinking. "Boat? It's mine."

"On a waitressing job? Come on. Be real with me."

"Trevor." Her voice was even, but there was a cutting edge to it, almost like a whispering warning. "You are such a dear friend, but it's been years since we have even spoken. You left. You never looked back. You never hesitated when we said we should split up to make the transition easier. And that's okay, but it means you don't get a say in my life now. You don't get to sit here and question me."

Her words were like ice cold drops of water, stinging and shocking him over and over. Sheepishly, he glanced down and nodded. "Sorry. Old habit." But he still wanted to know what was going on. Was it that man's boat, the man he had seen earlier with his arms possessively around Simone? Was it her boss's boat? Perhaps a married lover?

But he knew that flash in her eyes and the hardness in her voice, and he understood it was time to change the subject. So they talked about his college years and her discoveries out in the workforce. They exchanged updates on their families and laughed at stories from their joined past. It was all surface talk. He did not dig deeper for fear of chasing her off. She had cut her father out of her life, so Trevor had no doubt she would do the same for him. He had to tread lightly.

"Do you take the boat out every day?" he asked casually, his fingers dancing along the edge of her body, intoxicated by her trembles.

She purred, her eyes drifting shut as he massaged her shoulders. "Just about. Usually at night. I work during the day and have to do all the adulting. But at night…the ocean is mine." There was a random giggle, and then she turned toward him, her wide mouth grinning. "Hey, remember everyone talking about Bottlewood Benny?"

And Trevor returned her smile. "The sea monster? That everyone in our sixth grade claimed to see at one point? Yeah, why?"

"I think I saw him."

"Oh yeah?" Simone had always had an active imagination.

"Yeah. Majestic. Amazing. Powerful. I saw him." And then she was off, running down the beach, dancing through the morning's first rays, calling out a promise of another visit soon.

A few days later, Trevor went to the restaurant where she worked and watched as the men clamoured for a glance, a word. He understood. She was like a walking dream, a golden light dancing about an inch from every surface of skin. Her movements were smooth, connected, and those eyes shone with a youthful trust, an alluring innocence.

He waited until she had a break to approach her, shooing away a young boy that was trying to get her attention. When she turned, her eyes widened in surprise. "Trevor! Hey."

"Hey yourself. I…I wanted to see you again."

Her lips pressed together in a sympathetic smile, one he recognised as a smile given right before a girl would let him down easy. "Ah, it's always nice seeing you, but honestly, Trevor, I'm so busy I can barely breathe."

"How about one of these nights, you take me out on your boat?"

There was a switch in her eyes, a guarded shadow that told him his instincts were right. That was not her boat. It probably belonged to the man he had seen her with.

"Trevor, no. I'm sorry. I'm seeing someone. I don't think it would be right to take you out on the boat, especially as I can only go out at night."

Before he could ask more questions, Simone moved her lips into a semblance of a smile and mumbled parting words before skipping off to another area. It was equivalent to a slap in the face, being brushed off by a woman he thought of as the love of his life, whom for years was his best friend and confidant. But it only made him more determined to figure out the mystery.

A few nights later, Trevor borrowed a friend's boat and followed Simone at a distance. The air was dark and murky, almost impossible to see, and he knew if there were nautical patrols out there, he would be in a bit of trouble for keeping his lights off. But he could not risk being seen by Simone.

He watched her, that glow giving her away, as her boat bobbed up and down in a tranquil rhythm. Trevor tried to see through the fog and night more than just her illuminated figure, but there was not much to see. It appeared she was simply standing at the edge, staring over the railing.

The water gently rolled as he watched her, studied her, as he became mesmerised by her. But then he noticed his boat was rocking more frantically by the minute, and taking his eyes off Simone, he saw the inky waters curling into large, angry waves. Glancing up at the sky, Trevor saw the stars were blinking ignorance, the air still and warm. No storm. His attention returned to Simone just as she climbed up on the railing and dove into the distressed waters.

Confusion spread like smoke, causing him to cough and twist around, trying to make sense of it all. Did she really just jump in? Or did he not see it correctly through night's goggles? Did she fall? Replaying it in his mind, he saw her image, her body curve perfectly as she gracefully left the safety of the ship. She had jumped. Intentionally.

Simone was the best swimmer he knew, but the waves were overpowering even his boat, tossing it around like it were a mere toy. Trevor was thrown to the floor, crashing into the steering column. There was no radio to call for help, no way to communicate. Struggling to reach the edge, he pulled himself up, gulping for air as water smacked him in the face.

But he had to find Simone. She was out there in this water storm. He fought against the crashing waves and saw something near the surface of the water, something under her boat that was rising up. It was solid and shiny, a green object that he assumed was a monstrous turtle, but then he spotted the huge eyes, each one the size of his own head. They rolled in his direction, and when he was spotted, the creature rose up further, its body stretching out the length of both their boats, and Trevor realised it was this creature that was causing the waves.

"SIMONE!" he screamed, realising her fate. She had been consumed by this monster.

It rose up further, it's head now breaking through the surface of the water, its eyes solid and black. It continued rising, and that was when Trevor saw its thin neck. Bottleneck Benny.

It let out a squeal, its mouth flat and long on a flabby face. But when opened, Trevor saw rows and rows of jagged, gleaming teeth, as if it meant to display such a gruesome sight, as if it were warning him. He continued watching, holding on to the railing as the waves pushed and shoved his boat around. Then it reached up, multiple tentacles reaching up through the water and waving in a disoriented fashion. But this was no octopus; its body long and smooth like a whale.

Just as suddenly as it appeared, it was gone, dipping down into the water with one last scream, one tentacle splashing the water in front of his boat and drenching him further, threatening him one last time.

The waves slowly settled, and he sank to the floor, gasping and crying, mourning his love. The sea monster had taken her, the very monster they had tried for years to find, thinking it would be fun, an adventure. Never considering it would be the end of life as they knew it. This was a monster, after all.

There was a soft hum that gradually reached a higher pitch than the crashing of the waves and slowly, Trevor stood, his balance shaking, his breaths uneven. But he saw that familiar glow skimming the surface of the now-smooth water, and he cried out. Simone. It looked as if she were swimming, not floating. Not dead.

Moments later, she popped up, her hair clinging to her shimmering face. "What the hell, Trevor!" She impatiently lifted her hands, and he pulled her up, and then he found a towel to throw around her. "You're following me now?"

"Simone, what the hell was that? Are you okay?"

Her lips formed a perfect bow as she studied him, her eyes a soft caramel that pulled him in. The allure was so strong that he almost forgot the unforgettable. Almost.

"Trev, leave this alone."

"No. I can't. Are you okay?"

"I'm fine. In fact, I honestly have never been better."

"You were under water for several minutes." He stated this as fact, because he had watched, he had searched.

"I was."

"How?"

"Benny. Bottleneck Benny. I told you he was real. I said I'd seen him. But it is so much more than that. I...I love him."

The words took a moment to sink in, and as he tried to make sense of it, he reached out and took the towel. He dried her off, kissing her skin as he did so, savouring the taste and texture. Something about her was calling to him, and he hated the thought of her being in love with anyone, or anything, else. "You love the...monster?"

She did not try to correct him. Instead, she nodded solemnly. "I do. And he loves me. We can...we communicate. And when I'm close to him underwater, there is this...this part of his chest that I can rest my face against...I'm able to breathe."

Trevor shook his head. "No. This isn't...it isn't possible."

"You just saw. If he didn't love me, Trev, why didn't he kill me just now? And he didn't kill you. Because I told him to leave you alone."

He paused for a moment, studying her. Was it drugs? Perhaps there were drugs that could illuminate the skin, give off a glow that might look healthy but was actually dangerous. Maybe it was a radioactive glow. "But if you didn't tell him, he would have killed me?"

Simone nodded, casting her gaze down. "I-I feed him. That guy you saw me with the other night? I tricked him into going out with me, going on my boat. I took him out here to feed him to Benny." She glanced up, and that was when Trevor saw the tears, the desperation expressed in those soulful eyes. She was not lost yet. "I am not proud of it. But he… Benny needs that. And I need him."

"You need him?"

"Yes! All my life I never felt like I belonged. I always felt something was missing. I finally feel this is what was missing. He makes my heart race, he makes me feel beautiful."

"He has tentacles! Simone, just listen to yourself. You're basically killing people for this…this monster. Does it even have feelings? Awareness of what you are? Is it drugs? Are you on drugs?"

Her tiny features fell, sadness welling in those large eyes. He had disappointed her, but how had she expected him to react? "Trev, I lived the life so many others wanted me to live. My dad wanted me to behave, so for the most part, I behaved. You wanted me to be loyal and happy. So I was loyal and I acted the part of a happy girl. Everyone wanted a piece of me. Now I never expected anyone to believe me about Benny. But you…I thought you of all people might at least listen. I'm not on drugs. If anything, you're seeing *me*. *Me* for the first time. Happy."

"Delusional," he corrected gruffly, her words stinging him. All those years together, she was not happy? The promises and secrets and all she could say was she was someone other than herself?

Simone raised her eyebrows at him and then turned toward the water. She let out an ear-piercing shriek, and almost immediately, the water seemed to part and the creature jumped up, half of its body in the air. It was majestic and odd and scary as its tentacles flailed, and it screamed in return, an off-key love song only the two of them seemed to know.

Simone turned to him, and he noticed her glow was brighter, shooting out further from her body. With a wink, she jumped into the water and was gone. And that creature with the green, slick skin, round head and huge eyes, and the thin neck was also out of view, the waves slapping against the boat to remind Trevor of what he had just seen.

The next few nights, Trevor suffered from nightmares. He heard the shrieking, saw the creature watching him, plotting. And just as he tumbled from the boat into the waiting waters, he awoke with a start. During the day, he tried to find Simone, to warn her, to talk sense into her. But she was not at the restaurant, and the other servers were hesitant to talk to him. She must have warned them that he was stalking her, as they eyed him with disgust. He wanted to tell them she was in danger, and they were idiots for not seeing it.

Instead he went to visit the one person who might know anything about this.

Old Man Addington was a grumpy, blunt man that scared off a lot of people. But those that got to know him realised that as crotchety as he was, he was full of information about the town, the people, and the myths.

"Ah yes, Bottleneck Benny," Addington sighed, tipping back in his chair. He took a sip of coffee before continuing, "When I was just a boy, we were out at the beach. Just a bunch of us teenagers, getting into trouble. Oh, yes, we had trouble even back then, Trevor. I see that look you're giving me. It's true. Your generation didn't invent trouble."

"I never had a doubt," Trevor answered with a smile. "But about Bottleneck Benny…"

"Ah, always so impatient. As if you don't have your whole life ahead of you. But yes, I've seen Bottleneck Benny. Me and my friends. The one day we had skipped school and were out on the beach. Beautiful day. Not a cloud. Suddenly, the waves grew to the size of skyscrapers. It was crazy. There was no wind, the sun was out, but these waves were just astounding. And then…this…beast flies into the air, bigger than a house with this bobblehead set on top of a thin neck. Fluorescent green. Round black eyes that seemed to see us. And these tentacles that splashed the water. I'll never forget that day. My friend Yolanda was never the same after that. She became what we called a siren. Luring men to their deaths to feed that monster."

This caught Trevor's attention. "What happened to Yolanda? She ever snap out of it?"

Addington guffawed. "Snap out of it? This isn't some daydream. She got caught up in that world. I don't know what happened to her. I just knew she was not the same Yolanda. I knew to stay far away. So if you're asking me because of a similar situation, I'm here to tell you to leave it alone. Leave her alone. She isn't yours anymore. She belongs to the sea."

It was sound advice. Trevor knew there was truth in the story Addington told, and he knew there was good advice in his words, but all he could think of was Simone. Beautiful, untamed Simone. She belonged to him, not some creature that used women through the years to cause destruction. Simone was not a siren. She was much more than a weapon.

So it was with that frame of mind that he set out to find her. Surprisingly, she came right up on the beach, as if she had been waiting for him to arrive.

"Trevor. I'm glad you're here. I've missed you."

She almost appeared as if she were a hologram, her outline shimmering and skin flawless. He was afraid that if he reached out to touch her, it would just be static. But he was too enthralled to reach out, to feel if she were indeed real. Her voice seemed to carry him to heights that rendered him speechless, without any coherent thought or ability to fight through this fog she created. All he could think of was her scent, her eyes, her hair… He wanted her to touch him…

And as if reading his mind, Simone stepped forward and wound her arms around his neck. "Remember how we used to come out to the beach and dance to the waves? We'd stay up all night."

"I remember," he managed to breathe out. "Simone, of course I remember."

"You always treated me so good, Trevor. Like I was someone important. Dad would lecture me about being so flighty, about being impulsive. But you loved that about me. You loved the sense of adventure."

He stared into her eyes, mesmerised. Finally, he managed to nod. "Yes. You were fun. I love your spirit. I have always loved your spirit. I love you."

She nodded. "I know you do. I love you too."

"So everything that—"

"That's all over. I missed you. I couldn't stay away." Her fingers danced up and down his arms. He had to focus on breathing. "Have you missed me?"

"I have."

"Can we pick up where we left off all those years ago? I mean, have you stopped loving me?"

He gulped for air before managing, "No."

"Good." It was more like a breeze than an actual word, fanning over his face and bringing him in even more, carrying him closer, and then they were kissing, and Trevor could barely stand.

"Let's go out on the boat," she whispered, her breath curling around his tongue and intoxicating him further. "Let's go and stay out there. Forget everyone here. We can have each other."

Trevor found himself nodding, unable to look away. This was all he had ever wanted. Even if there was not this unexplainable pull, he would be willing to go anywhere with Simone. It had always been her. It would always be her.

There was nothing to do but follow her onto the boat. In the back of his mind was the image of Addington, his words trying to break through that thumping. But anytime any clear thought of that conversation broke through, Simone interrupted those thoughts with her image, her words, the feel of her skin.

The air was hot and still as they rode out to the middle of nowhere. The sea salt was almost overpowering, the blue water hypnotic as it slapped against the boat.

"When do you have to be back at the restaurant?"

Simone smiled at him, and he forgot that he had asked the question. "I don't work there anymore. Better opportunities await."

And it was then he noticed that this was a different boat, a better boat. Trevor recognised it as Warren's boat. Warren had been missing for a week. "Uh, this boat…"

Before he could finish the sentence, the waves grew, crashing over the boat, hitting him with salt and water. And he knew. He sensed the presence, saw the glow brighten around Simone.

"Trevor." She said his name calmly, and he turned to her, gripping the railing for balance. "I'm sorry."

He nodded. What else could he do? It was his own fault. For loving a siren. For falling for the words, believing her declarations. And as she shrieked, he tried to prepare. He braced himself, but it was over before he could fear the worst.

TRISHA McKEE writes romance, horror, sci-fi, and anything that pops into her mind. She started publishing her work in April of 2019, and in less than a year, her work has been featured in over 33 publications. She has earned the Story of the Month award, and her short story Where We Meet was nominated for the Best of the Net

2019 anthology. When she is not writing or talking about writing, she is fishing, dreaming, spending precious time with her handsome hubby and beautiful daughter, attending murder mystery games with her dearest friends, and hanging out with her bulldogs.

Already Paid For, Thirteen Press, 2020
Class Pet, Fantasy Short Stories, 2020
Evening Flea Market, Night to Dawn Magazine, 2020
Full Moon Date Night, Horror Magazine, 2020
Golden Boy, Black Hare Press, 2019
How to Break an Alien's Spirit, The Oddville Press, 2019
Late Fees, Sincyr Publishing, 2020
Lost to the Sea, Black Hare Press, 2020
Road Trip Buddy, ParABnormal Magazine, 2020
Screams and Shots, Youthful Imagination, 2020
Take That Chance, Breaking Rules Publishing, 2020
The Next Room, Breaking Rules Publishing, 2020
Where We Meet, Crab Fat Magazine, 2019

Website: www.trishamckee.com
Amazon: amazon.com/author/trishamckee
Twitter: @wordromancer

Blue Blood

By Zoey Xolton

En route to the Caribbean islands, the Queen Mary and her crew encounter the ancients that dwell within the tumultuous deeps of the Devil's Triangle; and for Duke Williams the cost of survival may be his very sanity...

The swirling vortex of the sky above flashes; a riot of magenta, blinding cerulean and midnight blue. Below, the sea boils—waves taller than the *Queen Mary* assault our gallant English vessel as we traverse the notorious Devil's Triangle. Bound for a chain of Caribbean islands, it is our charge to make bluff and trade common luxuries with the native islanders in exchange for information on the activities of the French. The Crown desires an outpost in the tropic region, and after years of French invasion and interference, is keen to gain the favour of the locals and establish a permanent British port for trade and exploration.

"Trim the sails," bellows Captain Blackmoore, "or we're going to lose them!" Nimble-footed sailors scurry up the rigging in droves, as foot-sure as rats up a rusty drainpipe. With the assistance of the men below, they hoist and secure the mainsails as best as they are able, before moving onto the fore and mizzen sails.

"Will she hold?" I yell over the din of the storm.

"Aye, if the weather is all we have to contend with!"

I cling to the quarterdeck's balustrade with frozen white knuckles. The sea and rain buffet me as if I were no more than a pinafore on a washing line. "What do you mean, man?"

"I mean, Duke Williams, that these deeps are known for sinking ships, strange disappearances, and unexplained happenings. This is the very eye of the Triangle—these are forsaken waters for good reason!"

"I don't believe in monsters, Captain," I say, masking my snort of derision with a cough.

"The beasts of the deep sea don't rely on your belief,

son. They lurk here, regardless."

I side-eye the old captain, before turning my attention back to the main deck. It's been a textbook journey up until this point. Moments later, as if my very thoughts damned us, a wave unlike any I have ever before witnessed crashes over the *Queen Mary*, snapping the mainmast and washing several sailors overboard and into the churning maelstrom of the sea. The cry rings out— *"Man overboard!"*—but it is hopeless. Those who have fallen are lost, there is no saving them.

I cross myself and pray. A shrill scream rips through the night, breaking my concentration, as one of the captain's lost men rises from the depths and up high above the crow's nest, encircled by a tentacle of mind-shattering dimensions. I feel a temporary warmth flood down my breeches as I watch an appendage of greater girth than the ship itself come slamming down across it, smashing the *Queen Mary* clean in half. The aft and fore decks splinter away from one another, and water rushes in to fill the fractured chasm that yawns open to greet the sea.

Another tentacle, then another, plucks gurgling men from the roiling waters, only to smash them like ragdolls upon its surface. The tentacles withdraw from sight, disappearing into the deep with their ill-gotten gains— before yet more would emerge—and the horror repeats like a waking nightmare. Over the deafening roar of the tropical storm, and the crashing of the waves, the sea devil's head emerges. Glowing yellow eyes with great slitted pupils rise above the carnage, followed by writhing, prehensile tentacles that coil and uncoil, as if scenting the air.

"Mother of God," I utter.

"Swim north!" the captain bellows beside me, seconds before he is snatched from the sinking ruins.

Without a coherent thought or plan, I do the only thing that I can. I throw myself into the sea, narrowly avoiding jagged pieces of the broken *Queen Mary*. Despite having been soaked on deck, the cold waters of the North Atlantic Ocean send shock waves rippling through me. The sea envelopes me completely, violently, driving the air from my lungs with brutal force. With all my strength I fight to reach the turbulent surface, but my limbs feel like lead weights, and my vision begins to darken.

A sound unlike any I have ever heard rips through the sea, splitting the fabric of existence it seems. A deafening, thunderous roar slices through my soul, causing the very water that holds me to bubble and pulse. Pale faces I scarcely recognise drift by on the turbulent undertow, vanishing into the gloom forever; damned to Davy Jones' Locker. A surge of fear ripples through me.

I will not die here! I swear to myself, to God—to the universe. And so I push, with whatever I have left, kicking, scooping with my leaden arms like a frog trying to swim through oil; and finally, I breach the surface.

I gasp, sucking in a great lungful of cold, briny air. I can all but taste the acrid, sizzling tang of the lightning streaking through the sky above. I turn, frantically treading water, surveying the sea—all I observe is darkness. I turn again. Open, violent ocean and all its chaos on one side…darkness on the other. Terror grips me as my mind reels. *Look up*, it whispers to me. I crane back my neck as the darkness seems to go on for an impossible distance. As the sea pulls me away, I slowly gain comprehension of the sight before me.

Squatting in the deeps is a beast—a creature, a nightmare—of such monstrous measure that I commend my own heart for not seizing in my chest at the sheer horror of it. Easily as wide as five ships, the beast's shoulders hang, hunched like a scaled gorilla, as it fishes dead men from the sea. Its great muscular arms end in gnarled and taloned hands. Its serpentine eyes are like ethereal beacons in the night, lit from within by some infernal florescence. Its mouth is surrounded by tentacles.

I watch as it passes a tiny limp body from hand to tentacle, and then in awestruck terror as its gaping maw opens. By the light of the storm-bright sky, I behold what can only be thousands upon thousands of immense, sharp teeth; like the vacuous gullet of a gargantuan lamprey eel, or leatherback turtle. The tentacle reaches in, dropping the sailor within, before retracting, and the maw closes...sealing his fate.

The beast's eyes blink, first one set of eyelids, and then another, as it searches the churning tides for more fodder. *That's me!* I suddenly realise with bowel-relaxing clarity. *God, help me!* But if there is a God, he has abandoned us all. I am alone, stranded in the vast, desolate expanse of the North Atlantic, with a being beyond the comprehension of mankind. In all my years of attending Sunday Mass, not even the Devil himself and his eternal Hell could hold a candle to the vast, boundless terror before me.

How can Man exist alongside such a creature? *Surely we have only thrived in its absence?* A whole fleet could not take down such a thing. Its scaled hide reflects the moonlight. No doubt no cannon, bullet or blade could penetrate it. What could Man do against such boundless terror? What are we, but bones to pick from its thousands of teeth?

As if the infernal powers of the universe have been dropping eaves on my dire musings, the water around me roils, and the beast's head turns, surveying the expanse before it. It fixes its gaze somewhere behind me, and as I turn, I am swept up in a great wave. As I am dragged along its crest, I gaze back. *Something else* is rising from the deeps… A sizeable piece of the *Queen Mary* rises up within arm's reach and I seize it, scrambling on board.

I realise this voyage may be my last, but my gut screams at me to be strong, to hold on—I must know what manner of entity could draw the attention of the tentacle beast. The sea beyond erupts in a mountainous spray, millions of gallons of salt water are displaced. An eerie white cocoon-like effigy bursts forth. Deep purple-blue markings zigzag across its pale, translucent flesh like lightning; hideous, bulbous, pulsating veins, pumping literal rivers of blood.

The tentacle beast cranes its neck as the bulging obelisk continues to rise, blocking the light of the moon. Then in a single fluid motion, the creature's likeness is revealed, as immense wings unwrap from around its body, and flare out, a ghostly canvas of skin and bone. I feel all meaning in life seep from my soul. Sailing, expeditions, the queen…what does it all matter in the face of such monstrosities? From what great chasm in the depths beyond our reach have these ancient beings emerged, hungry, sentient, and lusting for blood?

There is no mistaking the second creature…I have seen its resemblance drawn in picture books, in fairy tales written for small children, and in old, dust-laden tomes of mythological eras gone by. It is a dragon! Eyes like orbs, as black as the abyss, stare down upon the tentacle beast, overlooking my existence entirely. The dragon elicits an almighty, unholy, ear-piercing scream, more painful to bear than ten thousand burning hot needles through the eyes. I imagine my ears might be bleeding, but I'm soaked through, and I couldn't tell even if they were.

The tentacle beast rises from its squat, standing at its full height, as my wave bears me further away, to a somewhat safer distance—if there is even such a thing. The dragon is, without doubt, easily twice as large. I cower, clinging to my broken piece of ship. I am too afraid to utter a sound, but my mind races, a cacophony of word vomit. *We are nothing*, I realise. *How naïve and foolish; that we, as men, think that we rule the world. That we are its masters. That we are some omnipotent god's divine creatures chosen to walk this earth... We are nothing! We are infinitesimal in the shadow of such great, Hellish entities. We are but ants, busying ourselves with cities and roads, and storing food for the winter, while these titans of the deep slumber, seldom arising to contest territory and feed!*

The revelation washes over me, pouring salt into wounds that I didn't know existed. Half-drowned and losing my grip on the fabric of what I believed to be the only reality, I blink back into focus. The destroyer of the

Queen Mary roars in return, its prehensile mouth-tentacles flaring in rage. I look upon the behemoths of old, and I feel void; an emptiness in the recesses where my heart or soul should reside. Within me I feel a chasm as vast as the timeless boundlessness of the netherworlds these beasts must have originated from.

I am not a child of God. I am—I search for the right words—*a meat bag. A tiny puppet of flesh and impulse. Of what consequence is my life?* It doesn't matter. At least, not now. The beast rushes forward then, breaking my dour reverie. It reaches out, muscular arms gleaming in the darkness as it tries to gain purchase on the ghost-pale dragon. It seems an unmatched battle, and a thought terrifies: *Are there greater beasts than even these?*

The dragon rears back before unleashing what I can only describe as blue fire. White hot at its mouth, it blasts forward with the momentum of a hurricane—crackling, surging—I shield my eyes with one arm as it streams directly into the face of the beast. The beast raises its arms in defence, but its face is burned. I can smell the stench of its acrid singed hide on the air. When the beast lowers its arms, I see that its tentacles—those that are left, hang, limp and charred. One or two, I cannot be sure, plunge to the depths, burned clean off, the great meaty appendages causing waves of their own as they splash heavily into the sea.

The beast is deformed, and his stance is one of righteous indignation—if such feelings and descriptions can befit such a creature. Every line of its form is tense, its bipedal legs poised, ready to spring as the dragon spreads its membranous wings, revealing the terror and splendour of its true magnitude. *It's beautiful*, I think to myself in awe. *Beautiful and terrifying.* What god conceived of such a terrible beauty? Or perhaps there are no gods at all. Perhaps these mighty beasts are gods in their own right? Such power and immensity seems worthy of the title, and unlike the god of the Bible, these beasts are present, physical entities—capable of visiting their wrath upon the living, at will. Their tangible presence is mind-numbing. Not even in my worst nightmares could I have conceived of such things!

The beast leaps, moving faster than seems possible for an entity of such size. It reaches high as it leaves the ocean behind, burned hands enclosing around the dragon's throat. Gaining a firm hold, it attempts to clamber up the dragon like a bear up a great oak tree. Its clawed feet tear at white flesh, and an acrid, pungent odour fills the air, spilling into the sea. The dragon's ethereal blue blood is iridescent, glowing under the moonlight as it spreads like thick tarry oil upon the waves.

The dragon leans back on its long tail, and like a household cat, uses its back legs to defend itself. It kicks at the belly of the tentacle beast, over and over it strikes, and great splashes erupt around the gargantuan creatures as they battle. *They're scales!* I realise. Great black, smooth-armoured belly scales are plopping into the water like stones, as more of the tentacle beast's soft, under-flesh is revealed.

The dragon's blood reaches me on the tide, and I reach into the water with my hand. Slick with its otherworldly essence, I smear it across my salt-raw, wind-burned face, like war-paint, to serve as a reminder of my sanity. *This is real, and I am alive!* My face tingles with a strange, stinging sensation, but I have little time to dwell on such things.

Moments later, the tentacle beast screeches in ungodly agony. Its middle is torn asunder, its bowels and innards spilling into the ocean like a waterfall of gore, its gleaming black organs hang from the unsightly wound. It releases its grip on the dragon, its clawed hands instinctively moving to its abdomen. It clutches at its gut, hopelessly scooping its entrails from the sea. I watch in horrified awe, unable to tear my eyes away. The beast seems defeated—spent—and for several breathless heartbeats, I marvel that the battle is won…but it seems I am mistaken.

The tentacle beast suddenly draws out what appears to be its coiling intestines, as if it were a butcher at market, threading sausages. And in the most gruesome act of desperation and rage that I have ever witnessed, the tentacle beast launches itself once more at the dragon—wrapping its own entrails around its ghost-white neck. The tentacle beast loops them twice, then, like a monkey, clambers over the dragon's back. Planting its feet square into the dragon's shoulder blades, it heaves with all its god-forsaken, cosmic might, riding the dragon like a pale horse in the night. The sight of the titanic struggle before my eyes destroys any fear in my heart, or rational concept of the biblical Revelations; the proverbial End of Days.

Surely, this was more chilling in every sense possible. The devils, the demons, the gods—they are here now. They weren't coming, they never had been! They'd always been among us, slumbering, waiting…biding their time. Hiding in plain sight, in myths, folklore and legends, in the dark, far-off, hard-to-reach places of the world. *But they were here.* Terror was already here, in the flesh—these harbingers of doom were as real and tangible as I.

Was I its first witness? Had anyone who'd been lost to the Devil's Triangle seen and lived to tell the tale? *Some must have,* I reason. Writers, artists—those who depicted them on paper for history to dismiss as mere fiction. Did they come out of such a trauma unscathed, unscarred? Were they sound of mind? Were they able to assimilate back into regular society? The answer, it seems to me, is unlikely.

The dragon collapses its wings, tucking them in, and attempts to pull the choking bonds of flesh from around its throat with the immense fore claws at the tips of its membranous appendages. Seemingly unsuccessful, the dragon bellows lightening blue fire into the night sky, before launching itself and its ungainly rider towards the stars. I crane my neck, watching the otherworldly battle take to the air. The dragon's white form is visible high above, the tentacle beast's silhouette lost against the twinkling black.

The dragon reaches heights never before dreamed of by Man, and for one remarkable moment in time, the dragon and the beast present before the moon; the glowing celestial orb limning them in heavenly white fire. *Have they reached the known edges of the world?* I wonder. The dragon, bearing the full weight of the wounded beast, drops suddenly, a spectral calamity from the sky, spiralling at incredible speeds towards the sea. The beast is unseated, its roar like thunder echoes through the night. Airborne, it flies behind the dragon, clinging to its own entrails like reigns.

The dragon hits the water, nose first, in an elegant swan dive, while the tentacle beast trailing behind, smashes face first into the sea as if it is made of solid stone. The sea spray at their impact reaches the stars, and a great tidal wave, like a tsunami, radiates in a circular manner for miles. I am swept away, further and further, born towards nowhere, directionless and lost—a speck of flesh; fish fodder in a never-ending expanse of bottomless doom.

The tentacle beast flounders on the surface, as if stunned by the tremendous fall. His immense body floats, half submerged, unmoving, like a black, craggy, volcanic island in the growing distance.

The storm has settled as mysteriously as it begun, the sky unnervingly quiet—even the sea has lost its wrath. I feel my anxiety growing. *This cannot be right*, I think to myself. The dive of death was magnificent beyond comprehension, but where is the dragon? Has it returned to the Devil's Depths? Has it arisen, only to kill indiscriminately, without rhyme or reason? Surely the creature has its reasons, purpose?

As if the cosmos has again sought to answer my queries, the dragon bursts from the sea some distance away. Twirling, it spreads its great wings, the blood that covered it has been washed away, and the damage inflicted upon it by the tentacle beast seems to have miraculously healed. Its white belly is pristine and scarless beneath the starlight, as if it had not just engaged in a titanic battle of life and death. I watch in awe as it soars before hovering above the still form of the tentacle beast.

Moments later, an intense white glow grows with frightening speed within the dragon's colossal barrel chest, lighting up the night like a candle trapped inside a sconce of frosted glass. The glow rises up its moon-pale throat and erupts past the dragon's tree-sized teeth in a stream of godless, blue flame. The torrent of fire assaults the tentacle beast. The intensity of the glare burns my eyes, and I raise my arm too late. A nostril-searing stench fills the night as the tentacle beast's carcass ignites; muscle, flesh, scale and fat burning. One of the beast's dark limbs raises itself skyward—a final plea for mercy? Or does it goad its nemesis, begging for the eternal release of oblivion?

The dragon flaps its wings, buffeting the sea, and fanning the flames. Like a bellows in the forge of a blacksmith, it increases the horrific devastation and intensity of the flames. As the beast's clawed hand ignites like a torch, it falls back to the water, and the beast floats still—unmoving. Seemingly satisfied with its efforts, and satisfied that its emissary is well and truly dead, the dragon shrieks in triumph, its ear-splitting volume reverberating through my very bones.

The dragon swoops down, and rearing back like a falcon on the hunt, it snatches up the charred corpse from the ocean's hold and bears it toward the dark heavens, and into the distant beyond. I watch as the dragon becomes a pale, faint mark against the night sky, eventually indiscernible from the stars that pinprick the inky, endless black maw of eternity. I blink in the gloom, my retinas scarred, as errant flashes of light and spots distort my vision. I am exhausted. *How much time has passed?* I wonder. There is no sign of the dawn, no tinge of warmth on the horizon—just an incalculable, oppressive darkness.

Which way is north? How far am I from land? What else lurks in the deep beneath my leaden limbs? A sudden wave of nausea and fatigue washes over me, and I feel myself slipping, losing my grip…on reality? On the scrap which buoys me? I cannot know. I succumb, almost willingly, welcoming the overwhelming restful dark as it swallows me whole—mind, body and soul.

***

I would like to say that, in the nothingness, I prayed, but even in the absence of logic, of habit, I knew without a resounding doubt, that such a thing was an act of utter futility. If I was going to drown, I would. If it was my fate to fall prey to the lesser monsters of the sea, I would. I realised with a calm, but dreadful peace, that there was nothing I could do to stop the inevitability of the end. There would be no god awaiting me, no pearly gates, no smiling St Peter, no loved ones with open arms…nothing awaited me on the Otherside but the undeniable certainty of death, and its perpetual, cold and crushing embrace.

***

I know not how much time has elapsed, but when I next wake, I find wet sand beneath my fingers. I claw at the shifting granules, before instinctively rolling over—purging my lungs and gut of the salt water I'd imbibed. When the worst of it is over, I rest my forehead on the wet earth and shudder with the very effort of living. *How hard it is to merely survive!* I decide. Is it this difficult for all creatures? Do the ants, trodden underfoot, battle through life each day with this level of sheer determination and willpower? Do they feel the weary pressure of existence upon them, weighing them down with each tiny, insignificant step?

Rolling over once more, I look to the sky. It is dawn, and the endless expanse above is a mix of palest blue, brightest gold and the deep, but fading hues of a dying rose. *Where am I? Does it matter?* "I'm alive!" I breathe, my dry, cracked lips stinging with each word. The pain, though small, is reaffirming, almost pleasurable. I laugh then, drenched, bedraggled and spent on this godforsaken beach; like a maniac, or opium fiend. I laugh until I hurt all over. I laugh until my voice is hoarse with glorious, muscle wrenching pain, blood trickling from the corners of my mouth.

I feel the warmth of the sun give strength to my cool flesh, and I lay, broken and prone, arms and legs outspread, like a flightless bird. My navy coat shifts with the surge and lap of the sea as it lazily reaches up the beach, before receding once more. My coifed and curled wig is long gone, lost to the hunger of the waves when the *Queen Mary* was first attacked. In the distance, I hear voices, though they are garbled—the tongue unfamiliar to my ear. I hear the unmistakable shrill laughter of children, and a dog barking. I close my eyes in the knowledge that I am found, or that I have lost my mind.

***

"Duke Reuben Williams?"

I feel my eyelids flutter, and I strain to rise.

"Easy, man. You have been through Hell and back, give yourself time."

Slowly I regain focus, but dancing lights and blinking spots of white obscure the clarity of my vision.

"Where am I?"

A decorated officer with golden epaulettes stands beside my cot.

"You are in the naval infirmary of Fort Royal, Duke Williams, being overseen by Doctor Audric Baudelaire."

I ease myself onto my elbow and take stock, as best as I am able, of the man before me. His accent is unmistakable. "Are you going to kill me?"

"We may be at war, but the French are not monsters, Duke Williams. You were brought to us by the natives, having been swept ashore. You are here with our blessing and will come to no harm."

I relax but a little. "And who are you?"

"I am Vice-Admiral Jacque de Boyeir."

"Why are you helping me?"

"Your vessel, the *Queen Mary* was lost to the sea, and you are shipwrecked. Why would we not assist you in your recovery? You are a fellow man."

"But I'm British," I say, somewhat numbly. "We are at war."

"Again, we are not monsters," he says simply.

"Monsters don't exist," I whisper, voice trembling.

"The only monsters are men, Duke Williams, but we French count ourselves among the noble-hearted. We will see that you regain your strength and are returned to your precious England."

"Am I not a prisoner?"

"No, you are a free man, Sir."

"I could take my leave, now?"

"If you could stand, of course, but where would you go? We are on an island, Duke Williams. Martinique, specifically. It is a long swim back to the British Isles from here."

"No swimming," I utter as I allow myself to fall back onto the white-sheeted bed. "Never again."

"You aren't the first sailor to lose his sea-legs after a shipwrecking," says Boyeir, turning away. "And you will undoubtedly not be the last."

***

Forty-five days later I touched down on British soil. The French were true to their word, allowing me passage on the first vessel headed for England once I was recovered enough to travel. I had not meant to, but on the long return voyage, I lost my nerve, and my mind. Each night, and even during my waking hours, I found myself assaulted by bleak, terrible visions. With each rock of the ship, I felt the sea in my veins; churning, chaotic and dark.

I had nightmares and hallucinations of places I had never seen; secret, loathsome, and deep locations hidden beneath the waves. Trenches and splits in the far reaches of the earth, so cold and desolate as to chill my weary bones. I am but twenty-eight years old, yet I feel as though my soul is burdened by an infinite darkness, branded by the kind that bears weight—accrued only through countless centuries of time. There in the blackest depths of the sea, I have seen what I can only describe as a gateway—a glowing portal to another realm, like a tear in the very fabric of our world—a rift to places and things I can never unsee.

The magnitude of the entities that exist beyond our world had seen me feverish and catatonic for much of the journey over. The fear never leaves me. Its coiling terror has taken root within me, and I cannot dispel its hold upon me. With what sanity I have remaining, I have spent dwelling on the events of that night in the Devil's Triangle, and I have come to but one conclusion: The blood of the dragon has tainted and permeated every fibre of my being. I have become saturated and corrupted by its otherworldly power.

The crew are glad to be rid of me when the exchange is officially made. I am present enough of mind to know that I have frightened them. They think that I am a raving lunatic, another poor soul whose lost his mind at sea. Their conclusion is perhaps not wrong, but their reasoning is. The waves and the sky, the lightening and the sharks, those things when combined can put fear into the heart of any man, its true; but to be driven mad…is something else entirely. To lose one's mind is a sinister thing. To dance upon the knife edge of sanity and madness is the epitome of cruelty, and it would seem that this is my due—the price I must pay for acquiring such arcane and ancient knowledge. I set out an accomplished young man, a respected noble among my peers with a promising future ahead, and I return a wretch of a man— as broken within as the wreck of the *Queen Mary*.

As I am taken to my home in Winchester, in my moments of lucidity, I worry for my wife and daughter. I know I will be an affliction upon them and my household.

***

The sound of metal grating against metal jars my nerves and rouses me from my drug induced stupor. *They should oil the doors!* I think to myself in annoyance as two nurses come into my room. The door bolts securely behind them from the outside; an orderly awaits their call.

"Good afternoon, Duke," says the brunette. Mary is her name.

I struggle against the confines of the straight jacket.

"Now, now, easy, Duke," says Annabeth as she trundles the rickety trolley over to my bedside. "No use getting yourself all worked up."

"Any more of your dark dreams today, Mr Williams?" asks Mary.

I rock to and fro on my bed, cross-legged—all dignity long gone and forgotten. "Always," I murmur. "I am never alone…the dragon *knows* I can see. It can sense our connection."

"The dragon, again?" Annabeth says, shaking her head in dismay. "That nasty thing ought to leave you be." She hands Mary a pair of pills and signs off on her chart.

"Come now, Mr Williams," says Mary as she tips my head back.

I open my mouth and swallow the pills without complaint. The pills are relief. One, an anti-psychotic, the other a strong sedative, they grant me a deep, black, dreamless and visionless sleep—for a time. I find myself growing more and more resistant to their drugs with time. Each passing month that I am here, they are forced to increase my dosage.

On the bad days, of which there are many, they offer me a tranquiliser. As the liquid release runs through my veins, I become a drooling lump of once-humanity. I am left a mere flesh suit for a broken heart, a lost soul and a shattered mind; but it brings me peace from the nightmares.

Mary strokes my sweat-slicked hair and smiles gently. She knows what I have lost—what the fated voyage to the Devil's depths cost me. "There, there. Would you like the bee sting to see you through the night, Reuben?"

"Please," I whisper, my mouth dry.

She nods, and Annabeth pulls down the high neck of my stained jacket. "Hold still, then, it won't hurt for but a moment."

I feel the sharp sting of the large needle as it pricks my neck, and I relax almost instantly. "The pain is a promise of peace," I murmur. "For a little while."

Annabeth and Mary ease me back, and I feel the edges of reality darken. In the haze of my fast-fading consciousness, a voice like rolling thunder reaches out to my fragile mind.

I have tasks for you, Blood-marked. Soon, you will answer my summons, and the descent of Man shall begin. Rest now, it taunts. *For a little while.*

The ghost-pale dragon's smouldering eyes burn like dying stars in the growing darkness of my mind, and I feel my bowels involuntarily slacken as oblivion claims me.

ZOEY XOLTON is an Australian Speculative Fiction writer, primarily of Dark Fantasy, Paranormal Romance, and Horror. Her works have appeared in over one-hundred themed anthologies, with more due for publication!
She has recently celebrated the release of her debut short story collection 'Darkly Ever After'. You can find further details regarding her many publications on her website!

Bibliography
Bad Romance, Black Hare Press, 2019
Curses & Cauldrons, Blood Song Books, 2019
DARK DRABBLES Books 1-10, Black Hare Press, 2019
Darkly Ever After, Blood Song Books, 2020
Deep Sea, Black Hare Press, 2020
Deep Space, Black Hare Press, 2019
Divinity, Iron Faerie Publishing, 2019
Fable, Iron Faerie Publishing, 2019
Forest of Fear, Blood Song Books, 2019
Harvest II, Blood Song Books, 2020
Key to the Kingdom, Black Hare Press, 2020
LUST, Black Hare Press, 2020
Mythica, Iron Faerie Publishing, 2020
PRIDE, Black Hare Press, 2020
SLOTH, Black Hare Press, 2020
Spring's Blessing, Fantasia Divinity Publishing, 2019
Storming Area 51, Black Hare Press, 2019
Summer's Splash, Fantasia Divinity Publishing, 2019
Twenty Twenty, Black Hare Press, 2020
What If?, Black Hare Press, 2019

Connect
Website: www.zoeyxolton.com
Amazon: www.amazon.com/author/zoeyxolton

Acknowledgements

When we embarked on our Black Hare Press journey back in late 2018, we never envisioned the huge support we'd get from the writing community. We have been truly humbled by the number of submissions we've received (around 5,000 over ten publications!) and have loved reading every single one.

So, thank you to everyone who crafted tales just for us—from the tiny tales in our Dark Drabbles series to these monstrous beauties you have read here in Deep Sea, we thank you from the bottom of our hearts.

To our families and friends, collaborators, random strangers who took pity on us, and everyone who has helped us on the way: we couldn't have done it without you.

And to you, our discerning reader, we and these fifteen talented writers did it all for you. We hope you enjoyed these tales of magical alternate history. If you did, don't forget to leave a review.

Thank you all, and see you next time.

Love & kisses

Ben Thomas & Dean Kershaw